FRAN'S WAR

Fran's War

Sally Trench

Hodder & Stoughton
LONDON SYDNEY AUCKLAND

Copyright © 1999 by Sally Trench

First published in Great Britain 1999

The right of Sally Trench to be identified as the Author of
the Work has been asserted by her in accordance with the
Copyright, Designs and Patents Act 1988.

10 9 8 7 6 5 4 3 2 1

British Library Cataloguing in Publication Data
A CIP catalogue record for this title
is available from the British Library

ISBN 0 340 74560 6

Typeset by Hewer Text Ltd, Edinburgh
Printed and bound in Great Britain by
Clays Ltd, St Ives PLC

Hodder and Stoughton Ltd
A Division of Hodder Headline PLC
338 Euston Road
London NW1 3BH

Our deepest fear is not that we are inadequate
Our deepest fear is that we are powerful beyond
    measure.
It is our light, not our darkness, that most frightens us.
We ask ourselves, who am I to be brilliant, gorgeous,
    talented and fabulous!
Actually, who are you not to be?

You are a child of God –
Your playing small doesn't serve the world.
There is nothing enlightened about shrinking
so that other people will not feel insecure around you.

We were born to make manifest the glory of God that
    is within us;
it is not in just some of us; it is in everyone.
And as we let our own light shine,
we unconsciously give people permission to do the
    same.

As we are liberated from our own fear,
our presence automatically liberates others.

Nelson Mandela
Inaugural speech, 1994

ACKNOWLEDGMENTS

Bosnia 1991–1996 was a huge endurance test for all convoy drivers. For myself, I know that I could not have returned month after month, had it not been for the support and tender loving care of a group of people I feel privileged to call my friends. They did not deserve the involuntary imposition of a mad passionate delinquent into their lives and no doubt felt deeply unprivileged. So both sorry and thank you to Diana and Mike B, Teresa de B. and Sally D.H. for always being there.

INTRODUCTION

My eldest son walked in.

'I'm going to Bosnia,' I announced.

'There's a war there,' he replied, peering at *The Times*.

'That's why I'm going.'

'Mother, for heaven's sake, grow up. Manchester United won again. They have a good chance of winning the cup.'

'Good, I'm very pleased for you. How do you think I should go about getting to Bosnia?'

'Ask Jan. I'm sure he would parachute you in.' His half-brother was a helicopter pilot with the RAF.

'Don't be so facetious.' My eldest put down the newspaper.

'What the hell do you expect? What mother in her right mind would go into a war-zone to get her head blown off? Anyway, do you know where Bosnia is?'

I went into my office and peered at the atlas.

'Between Croatia, Serbia and Montenegro,' I shouted. 'It's very mountainous. I wouldn't want to parachute in.' His six foot three frame lounged in the doorway. He was staring at me.

'You're serious about this?'

'Absolutely.'

'What will you do when you get there?'

'Find out what I can do to help.'

1

He grinned. 'Mother, the best way you can help is to stay well away. The United Nations really don't need you.'

'Go and have your breakfast, I have phone calls to make.'

In my heart I knew I could not sit back and do nothing. What I had seen on the six o'clock news in November 1992 was a travesty. Like the rest of the world I had watched the satellite pictures of a small insignificant country called Bosnia being plundered and raped, similar to the current situation in Kosovo as I write. The haunted and hunger-ravaged faces of the children fleeing from their burnt-out villages pierced my heart and my passionate sense of justice. I switched the television off. It was not my business. I threw a log on the fire, drew the curtains and curled up on the sofa with a book. But it was too late! I had no sleep that night. I found myself watching the breakfast news. It showed pictures of women and children being herded, whimpering, into trucks. Other victims squatted in burnt-out buildings, cowering in terror. The voice of materialism insisted that I had no money to spare and that I couldn't just shut up my house and depart for a foreign land. Admittedly, my youngest child was nineteen and had flown the nest, but what would I do with my dogs if I went off into the blue? What could a late middle-aged grey-haired woman do anyway if she started off from her middle-class home in middle-class rural Oxfordshire? Maybe my eldest was right. What mother in her right mind would go into a war zone to get her head blown off? Having convinced myself that I was too dull and boring to do anything at all, I began to hear the unwelcome murmur of challenge. Where was my self-determination? Was I truly prepared to be a mere cog in an uncaring society?

I phoned the Foreign Office and listened to some dismal bureaucrat informing me that all the borders were closed and that no civilians were being allowed in or out of Bosnia. I phoned the Croatian Embassy who were equally negative. I phoned the United Nations, who passed me from department to department and eventually suggested that as I was totally unqualified and therefore useless, I should ring the Red Cross. The Red Cross suggested that I should collect blankets.

At dinner that evening, my eldest commented: 'I see you're still with us. Haven't gone to Bosnia then?'

'Not yet, but I will.' He knew that tone of voice.

'Look, Mother. It's a crazy idea. First of all, you haven't got the money to get there. If you get across the border, what will you do? You don't speak Serbo-Croat. How could you help?'

'That's why I'm going. To find out *how* I can help.' He cut his roast lamb as if he was slicing his mother's head from her neck.

'I've worked it out. If I fly to Split in Croatia, where all the journalists are based, I'm sure I can persuade someone to take me across the border. All I need is a plane.' My son chuckled in disbelief. I thought of Richard Branson and Virgin Airlines.

In bed that night I began to scheme. I realised a letter sent to Richard Branson's office would pass no further than a secretary. I remembered, suddenly, the saying that behind every powerful man was an even more powerful woman. I screwed up three attempts and finally wrote: 'Dear Mrs Branson, As a mother of young children you must be as horrified as I am at what is happening in Bosnia. I want to help but don't know how to help. I do believe that if I could get there and experience the problems first hand, I would then be able to make a worthwhile contribution to the well-being of the children. I have no money for an air fare to Croatia and your husband has a plane. Please would you ask him to consider flying me into Split as soon as possible. Yours sincerely, Sally Trench.' I slept that night.

My problem next morning was the discovery that Richard

Branson's phone number was ex-directory. But I had read that he owned a house near Oxford. I assumed he must own a private plane, so I drove to Kidlington Airfield and parked outside the security barrier across the entrance which had to be opened manually by an officer. I waited and hoped. A green catering truck was blocking the entrance. The officer was talking to the driver and couldn't see me. I slid under the barrier and ran like hell. Eventually I found the ops room and walked in.

'Can I help you?' enquired a man in a crisp white shirt and blue tie.

I decided that truth was prudent and he listened patiently to my story. 'So you see I need Richard Branson's address.' He smiled at me sympathetically. 'I'm afraid you're out of luck. He doesn't keep a private plane here – Sir Frank Williams of Formula One does, but not Richard Branson.' My disappointment must have been obvious. 'Wait a minute, I think there is somebody who can help you.' The man put his head through a glass door behind him and called for Sharon. He repeated my request. 'Oh yes, he's our neighbour. He lives along a driveway off the main road. It's not marked. I'll draw you a map.'

Some would say that this was extraordinarily good fortune, but I believe in Providence which is perhaps an easy justification for faith. I found the house amidst stunning grounds. It was empty, and with a prayer and a light heart I posted my letter through the box.

Richard Branson rang me two weeks later and within forty-eight hours I was on my way to Croatia with my haversack full of letters of introduction and the names and addresses of contacts. However, I was not, as I had hoped, on my way to Split. The Boeing 747 carrying fifty tons of aid and four passengers was too big to land at Split runway. We were on our way to the Croatian capital, Zagreb. Richard Branson had failed to inform me of this minor diversion, or I had forgotten to remind him that I had wanted to go to Split. Instead, I found myself in a high security airport in Central Croatia surrounded by warplanes and thirty miles east of the front line at Karlovac. With no official contacts I decided to look up the address of the British Embassy in the phone book and to make my way there. It was lunchtime and the staff were unimpressed by my demand to see the Ambassador. 'I'll wait,' I said and promptly sat in a chair, joining a row of bedraggled refugees.

'Mr Sparrow is a very busy man and has appointments all afternoon,' the harassed secretary told me.

'That's OK. I'll wait till he's finished his appointments. I'm staying until I see him.' Over the next two hours the refugees and I stared silently at one another and I noted the room into which the secretary was taking letters to be signed. At about four thirty a well-groomed heavy-set man appeared, dark weals beneath his eyes. With nothing to lose, I leapt to my feet.

'Ambassador, Mr Sparrow, Sir, I need to talk to you.' If he was surprised he clearly did not show it. He looked too exhausted to show any emotion. With a grave dignity Mr Sparrow shook me by the hand and said 'And you are . . . ?'

'Sally Trench. Please can we talk.' He ushered me into his office and asked the enraged secretary to bring a pot of tea.

During the two hours in which we talked I found Mr Sparrow to be a gentle and compassionate man torn apart by the hatred and evil of war. I remember him carefully putting down his cup of tea and opening his arms as if to embrace some ghost. 'All my friends are Serbs, Croats, Bosnians. And now they are killing one another.' His eyes brimmed with tears. I felt his anguish.

'Please, I want to help. How can I help?' He smiled weakly. I knew what he was thinking. What could one unqualified middle-aged woman do to help in a tyrannical bloodbath of mutual hate.

'The most urgent need is food. It's November and there is a very long winter ahead. All sides are starving.'

'What about the children?' He shrugged his shoulders.

'Many of them will die this winter. Even the refugee camps are overwhelmed by the numbers.'

'Can you get me into a refugee camp?'

'I can write you a letter of introduction. The nearest one's at Karlovac but that might have fallen by tomorrow. This morning the Serb front line was only three miles away.' From my haversack I produced a pen.

'Please, I would be very grateful.'

The next morning, clutching my precious letter, I caught a bus to Karlovac. It was a dismal town with signs of bombing. As soon as I disembarked on to the empty street I could hear the reverberations of distant shelling. I had been born just after the end of the Second World War, so this was a new experience. I was scared. There were very few civilians on the street, just groups of gun-toting soldiers, their Kalashnikovs thrown idly over their shoulders. Sandbags were propping up every building and I could sense eyes staring at me. I felt intimidated and wished I had turned round with the bus and returned to Zagreb. There was an army post ahead, so with all the confidence that I could muster, I strolled across to the unshaven soldier and pointed to the address on the Ambassador's letter. I was directed to what appeared to be the town square. With enormous relief I saw a United Nations High Commission for Refugees poster with the words 'A refugee would like to have your problems' emblazoned across it in large black capital letters. I walked into a building which turned out to be a transition camp for male refugees. Each room had eight bunks and the skeletal figures lying on them were barely recognisable as human beings. After being shown around by an official I asked where the children were. At another camp about a mile away. Would I like a lift in a UN jeep? Indeed, I would.

The children's camp was even closer to the front line. It had been a school and was now desperately overcrowded, forbiddingly cold and thoroughly insanitary. My heart crumpled as I was faced with hundreds of children, half clothed and half starved with nowhere to go and nothing to do. The few staff and mothers were themselves skeletal and exhausted. If the children in a camp were like this, what were the horrors being experienced by children behind the front line? At last, I knew what I had to do in the nightmare of this tragedy. My single objective must be to take food into the war zone in order to keep at least some of the children of Bosnia alive. In fact the very word 'tragedy' implied a moral elevation which was totally lacking to this business. What was happening in Bosnia was barbaric – it was the work of liars and cynics manipulating tribal prejudices with atrocity propaganda and the resurrection of ancient blood feuds in order to bring about ethnic cleansing. The displacement of over three million innocent civilians, turned refugee, was not a consequence of war, but precisely its purpose.

I returned home by bus and train in time for Christmas to gorge myself on turkey, mince pies and Christmas pudding, while the victims of war had nothing.

For fifteen years I had been running the charity Project Spark which I had set up in 1972 to help deprived and disadvantaged children.* I now decided that our energies and assets could best be used in the transportation of food to Bosnia. With the

* Sally Trench, *Somebody Else's Children* (Hodder and Stoughton, 1990).

agreement of my trustees, I bought a truck and became a truck driver. Angus, Tariq, George and other young friends joined me and we began to take convoys across Europe and into Bosnia. During 1993 we made five trips and between journeys, I went to speak in schools in order to motivate the children to raise the necessary money to buy more food. My idea was simple: we needed to inspire the children of the UK in order to persuade them to help children less fortunate than themselves.

The children of the UK responded magnificently and I kept the schools briefed on the destination of their generous gifts, always hoping that my circulars would inspire them to greater efforts, which was frequently the case.

The children organised sponsored bike rides, sponsored football matches, concerts and plays. I had been fortunate in capturing their imagination and they gave their all. The response was fantastic. One nine-year-old raised £30 in sponsorship money by running non-stop round his school football pitch thirty times. Their meagre pocket money provided endless food and in order to involve them as fully as possible, I would drive a truck to the school and the children would form a human chain in order to load it. I found it a very humbling experience and tried to pay adequate tribute to the immense dedication of these children in my 1993 annual report:

The dramas in Bosnia we have experienced could well overshadow the importance of the vital hard work put in by the young here on our own doorstep. For instance, in the month of October I visited 38 schools, spoke to nine thousand children and through their sponsored bike rides, swims, runs, canoe races, twenty-four-hour music play-ins and many other individual efforts, over thirty tons of imperishable food was collected and monies raised. One Church of England primary school with only seventy pupils aged 5–11 years gathered two tons of tinned food from their own village. The diligence and motivation of the children in helping those of their own age group less fortunate than themselves has been an example to us all.

Unprompted letters, home-made cards, drawings and presents poured in, revealing self-giving and a generosity of spirit which was inspirational.

Between 1992 and 1993 three and a half million people became displaced in Bosnia and thirty-six journalists were killed, 1,500 foreigners were detained by Croatian police. As fighting approached Sarajevo, workers at two aid institutes fled, leaving 230 children on their own. Several died. In August, we discovered 1,100 Bosnian women and children detained on an island by Croatian soldiers in heat of just under 100°F. The children had no shoes and were allowed access to water for one hour a day. As for the children of the besieged town of Srebrenica, the lack of proteins and vitamins they suffered was critical.

An estimated 55,000 Muslim refugees in Mostar were starving to death; water supplies had been cut and vital services such as the bombed-out hospital trying to function in its own basement were without medicines. Doctors were performing amputations without the benefit of any form of anaesthetic.

On one occasion we were captured at dawn two miles out of Mostar crossing the final checkpoint behind the front line. We had been trying to take eight tons of food and two tons of medical supplies into the besieged city. Soldiers held us at gunpoint for the rest of the day. We were among the fortunate because we were released. That same day three Italian aid workers were shot.

The devastated Bosnian capital of Sarajevo suffered a massive barrage of mortars overhead – in excess of 3,000 shells a day. The one and only bakery left ceased to operate and women and children were hiding in the safety of sewers and dark cellars starving to death. There was no electricity, no gas, and no water.

Prospects for the winter were extremely bleak. Our trips to Bosnia were an endurance test. During 1993 I wrote in my diary:

'It's D-day. Packed my haversack last night in preparation for three weeks away, keeping in mind that the mountains in the war zone will be below zero. So three thermal vests, three pairs of trousers, three sweaters, three pairs of socks, maps, prayer book, tin opener, torch, Swiss penknife, packets of soup and tea bags. Well protected and overloaded with crucifixes and rosary beads in my pocket, I rattle like a nun. Despite all this protection, I feel quite nervous, a sense of anticipation. On the one hand I must be cautious and responsible, but risk and danger go hand in hand with war. I am totally aware that I must keep a cool, rational mind; what fears I have, keep to myself, and truly try and leave the rest to God – for the "rest" will not be in my control. Indeed it is not anticipation I'm feeling, but a base undiluted fear of the unknown. If I knew absolutely nothing of what I was about to enter, then ignorance and innocence would be a good substitute for courage – as it is, from my last trip I now know just enough to fear the worst.

Saturday, 23rd. Five days of endless patience. Five nights and days of total exhaustion. We are in Split. Angus and I are sharing a bottle of vodka. Wasted a day in a queue of lorries at the Austrian border. Had to produce endless paperwork for the officious Austrian customs, who endlessly stamped everything but my toilet roll. Then into Slovenia feeling that we were almost there, but knowing full well from previous experience that the most horrendous drive down the Croatian coast was still to come. It is, without doubt, the worst drive on earth, down and up winding mountainous roads for nearly three hundred miles of hell with each truck laden with five to seven tons of aid. I have now developed an agonizing razor-sharp pain behind the back of my right shoulder – whether it's tension or I have pulled a muscle turning the non-power steering wheel of Slug I do not know, but I am suffering. Stopped at 5 p.m., heated up our tins of stew and commenced the dreaded mountain drive – bridge blown up so have to take the twenty-minute ferry across to Paag – blissful interlude – then back to driving. At 10 p.m. coming into Zadar we found that police had blocked off the road and we're sent on a detour across stony fields. Only today at the UN press briefing did we realise how close we had been to failure. Half an hour after our arrival in Zadar, the Serbs moved in and shelled it. We are now blocked off and cannot get out of Croatia. I've decided not to worry about anything until I have fulfilled my goal of reaching the children in Mostar with our aid. If the devil himself appeared, I wouldn't notice. I am too bloody exhausted and can hardly see what I'm writing. I suppose it could be the vodka!

Sunday, 24th. A few hours' sleep and then the daily press conference in Room 435 at Hotel Split. We were given the latest details of the war and of roads which are mined or closed by shelling. Meanwhile George is going to the airport and collecting some press passes! Wonder if that will be beneficial? Hotel Split full of foreign journalists, UN officials and the army. I speak to a Major who advises us not to go on to Travnik after we have been to Mostar. Tensions are mounting, most roads are being shelled. Mostar shelled last night and now under curfew between 4 p.m. and 7 a.m. It's not the best of news. We are all apprehensive but everyone determined to get the food and medical equipment to Travnik. Spoke to Tariq last night, who has just come back from a camp behind the lines. He says fifty people a day are dying, just keeling over from starvation. His story has strengthened our resolution to continue. The last week has been gruelling but what lies ahead is going to sort the men from the boys – we either make it or get killed. If we're captured, it will be the Muslim drivers who will be given the worst time. I will be systematically raped I suppose. I must find a level of composure with my God, entrusting myself to Him: his most affectionate and disobedient servant!

25th. Have decided to wear three pairs of knickers, alternating them each day that is if I get the chance of any privacy. Thank goodness my period has just finished. Imagine all my pockets stuffed with sanitary towels! Make good field dressings though! We're not carrying anything except what we're wearing and what is in our pockets as the soldiers at the checkpoint steal everything. Can't get my diamond ring off my finger – will have to put a piece of plaster over it and hope for the best. Tonight has a new quality, realising that life might not continue – that one wrong move could end it. Some deadly sniper could extinguish me. Why the hell am I not back home by the log fire reading yesterday's Sunday papers? What am I doing involving myself in a dangerous war between people I know little about? It's about the children – not the immorality of war – but the morality of their birthright: their right to a decent world for their future. Bugger that bloody pain in the back of my shoulder – it's razor sharp like a knife stabbing. Have made a decision not to take my flak jacket. It's too rigid and too constricting. I'm just going to have to rely on my God and the good common sense He gave me. I hope that we get there and back. I am looking forward to the bottle of vodka I'm leaving behind! But if it is to be death I only hope and pray that it happens on the return journey, after our mission to get the aid to Travnik has been accomplished – then our lives here won't have been in vain.

Midnight. I remember a scene in an RAF war film, where the young pilots are sitting around waiting for the phone to ring, for the order to take off. I sense that same chilling apprehension in myself, not quite knowing what to do or where to place my keyed-up body. I drag at my hundredth cigarette, hating it as it rasps my throat, but needing to do something with my hands and hiding my strained face behind the curling ringlets of smoke. Learning to wait and do nothing is the quintessential act of faith.

OK. We're leaving in an hour. Have faxed the UNHCR with our inventory of aid and informed them of our destination, etc. Have had a briefing with all the drivers, talked over the risks and contingency plans. We are psyched up, each one plainly controlling his own vulnerable infra-structure. Each of us masking our insecurity, appearing calm, smiling reassuringly at one another and then suddenly breaking into hysterical laughter at some completely fatuous remark. We are just like amateur tightrope walkers, swaying, swinging, but at the last moment finding the balance to stay erect and strong: a trapeze team juggling our emotions to make the best public act. Each one so aware that our personal 'act' is dependent upon the others in order to make the performance work. At this point I need three basic ingredients – faith in my God, immense stamina and a crazy sense of humour. I feel I am losing all three as the minutes pass. I decide to ring the UN for an update only to be told Mostar is being heavily shelled and is still under siege. I'm lighting my one hundred and first cigarette which I don't really want. I think of my dogs back home. I visualise the faces of my children.

1 a.m. Tariq's having a cold shower. Angus is alone on the balcony looking at the stars. George is lying on the couch listening to Mozart on the radio. I finalise my preparations. Empty my pockets, hide money in my sock, tape up my ring and

finally remove my watch. I write out my home address and
leave it with my personal possessions. I carefully put on my
boots – it is a time for seclusion, raking up every ounce of
human effort and every tiny element of spiritual support. We
all know that what we are about to enter is insanely dangerous
– anarchy at its worst and possibly death for one or all of us.
God please go with us.'

'If there is any kindness I can show, or any good thing I can do
to my fellow being, let me do it now, and not deter or neglect it,
as I shall not pass this way again,' said William Penn. I
remembered his words as the politicians returned from the
USA after implementing peace in the Balkans in Ohio at the
end of 1995. Bosnia had been decimated, but most roads were
now passable and the airports were open to commercial flights
bringing in aid. Our convoys were therefore redundant and
many of the aid workers and non-governmental organisations
withdrew – Rwanda had superseded Bosnia as flavour of the
month! Yet there were thousands of Bosnian children lan-
guishing in refugee camps, displaced and homeless. Their
homes and schools had been destroyed. Their teachers had
fled abroad or been killed. They had endured the harshest of
difficulties in order to survive. For many Bosnians, whose way
of life had been irretrievably destroyed, there was nevertheless
a deep drive towards seeking help for their children. 'Give
them an education,' they pleaded with me. 'Take them to
England. Keep them safe, so that when the war is finally over,
they can come back and help in the reconstruction of our
country.' I returned to England and set about locating schools
willing to offer a tuition-free place to a Bosnian child.
    In the spring of 1992, there had been 30,000 Bosnian
students attending university in the country. By autumn
1994, the Bosnian Student Project USA were able to locate

only about 1,000 who were still alive and studying. Most of the children of elementary or secondary school age had missed at least three years of education. The next step for Project Spark was the decision that we should sponsor bright English-speaking Bosnian sixth form students to attend schools in the UK. Ardingly College and Christ's Hospital in Sussex were the first to offer boarding places and others followed. Host families had to be found for those attending day schools such as Skinners in Tunbridge Wells and Tewkesbury Comprehensive. Funds needed to be raised for fares from Bosnia, clothing, pocket money, food and books. I decided that the best way to raise the money was through speaking tours in the USA, Australia, New Zealand and South Africa, and once again it was the schools and the children of those countries who raised most of the money.

In the summer of 1996, after six months of endless bureaucratic paperwork, my first four Bosnian children arrived at Heathrow Airport on educational visas. My speaking tours had provoked further offers of school places in English-speaking countries and two more children had gone to New Zealand, a further two to Australia and four to the USA. The first four completed their 'A' level courses in the UK in brilliant style and are now back home attending Sarajevo University. Danjela, who attended Tewkesbury Comprehensive, is the first Bosnian to be awarded the Duke of Edinburgh Award Scheme gold medal. In the summer of 1998, Andela left her boarding school in Connecticut with honours, having won a full scholarship to an Ivy League University to study Astrophysics.

The year's highlight for me was preparing for the Christmas festivities, which are not normally celebrated in Bosnia. Carols, Christmas stockings, cards, presents, stuffed turkey and Christmas pudding flambé were all novelties, but the children came into their own when they celebrated the New Year Bosnian style, eating, drinking and dancing into the small hours. I crawled into bed with the firm belief that I was back in Sarajevo. It all seemed a lifetime away from that day in 1992, when I had watched the television news of a small country at war somewhere in South Eastern Europe.

But what had happened to me during the war itself? I have seen too much and I have judged. No one has the right to create such a mortal obscenity. I have seen death on two skeletal legs, bones protruding through transparent skin like the barbed wire behind which he stands, eyes like sunken black raisins peering from a hollow cavernous face, staring indifferently without understanding. The exile of these people is without remedy, since they have been deprived of their families, their homes and their dignity. They have been dehumanised. This is a modern war and these are modern atrocities taking place today in Kosovo.

I have seen so much that I am scarred for life. I find I cannot talk about it, for I believe that no one would understand: as I cannot understand what it is like to walk on the moon. How can one person understand what another has seen, experienced, and suffered in a war of anarchy in which daily atrocities have been practised? Sleep, food, freedom to move, the security of a home – all that is normal to most of society – my Bosnian children were dispossessed and divested of these things. They, like me, do not talk about it. The pain is too great.

As a member of the human race, I feel that it is my responsibility to scrutinise and challenge first myself and then society. The 'contradictions' within me have too frequently been labelled as rebellion – but this is a devaluation of my spirit, which struggles to seek the Truth and then to preserve it. It is an unceasing struggle, an unceasing confrontation through which I try to maintain hope.

Albert Camus wrote: 'The two qualities in man worth

cultivating are intelligence and courage . . .' The first enables one to recognise one's own precariousness and the second prevents one from being abashed by it.

My own sense of vulnerability and precariousness leaves me unable to express my experiences of war, so I have written about them through the eyes of a child called Fran.

This is Fran's War.

Fran's War

CHAPTER ONE

My name is Fran and I was born in a small village twenty-five
miles from the city. I believe that I am fifteen years old. I am as
uncertain of my age as I am of the year. There is no time in war.
Sometimes there is light, but the black smoke from the shelling
creates its own darkness. I can only be sure that it is night time
when I see the stars but when they are visible, there is too often
a moon. The moon is my enemy for my shadow in the
moonlight can be picked out by snipers as I dart across the
rubble, avoiding both soldiers and UN peace-keeping troops.
There used to be a group of us but the others are dead now. My
dearest friend, Assad, was shot some time ago. I remember
taking his watch and his holy beads. I sold the watch for food.
Dog wears the holy beads as a collar. My English friend is
convinced that that is why dog is still alive and was never
eaten. But I know that the reason my four-legged friend is still
alive, is because Mamma called me after Francis, the Saint,
who loved animals – she had hoped that I would be the male
heir. It was I who found dog.

Our life had been peaceful. My earliest memory is of Mamma
kneading dough, her thick podgy fingers on the wooden table
in the kitchen, brushing her hands on the side of her bulbous
hips leaving prints of white flour on her apron as she kissed me
goodbye when I trotted off to school. Dadda was lean with

broad shoulders and hands the size of his feet. He was always outside with his tools tinkering with the car before driving to work – oiling, polishing, loving his car. Every Sunday, Dadda drove us into the city to go to Mass. Mamma said we were going to see Jesus but Dadda always went to see Mladin in the bar. I hated church because I never did see Jesus and the priest always called us sinners and would make the sign of the cross speaking in some foreign tongue. Mamma said it was Latin and that one day I would learn it at school.

'Do all sinners have to learn Latin?' I had asked. Mamma smiled and rubbed my cheek with the back of her scaly hand.

'No, my angel. Latin used to be the international language for priests across the world in the Roman Catholic Church.'

'Does Jesus speak Latin?'

'Jesus was a Jew and spoke Aramaic – Good morning, Mrs Minic,' Mamma embraced the old lady in black. So Jesus, who I came to see every week, but never met, was not a sinner like me but a Jew who did not have to learn Latin. I was baffled by this and after Mass, when Dadda came across to pick us up, his breath smelling of stale seaweed, I continued.

'Mamma, why didn't Jesus learn Latin? I have to.' I saw Dadda raise his eyebrows as he lifted me high in the air and swung me round on to his shoulder.

'Fran,' Mamma said, 'Jesus is the Son of God and God speaks all languages to all people.'

'Does he speak our language?' I meant of course the sinners' language.

'Yes, Fran, he even speaks our language. Now, Dadda's taking us to the Pizza House for lunch and if you're good you can have a Coke.'

Those were good days. In the winter, the timber house flaunted its charms. It protected us from the fevered winds that brought the snow every year, crowning the hills, like icing on the Christmas cake. The smell of spices, peppers and onions pervaded the kitchen, overriding the gentle scent of the weeping pine logs glowing and hissing on the open fire. Around all that warmth and solidarity, the adults clustered together like jewels, talking, laughing, reminiscing over glasses of slivovitz and thick black coffee served in small doll-cups, while the children vanished into the television room. As dusk descended, the Nannas gathered the tiny ones into their arms, small brown legs punching the air, rocking them to sleep, muffling them in their long black skirts of widowhood. Mamma, surrounded by friends and neighbours, would play folk tunes on the piano whilst the men lowered their voices and played cards: the evening flowing as freely as the slivovitz.

The summer was magic. Assad lived next door. We would rise before light and leap the rocks, playing tag beside the swift-running river until we reached the gorge overlooking our village. Here, the hazy dawn turned silver over the rapids, when the watery sun burst upon the spray and the air tingled. Later, we would bike up the snaking road to the spring on the other side of the mountain where, gasping, we would breathe the purest air and lie weakly amongst the wild flowers and sweetbriar. Once revived, we would cast off our clothes and stand, unyielding, under the freezing water counting the goose-pimples that now covered our small statuette bodies, seasoned by the sun. Sometimes I would be allowed to join the older children down by the ancient bridge where the birds nested in the invisible cracks opened by time. The older boys prided themselves on their youthful ability to stand on the balustrade before leaping into the river below, with their knees pulled tightly under their chins. I promised myself that one day I would be big enough and brave enough to do that. When the geese began to mass above the plum orchards, Dadda would spend the evenings chopping wood and I would become silent and downcast, realising that the carefree days of summer were over. It was back to school and waking in the mornings to the game of pulling my clothes on fast enough to beat the hangover of the night's eternal cold.

It was on St Nicholas's Day that I first met god. It was the day that Dadda gave me my first pair of skis. We drove through a milky mist to the slopes where Dadda clipped them on.

'Okay, Fran, we're going up there,' Dadda said, pointing to a tow rope. He held me between his legs, his skis outside, parallel to mine. He gripped the moving tow rope and we glided to the top of the hill.

'Right, Fran, put your skis together, bend your knees and push off, like this,' he demonstrated and was down the hill before I had had time to pull my bobble hat firmly over my forehead. I pushed with my sticks and began to slide through the snow faster than I cared. I sat down on the back of my skis but instead of stopping, the skis carried me on down to the adult ski-lifts. Dadda and his friends were queuing there and laughed at my ignoble efforts. As he brushed the snow off me Dadda said, 'You just keep practising on that tow rope and by the time I come down, you'll have it sussed. It's all about balance and changing your weight. Remember to keep your knees bent.' I felt my bottom lip quiver and held back the tears. He was going to leave me! Suppose I fell? Suppose I hurt myself? But Dadda had disappeared up the chair-lift by the time the first tear fell. I never wanted to ski anyway, I muttered miserably to myself as my left foot skewed out from under me and I found myself horizontal in the snow. My quiet tears were uncontrollable when I discovered that I had not the strength to pull myself up. Someone was approaching and through my blurred vision I studied him. He was gigantic, his movements languid but resolute. There was no timidity, nor uncertainty. His young face was ruddy beneath the downturned horseshoe moustache that tangled into a dishevelled beard. Without hesitation, without words he lifted me onto my skis and I was deeply moved that he was aware of my distress but I hesitated in confusion. Not wanting to draw his attention to my tear-besmirched face, I averted my eyes and it was only then that I saw the small red, white and blue emblem sewn onto the sleeve of his blue shetland sweater. When the winter Olympics had been held in our country, we had learnt the flags of the nations in school. I knew that the red, white and blue one was called a Union Jack. So this was a foreigner. Perhaps a Jew like Jesus, but certainly not a sinner like me. I stared into his blue eyes, round as water-melons and saw the tenderness and pain of a wounded bear.

'Don't be afraid – after all, you haven't got as far to fall as I have.' I looked at him in complete disbelief. He registered the surprise on my face and laughed. 'Have I said something wrong?' All I could remember was Mamma's words, 'Yes, Fran, He even speaks our language.' Indeed, Mamma had said that God speaks all languages to all people. So this was He. If I had not been on skis I would have curtsied. As it was I stood in dumb astonishment.

He looked over his shoulder. 'You're not here alone, are you?' he asked gently. I nodded my head wondering whether I should bow. 'Are you with your parents?' Again he was looking round. Again I nodded. He crouched down, his hairy face level with mine.

'Are you okay?' I wanted to reassure him but my heart was pounding so fast that if I spoke, the words would have exploded into an inexpressible disconnected noise. I quivered under the powerful current of my own anticipation, for I knew my life was being interrupted by a force nobody else was perceiving. Words failed me. He put up his gloved hand and pulled at my nose.

'You're all right, aren't you?' he repeated. So this was the

Father of Jesus, the Jew. I bowed stiffly and clumsily, lost my balance and fell face downwards into the snow, my heart now beating where it should not have been.

'Hey, you seem to spend more time under the snow than on it.' He was lifting me up. I felt confused and ashamed. 'What's your name?'

'Fran,' I replied humbly, blinking in incredulity. No words could ever express the importance of this moment.

'Well, Fran, will you share some chocolate with me?' It was a moment in which the smallest and most ordinary thing – a chocolate bar – became a majestic vision, filling the moment with hushed wonderment. He stood upright, towering over me and chewing the chocolate. I felt hugely rich. No eternal abundance could have provoked such intense pleasure. An endless paradise of happiness opened before me.

'Thank you, God.' At least I had remembered my manners. I bit my lip. His liquid blue eyes were as deep as the inkwell on my school desk.

'What a strange little girl you are,' he chided good-humouredly. 'You okay now?'

'Yes,' I sighed, 'thank you for the chocolate.'

'You're welcome. Perhaps see you around. Take care.' With a quick push of his ski sticks, he glided towards the adult ski-lifts, his gigantic body gracefully co-ordinated. Five years would pass before we were to meet again.

Dadda collected me and we drove home. 'You're very quiet,' he remarked. 'Did you enjoy the day?' Could I speak of all that had taken place that afternoon? Could I explain and express my extraordinary encounter? Could I describe the swirling current that had touched a sphere within my child-world? Something I had never experienced before. Could I trust Dadda not to laugh at me? I loved Dadda with all my heart. I had never kept secrets from him before.

'I met God today,' I blurted out.

'You did?' he sounded surprised. 'And who was that?'

'It was when you'd gone up the chair-lift.' Dadda changed gear as we sped around the bend approaching our village. He was silent. I was silent.

'Did he speak to you?'

'Oh, yes, and he gave me some chocolate.' More silence.

'Fran, what makes you think it was God?'

'He was a foreigner and he spoke our language.' Dadda slowed the car and parked it in the siding beside the pine wood. He released his seat belt, leant towards me and placed the lightest kiss on my forehead.

'Young lady, I'm quite lost. What are you talking about?' Now the words tumbled out in my excitement. I explained that I was a sinner. Like Jesus was a Jew, and at Mass Mamma had informed me that God spoke our language – the sinners' language, despite being a foreigner. Dadda, wide-eyed, listened patiently. When I had revealed all, he pursed his lips and remarked 'Jesus, preserve us from religion – it will be our downfall, surely!' He patted my head, put on his seat belt and turned on the ignition. As we reached the house, he smiled at me. 'Better get upstairs into the bath, it's past your bedtime. I'll send your Mamma up, she's got quite a lot of explaining to do.'

'Is Mamma in trouble?' I asked anxiously.

'No, Fran,' he grinned, 'she's not in trouble. It's just a misunderstanding, but best to be sorted out and sooner rather than later. Go on with you – upstairs now – I'll deal with your skis.' So it was that I eventually learned the truth about the Father of Jesus and about our human frailty that created sinners. Mamma often spoke about the power of forgiveness, which seemed pretty incomprehensible to me at the time. As the years passed I listened to my parents in their wisdom, I listened to my teachers with their knowledge and I listened to the priest berating his parishioners, petitioning us to pray harder. The plundering and turmoil of our land were not far away.

CHAPTER TWO

As the years passed, I dwelt in the shelter of my childish innocence, shielded by the deep abiding love of my parents.

One afternoon Assad and I took a short cut home from school along the dirt path, now covered with nettles and cowslips. It led us in a curve round the top of the hill from where we could look back on our village. Sprawled out at the base of the valley lay our small community divided by the river. Wisps of blue smoke rising from the chimneys curled upwards and lost their way in the evening mist. Assad was stationary, gazing into the middle distance, his hands dug deep into the pockets of his shorts. Almost abstractedly he asked, 'Fran, have you noticed anything?'

'What's anything?' I flopped onto the grass in abandonment. I had no wish to be serious. After all, the school holidays began next week.

'Well, little things,' he kicked at a stone.

'No. What little things?'

'It's hard to explain.' He took a deep breath. 'But something's going on and . . .' his voice trailed off. I closed my eyes and wondered whether I wanted to be a part of Assad's mystery. I heard an automobile struggling in low gear on the main road. 'Go on,' I encouraged.

'Well, it's hard to pinpoint it. My parents are behaving

oddly.' I visualised my Mamma and Dadda in the kitchen right now. Dadda would be reading the paper and chewing garlic whilst Mamma would be preparing supper. 'Come on, I think we should be going,' Mamma always wanted me home directly from school.

'So you haven't noticed anything?'

'What's there to notice? Come on, race you to the old barn.' It was that same evening, alerted by Assad's reflections, that I, too, noticed that my parents were acting out of character. Always after supper, they would come into the television room to watch the news, while I finished my homework there. I glanced at my watch and realised the news was over. Mamma shouted from the kitchen, 'Fran, it's time for bed.' I closed my books and placed them in my satchel ready for the morning and went and stood in the doorway of the kitchen. 'You didn't watch the news tonight?' Mamma gave my father a furtive look. She looked strangely nervous.

'We'll watch it later. Now off you go. Don't forget to clean your teeth.'

'But you always watch the early evening news.'

'You heard your mother. Go to bed, Fran.' Dadda said it so brusquely that I was taken aback.

I could not sleep; a peculiar foreboding hung over me as I lay in my pitch-black room. My parents rarely argued and never with raised voices, but I could hear raised voices from the kitchen. I knew they were talking about me. It couldn't have been about my school report as I had been placed in the top three in every subject and Dadda had told me that Mamma had given birth to a genius. I strained my ears to hear and was about to tiptoe to my closed door, when I heard them retire to the television room. I turned over and fell asleep.

The following weekend we drove to the city, as we did every Saturday to visit the market, where we would buy provisions for the week. Dadda always bought the meat from Idris, who owned a butcher's shop in the cobbled street overlooking the river. Mamma and I would scour the stalls for vegetables and fruit, though we grew much of it in our own garden. When the shopping was finished we always went to Maria's pâtisserie where my parents would drink coffee and I would choose an ice cream. But not this morning. We headed back to the car with me complaining, 'But we always go to the pâtisserie.'

'Well, we're not going today, Fran,' Mamma replied firmly.

'But why not? Have I done something wrong?' Mamma stopped suddenly, put down her basket and swooped me up into her arms.

'No, darling, of course you haven't done anything wrong.' There were tears in her eyes as she clasped me with such fervour. 'It's just that now you're older and growing up so fast, you don't need childish treats.' I wanted to point out that adults ate ice cream and that there was nothing childish about it but Dadda arrived. He was not carrying meat but two large petrol cans. Wordlessly, he put them in the boot of the car.

'Idris is coming over tomorrow. He'll bring the beef then,' he said eventually. 'The others will be coming too.' Mamma nodded in understanding.

'Who's coming tomorrow – are we having a party?'

Dadda paused before replying and then said casually, 'Actually, Fran, Mamma and I thought you would like to go on a picnic tomorrow with Assad and all the children from the village.'

'All of them?' This was unprecedented. We saw each other every day in school and nobody had mentioned a picnic. I was baffled.

'Yes. Mrs Ahmed thought it would be a fun outing for the end of term.'

Mrs Ahmed, my class teacher, never thought anything

would be fun and we had never before been given an end-of-term outing. None of it rang true.

'Why aren't we having it next Friday then? Why is it being held this Sunday?'

'Mrs Ahmed didn't want to take you out during lesson time.' That rang true. 'Anyway, you're all to meet at the bridge at eleven thirty.'

'But Mamma and I go to Mass then.'

'Well, tomorrow you can miss Mass,' Mamma said quickly. It was then I knew that Assad was right. The adults were behaving most suspiciously. Never had I been allowed to miss Mass on Sunday.

'Dadda, will you take Mamma to church?' I climbed into the back of the car.

'Not tomorrow.' Our eyes met in the driving mirror.

'So you won't be meeting Mladin in the bar?' Dadda threw his arm over the back of his seat and twisted round to face me. His handsome features seemed distorted. He looked haunted. My mother placed a calming hand on his knee and hissed between clenched teeth 'Dadda.' He turned back and stared through the windscreen. For a single instant I felt his fear.

'You'd better watch that tongue of yours,' Dadda snapped. 'Things are going to change around here and you're going to have to start growing up.'

I could not restrain myself from quipping: 'I thought I had grown up and that's why I wasn't getting an ice cream.' I saw his neck muscles tense as anger welled up.

'For goodness sake, you two. You're like a couple of sparring bullocks. Now let's go home and Fran and I will bake a carrot cake for tea.' Mamma was always conciliating and always forgiving, whereas there was a dark side to my father which I had never encountered personally. But I had witnessed it one evening when he had returned from the local bar and found the

Muscavic boys in our yard engraving their initials on his car. On that occasion Dadda had not only sworn in front of Mamma and me but had boxed the ears of both boys and marched them home, reminding them that the first duty of a Muslim was unquestioning obedience and submission to Allah who certainly would not want them carving their initials on Dadda's car. They should be grateful that Dadda was not Allah as Allah would show them no mercy. I liked the Muscavic boys and felt very sorry for them that evening.

The following day all the children from the village met at the bridge at eleven thirty. We picnicked beside the river and then started to walk up the neck of the gorge to the pine forest. By late afternoon the sun would have passed behind the towering granite rocks on either side leaving the gorge in deep shadow. The children were scattered along the rugged path chatting softly to each other, flanked by Mrs Ahmed and a few of the mothers who had joined us. As we reached the pine trees, Assad sidled up to me and gestured to me to sit down. We had not yet spoken because he had been playing football with the older boys.

'Fran, do you know what nationalism means?' Assad asked. His deep brown eyes were serious. It seemed a long word.

'No.' I was searching in my rucksack for a drink. 'What does it mean?'

'I don't know.' Assad paused. 'But it rhymes with fascism.' Since I did not understand either word, I was not very interested in the conversation. 'Do you want some lime juice?' I offered. Assad ignored the lime juice and seemed to be getting impatient.

'Fran, I overheard my parents talking last night. The reason this picnic was organised was to get all of the children out of the village so that the parents could have a meeting.' I peeled an orange and handed him a segment.

'Why should they want to get rid of us?'

'So they can decide what to do.'

'What to do about what?' It was my turn to feel impatient. Assad was picking a scab from his knee. 'Well, go on, tell me,' I demanded.

'There's going to be a war.' I felt his excitement.

'Don't be so stupid, Assad.'

'There is, and that's why they're all meeting. To discuss how they're going to defend the village.'

'I don't believe you.' I was closing my knapsack. Assad put out his hand. 'OK, follow me and I'll show you something.' He jumped to his feet and pulled me up. I checked where Mrs Ahmed and the mothers were. Still half-way down the gorge. Assad led me into the pine forest. It was dark, with slivers of daylight piercing the coarse branches which obscured the mountains.

'Look,' he pointed triumphantly.

All I could see was a freshly dug hole, large enough for four people to sit inside it. The sides were secured with wooden slats. I felt Assad's eyes watching me. I looked at him steadily. 'This doesn't prove anything.'

Grabbing me by the waist, Assad pulled me after him. We stumbled through the forest until we came across another hole and then another. 'They're fox-holes for soldiers – I'm telling you there's going to be a war.'

In school we had been taught about the last world war and about our own troubled history. We were informed that our country was a mosaic of peoples and religions. We knew that under the Communist system, religious teaching was banned in all educational institutions, but it was self-evident that our community shared and joined in the special holidays and celebrations held by Muslims and Christians alike. We prided ourselves on being both multi-cultural and tolerant. As we ate and drank together in one another's houses, toiled on the land helping each other bring in the summer harvest, there was complete harmony in our small community. Mamma would share out the fruit from our orchard, whilst Assad's Muslim family, who owned the cows, gave us large jugs of fresh milk. Money never changed hands. All the children of course knew that the various religious faiths had been enemies during the Second World War, but that was the distant past. Former enemies, now reconciled, had become good friends and encouraged their children and grandchildren to be friends too. It was a good life as we reached out to one another, and nobody went without. I therefore reasoned that Assad's prophecy of war was beyond belief.

'Who's going to fight us?' I asked.

'Foreign soldiers that invade us.' Assad was prancing round me in his excitement, pointing an imaginary gun at my head.

'But what for?'

'According to my father, they want our land, but my mother reckons it's an excuse for ethnic cleansing.' I felt perplexed.

'What's ethnic cleansing?' I imagined it must be the name of a disinfectant. Assad was unprepared for my question. He stopped buzzing round me like a demented bee and thought carefully before replying.

'I think it is about the majority extinguishing the minority.' I knew that Assad was very clever because he was two classes ahead of me, but he was showing off his intellectual superiority at my expense.

'So who's the majority? And are the minority the enemy?'

'No. In this case, it's the majority who are the enemy.' I was confused.

'That doesn't make sense! Why should the majority want to be the enemy?'

'Fran, you're being thick . . . Each side thinks the others are
the enemy. Put it this way: the minority will be the victims.'
  'So who are the victims?'
  'You or me, Fran, perhaps both of us.'

That was the day our lives changed. After the secret meeting
between the parents our sleepy little village became a hive of
frantic industry. Dadda was out every evening at meetings in
the city, meetings in the village hall, meetings in the bar. Mr
Sahovic, who was a carpenter and the father of Ben, would be
seen from dawn to dusk reinforcing the doors on all the houses
and adding shutters to any windows that did not already have
them. The older boys were taught to dig trenches in the
paddocks from north to south and from east to west. Assad
and his father busied themselves building a cowshed up in the
pine forest. They believed that if they moved the farm animals
up the mountain and concealed them in the forest, the soldiers
might not find them. Convoys of trucks arrived in our square
and deposited thousands of sandbags for us to pack around our
homes as protection against bombs. I observed all this quite
calmly for I did not associate the extra activity with the
possibility of war. And my parents took every precaution in
order to keep my home and school routine undisturbed. In fact,
the only unusual event in terms of my routine was the weekly
gathering in the square when we all learnt to familiarise
ourselves with every kind of gun. We learnt how to dismantle
them, how to put them together, how to clean them and of
course how to fire them. By the end of the year we were all
crack shots, from the smallest child upwards.
  The summer holidays passed and it was only when we
returned to school for the new academic year that I was struck
with a fear I had never previously experienced. The fear of
losing my family, my friends, my own special way of life – for

our school was half empty. The boys of fifteen and above had all been called up. Until now there had been one year's compulsory conscription after school, followed by regular periods in the reserve forces up to the age of twenty-seven. But teenage children were now being press-ganged into the military. All our male teachers were missing and Ben Sahovic, who belonged to one of the four other Catholic families in our village, told us that he had heard that the teachers had fled the country to avoid conscription. Although it seemed cowardly, I reasoned that the teachers had experienced a year of military life already and were aware of the hardships.

As autumn unfolded, I heard the cries of the wild geese flying away to warmer waters. As they scaled the gorge, I would see them drop like rag dolls: trophies for the hunters. Dadda had been out killing wild boar throughout the summer and joints of salted bacon now hung from the beams of our cellar. Food had become an obsession in the village. Tons of vegetables were pickled in vinegar and spices, and placed in large jars. They lined every basement like rows of soldiers standing to attention. Mamma now spent her days bottling and preserving. Huge pans of fruit bubbled day and night on the Aga. As autumn turned to winter, the markets everywhere became wastelands emptied of people and food. There was now petrol rationing, so we rarely visited the city and only when Dadda's butcher friend, Idris, visited us did we have meat in the evening. Dadda explained that all the food and petrol had to be given to the army.

Although I could not understand why there was no longer enough for everybody, the worsening conditions barely affected us children. We continued our schooling, played hop-scotch in the square and listened to the hushed whisperings of our parents, who clustered endlessly together to talk about war. For us, war was another country, another world, another planet. Every night families would hug their log fires and watch the news on television. No longer was there laughter; instead, a pervading gloom sank its teeth into our small community. Mamma was now making beeswax candles and knitting socks for 'our boys' on the front line. Dadda spent hours chopping wood and would only deign to consider coming in for the evening meal after dark, when he could no longer see. He reeked of sweat and breathed heavily after his exertions, sweating around the lips. But the only lasting evidence of his worries – apart from the chain-smoking of course, was a constantly hunched appearance and the dark rings under his eyes.

One evening as we sat silently around the kitchen table eating cabbage soup, there was a knock at our front door. This in itself was unusual as we all walked into each other's houses quite freely. Dadda gestured us to remain seated. He picked up the gun resting beside the sideboard, and went out into the hall. Mamma and I could hear voices, but could make no sense of the words until we heard Dadda swearing. Mamma gripped my hand with both of hers and pressed it. Dadda was pleading with whomever it was on our doorstep. Finally, we heard the door slam and Dadda came back into the kitchen cigarette in hand. His eyes were on fire. Mamma instinctively ran towards him and he threw her back into her chair, but not aggressively. He waved a photocopied sheet of paper in the air. 'The bastards have requisitioned my car. They want it for some bloody army officer. They're actually taking my car.' He flung himself into his chair and threw the gun across the kitchen.

'Are they paying us for it?' Mamma was always practical.

'Not a bloody cent.' Dadda sounded savage.

'Can they do that?'

'For the good of the Nation, they can do what they bloody well like. I don't believe it! There's no bloody war here and yet we have military occupation.' He put his head in his hands. 'I tell you, Mamma, this is only the beginning.'

That was the night I awoke to the powerful drone of tanks advancing along the main mountain road. The following morning I expected to see a complete army encamped in our village, but there was nothing. I dressed for school and went downstairs. Dadda, looking dishevelled, was listening to the radio.

'Fran, all the schools have been closed. From next Monday, we'll take it in turns round the houses to give you children two-hour tutorials. Mrs Ahmed is organising a schedule.' War had its advantages! Only two hours of school each day! I put on my outdoor boots, suppressing my excitement.

'Why are you wearing your boots?' Dadda asked.

'I'm going to see Assad.'

'No, no, Fran, I'm afraid you can't go out.'

'Why not?' I gasped.

'It's not safe. Did you not hear the tanks last night?'

'I'm only going next door, Dadda,' I explained.

'Fran, read my lips. *You are not going out today.* That's final.' This was the first time my freedom had been restrained. The claws of deprivation hung ominous.

'Bloody war!' I only meant to mouth it but the words were audible.

'What did you say, young lady?' Dadda turned off the radio.

'I said "bloody war". Like you said it last night,' I added. Dadda appeared bemused. Mamma came in holding a loaf of bread and smiled meekly. I noticed her hands, sinewy and with the veins prominent. She had lost weight.

'Fran,' Mamma crinkled her forehead, 'There is a right and a wrong in life and swearing doesn't make any difference to either. So best to forget those swear words. Now, this morning Dadda is going to start the conversion of the cellar and you and

I are going down to the village hall to help Ben's mother make bandages for the field hospitals.' I was disappointed.

'If we can walk to the hall, why can't I go and see Assad?'

'Dadda will walk us to the hall and collect us at midday. Assad could well be there helping as well.' Mamma placed a clean tablecloth over the kitchen table. 'Or, if you prefer, you can help your father convert the cellar,' she offered.

'Convert the cellar into what?' I asked.

Dadda answered me. 'Into a snug hiding-hole that will protect us from the shelling, should it come.' His face was etched with worry. Why did he always assume the worst? He never used to be like that.

'I'll come with you, Mamma.' At least I might see Assad at the village hall.

But it was only the women who were there. Some had brought their sewing machines and were tearing bed sheets into strips with which to cover sanitary pads. Ben's mother, Mrs Sahovic, explained to me that these were very absorbent so would make excellent surgical dressings. How I wished I was at school, instead of rotting away in this hell-hole covering sanitary towels. I was beginning to hate this invisible war. It was changing all our lives. The day was not progressing well, but I was not prepared for what happened on the walk home. Dadda collected us from the hall at midday and we were walking past our friend Mr Ahmed's house when Mr Ahmed appeared on the front porch. 'Hello there, my good friend.' He grinned, addressing Dadda. 'Come in and have a coffee.' Mamma began to walk over to him but came to a sudden halt when she heard Dadda's reply.

'Sorry, not today. By the way, the army requisitioned my car last night. Did they take yours?' The answer was obvious since we could all see Mr Ahmed's car in his yard.

'No, but I heard they had taken yours and the car belonging

to the Sahovic family. Please, we've just made fresh coffee, do come in.' The invitation was genuinely friendly and in no way out of the ordinary. My father looked up from the ground and I noticed the veins in his neck bulging. I glanced at Mamma who was now climbing the steps up to Mr Ahmed's verandah. 'Mamma, that's far enough.' His voice was steely. 'We will not be drinking coffee with Ahmed today.' Mr Ahmed, Mamma and I stared at one another in embarrassment.

'I'm sorry you feel like that. Is there a problem?' Mr Ahmed seemed more astonished than hurt by Dadda's rudeness.

'Since you ask, yes there is. Have you asked yourself why the army has only requisitioned cars belonging to Catholic families?' Mamma gave a cry and rushed to her husband. Mr Ahmed stood perfectly still wringing his hands.

'I'm sorry you have interpreted it like that. We just assumed that they had taken the reliable new cars. After all our car is over ten years old.' Mamma was trying to pull Dadda away, but he wouldn't be pulled.

'Come, come, Ahmed, my so-called friend! Not a single Muslim car had been requisitioned. Can you give me an explanation for that?'

Mr Ahmed was distressed.

'I'm afraid I cannot. I'm sure you're seeing too much in this.' In almost the same pleading tone he continued, 'I was under the impression that you yourself were not in fact a Catholic although your wife is. That surely proves that your car cannot have been taken for the reason you think.' But Dadda was not to be moved and I could see that Mr Ahmed was now beginning to get angry. Mamma was standing between the two men.

'Dadda, let us go home. Do you want to set neighbour against neighbour?' My father brushed her aside and replied heatedly.

41

'You're right, Ahmed, I'm not a Catholic. I don't feel that I have to hide behind a religion or to mix myself up in either its politics or its intrigues. Whereas you Muslims . . .' There was an anguished scream from Mamma, as tears of reproach flooded down her face. I did not blink. I was fascinated by the ugliness of the moment. Dadda was now extracting pleasure from Mr Ahmed's horror.

Suddenly and swiftly, Mr Ahmed left his verandah and closed his front door behind him. I walked behind my weeping mother, now leaning heavily upon her husband's arm.

War had come to our village without a single shot being fired.

CHAPTER THREE

Mamma was so distraught that she went straight to her room. Dadda slammed around the kitchen making coffee. I sat watching him miserably. Dadda lit a cigarette and patted me on the shoulder. I did not really understand but I knew Mr Ahmed had been accused unjustly and that my own family was now divided. Dadda sat opposite me drawing on his second cigarette. He spoke calmly, but sternly.

'Fran, war changes people – it changes attitudes and, consequently, actions.'

'Mr Ahmed was only being friendly.' I felt that I was sitting in the dark, sitting with someone I loved, but with no contact between us. 'Mamma's very upset.'

'Your Mamma's naïve. She always sees the best in everyone.' Dadda flicked his ash.

'But Mr Ahmed has done nothing to harm us. You keep talking about war, but there is no war here, so why were you so cruel to Mr Ahmed?'

Dadda inhaled before stubbing out his half-finished cigarette. 'Fran, you're too young to understand all the implications. It's very complicated.'

I considered whether or not I should tell him that I understood about ethnic cleansing, but decided he was not in the mood and I had better stay silent. Yet, deep inside me, I knew that when others suffered, when human dignity was threatened or violated, a sense of our common humanity would always compel me to stand up for the truth. I knew that my father's behaviour was wrong. My mother knew it too. But we loved and respected him and by that very fact, a solidarity was created between us. We were able to dismiss Dadda's behaviour as a mini-state of war panic.

After that episode, Dadda would only allow me to continue my schooling with children from the other Catholic families in the village and even that he only permitted because Mamma pressurised him. If Dadda could have had his way, I would never have left the house at all! Whether it was genuine fear of the real war some distance away, or because of his own personal war with the Muslims in the village, I was never to understand, but from that day I had lost my freedom. War became my enemy.

When I was not being tutored in the mornings with other Catholic children, I would help Dadda in the cellar. We shifted hundreds of sandbags, putting one on top of another round the walls. Dadda built a false wooden floor raised on bricks above the concrete. In the two-foot space beneath the wooden floor he placed Mamma's preserved food and the tins we had been collecting over the summer and a small battery radio covered in cellophane. Ammunition was taken out of cardboard boxes and placed in tins which were wrapped in plastic bags. Mamma's beeswax candles were similarly wrapped and placed under the floorboards.

I did not see Assad Sedlarevic at all and I fretted. We had grown up together, like brother and sister. Until Dadda's fight with Mr Ahmed a day had never gone by without one of us being in the next-door house. I decided to tackle the issue with Mamma, alone. The opportunity arose when Dadda departed for one of his meetings.

'Mamma, can I go next door and see Assad?' The direct approach was always best with Mamma. She looked up, her eyes showing great agony.

'You miss him, don't you?'

'You can't believe how much,' I replied dramatically. 'Please, Mamma, Dadda doesn't have to know.' Mamma uttered a deep sigh.

'Darling, these are difficult days for you, I know. Your father's only doing what he thinks is right.'

'Is he right, Mamma?' She appeared to be in the grip of great pain as she sought for words.

'Your Dadda is a good man, Fran. Whatever he does is for the best.'

'Do you think he's right, Mamma?' I persisted. I was tearing her apart. It seemed an eternity before she replied.

'He doesn't mean to hurt you, Fran. It's not what it seems. He loves you very much.' Once again Mamma had avoided the question. I was about to confront her but she spoke first.

'It's not all one-sided, my darling. Assad hasn't visited us either.' There was a brief pause and she remarked sadly, 'Neither has his mother.' Only then did I realise that Mamma and I were sharing the same pain. I rushed into her arms.

'Oh, Mamma, I'm sorry. What shall we do? I hate this war.' We stood in the middle of the kitchen consoling one another in our loneliness. How stupid I had been, how insensitive.

'Dear Fran, please don't put me between yourself and Dadda – the two people I love most in the world. Don't let the war do that to us. Life is hard enough without that.'

'Mamma, I'm so sorry; will you forgive me?' I wept.

'There is nothing to forgive. You were asking for the truth and that is to be admired. Now wipe your tears and wash your face and we'll go next door.' She took off her apron and glanced quickly in the mirror. 'They've probably missed us as much as we've missed them. Come on. All this pride and anger will achieve nothing. Well done, Fran, for bringing me to my senses.'

Mamma did not hesitate. We left our house and Mamma boldly opened our neighbour's front door. We walked into their hall and came face to face with Assad. He had been bending over his upturned bicycle mending a puncture.

'Fran!' Assad's brown eyes lit up when he saw me, but when he turned to Mamma he winced and looked awkward. Mamma intervened.

'It's all right, Assad. I'm aware of the problem. Where's your mother?' Assad pointed to the kitchen and Mamma walked toward the door. We followed. Assad's mother looked much younger than her years. She had black hair reaching to her shoulders. Her olive skin was as clear as her dark brown eyes. She was very beautiful but she could never be as beautiful as my Mamma. Mamma was beautiful inside. They fell into each other's arms weeping with joy. Assad tugged at my arm and nodded towards the kitchen door. We went back into the hall and closed the door behind us.

'Oh, Fran, I've been so miserable. I kept hoping we'd pass in the village on the way to lessons. Papa wouldn't let me come round. I'm sorry.' He looked down at his punctured tyre, obviously feeling ashamed.

'I know. Dadda only lets me out to go to lessons. I don't know what's the matter with everybody. They keep blaming the war.'

'After your Dadda's row with the Ahmeds, Papa ordered me not to see you. He said it would only make things worse.'

'Worse!' I shrieked, 'How can they be worse?' Assad put his arm over my shoulder.

'Fran, don't cry. We're friends. We'll always be friends,' his noble words fell on deaf ears. I choked in my despair.

46

'Promise me,' I grabbed the front of Assad's shirt, feeling that I was drowning in a sea of overwhelming desolation. 'You've got to promise me we'll always be friends whatever happens in this bloody war.'

Faced with my profound distress, Assad began to laugh. I was speechless and then said, 'There's nothing to laugh about.'

'Oh, Fran, I've never heard you swear before. Yes, I promise we'll always be friends. We don't have to be like our parents, you know.' Assad placed my hand in his and led me across the hall and into the family prayer room. 'You sit on that prayer mat,' he directed. I sat opposite him cross-legged. 'No, Fran, turn and face Mecca.'

'Where is he?' I was scouring the walls, not quite sure what to expect. A picture? A crucifix? A portrait?

'You don't know anything, do you? We Muslims pray to Allah five times a day but we have to face the holy city of Mecca in Saudi Arabia.'

'Do you carry a compass?'

'Don't be facetious,' he wagged his finger at me.

'I wasn't being fass . . . fass . . . whatever that means. But it doesn't matter. Why have you brought me here?' Assad was washing himself in a bowl of water which was on the floor. 'What on earth are you doing?' War seemed to have brought insanity as well as everything else.

'I'm purifying myself because I'm going to make an oath to Allah. You do know who Allah is?'

'Of course. He's your Jesus.' I replied confidently.

'No, Fran, Allah is our God.' Before I could stop myself I heard my own voice: 'I met God on the ski slopes when I was much younger and he gave me a bar of chocolate. Well, I thought he was God anyway.' I saw the confusion on Assad's face. 'Don't worry about it, Assad. I know who you mean by the real God.'

'Good. Well I'm going to promise Allah that I will always be your friend.'

'But shouldn't you do that on the Bible, like when they take an oath in court? I've seen it on the television.' Assad shook his head.

'No. We have the Koran instead. But if you want me to swear on the Bible . . .'

'No, it's OK. If you say it to Allah, I'll believe you, Assad. I'll believe you anyway without you having to promise Allah.' It all seemed a bit over the top to me. Assad's word was good enough for me, whether or not he made a special promise to Allah. Nevertheless, I sat dutifully on my prayer mat while Assad recited some mumbo-jumbo, before prostrating. In truth, I felt extremely honoured that Assad should be performing this ceremony to confirm our friendship and wondered if he expected me to do the same thing for the Roman Catholic God. I hoped most sincerely that he didn't. Good fortune saved me because our two mothers suddenly appeared, arm in arm. They were mildly surprised to find us sitting on prayer mats, admittedly no longer facing Mecca, as we were now making plans about how we were going to meet in the future without the parents knowing.

When we were back home, I asked Mamma whether she was going to tell Dadda about our visit. 'I have no wish to incur your father's wrath and I have no wish to lie to him. On this occasion, I believe that discretion – that is to say silence – is the better part of valour.' Mamma was a realist.

During the following weeks we were led to believe that the war was escalating. Partly because we could hear the movement of tanks driving across the mountains during the night, but also because the television told us so. It was never turned off, except when we were asleep, so that we wouldn't miss a single news bulletin. In the kitchen, the radio was also on permanently, bringing local news flashes. Newspapers did not reach our village any longer because of petrol rationing and the post had been axed for the same reason. Dadda was very upset when it was announced that our passports were now regarded as obsolete by the government. Mamma was quick to point out that we had not been intending to flee the country, so it was of little personal concern.

There had, of course, been lengthy discussions in the village hall as to whether or not the families should move to the city where there were undoubtedly greater defences and therefore greater protection; but families like my parents and their grandparents before them had always lived in the village. After the last war, they had all rebuilt their houses. Their farms, their culture, their memories, their emotional and financial well-being were all centred on the village. Nobody wanted to move. There was further discussion as to whether the women and children should leave; but the women raised hearty objections and went a long way towards swaying the vote by pointing out that our families had been together for decades, sharing and working the land, celebrating births and mourning deaths and it was only right and proper that men, women and children should stand together and defend their village should it be necessary. Like me, they could not accept the fact that war was on their doorstep, despite all the preparations for defence.

We had known nothing but harmony in this village for nearly fifty years. The idea of war was anathema. Despite television images of carnage, reports of genocide, rumours of ethnic cleansing and mass murder which reached us daily, we somehow seemed to be unable to confront the evil. We believed that in some way we would be protected. Dadda, perhaps, had assimilated the wider issues, hence his despair when our passports were declared obsolete. He certainly cheered up when the television showed United States officials entering our capital, but sank into deep depression again when it was announced the following day that Western Europe would not support military intervention in our country. According to the late news, European governments had agreed that they were not going to do anything beyond providing humanitarian relief. From that day onwards life deteriorated. In this war I learnt that things can always get worse.

We had now moved our mattresses and sleeping-bags into the cellar. Dadda had rigged up a camp stove for cooking and two gas rings running off butane gas. This invisible war dominated every hour of every day, but I was confident that we were well prepared if it should actually reach us.

It did reach us. The first major sign was when refugees started to pass through the village, like long lines of ants. Old men, old women and mothers with children. The fortunate ones had horse-drawn carts bulging with their few precious belongings. Others carried what they had hastily packed into bags and suitcases. The refugees came from villages north of our mountain. I remembered watching American cowboy films on television and seeing similar cavalcades of wagons heading west to discover new lands. Our people were fleeing south seeking safety and protection from life in our towns and cities. They talked of massacres, rape, the burning of their houses. I looked at Mamma in disbelief. As I listened to their wailing, it was beyond my comprehension that man could turn on man in such an evil way. We gave them bread and water and Mamma made more bread and even more bread, until Dadda not unsympathetically ordered her to stop. 'We can't feed them all and there will be no flour left for us.'

'But we have plenty. We can't let them keep journeying on without food and water,' she pleaded, tears pouring down her cheeks. Dadda pursed his lips and shrugged his shoulders. For the first time in my life I saw him cry. He seemed to be losing his control of life, sensing his impotence to help. Dadda sat and wept, whilst the tide of refugees surged past our door. Mamma no longer gave them bread. What surprised me was the refugees' acceptance that they had lost everything in life. They weren't angry, indignant or even annoyed. Upset, yes, but not the raging wrath that I felt within myself at such injustice. Mamma said they had seen too much to feel any longer: that suffering brought death to their hearts and that all this fighting and pain bred indifference and apathy. I wondered if I myself had previously been suffering from indifference and apathy. I had always been so detached and aloof. But then, I reasoned that my detachment and aloofness must have been bred from security and contentment as I, unlike the refugees, had never suffered. How strange that their suffering and my security could both result in apathy and indifference. On the first night that the refugees poured through, Dadda moved us into the cellar to sleep, whilst he rested in the hall with his gun. 'But why, Dadda, they won't hurt us,' I shouted.

'Fran, they're hungry, they're homeless. We still have what they've lost.'

'No, Dadda,' I was indignant. 'It's because they're Muslims, isn't it?'

I thought he was going to hit me and so he might have done if Mamma had not swept in front of me with a cup of coffee. 'That's very stupid, Fran,' she said. 'How do we know what religion they are? They don't carry dog-tags round their neck saying Catholic, Protestant, Orthodox or Muslim.'

I felt choked.

'They're our people. We are no different from them. We must help them,' I cried.

Dadda lit a cigarette. 'Mamma, you talk to her. After all you brought her up with this do-gooding Christian attitude.' He departed with his coffee and ashtray. I looked in horror at my

51

tortured mother. What was happening to our family? We never used to fight. How come religion was now such a problem when it had been just a small part of our life before? All the standards and values of previous years were crashing in splinters before my eyes. I blinked back angry tears of disillusionment and heard my small pitiful voice as from afar.

'Mamma, you've always helped everybody.' She put her hand through her grey hair, her pallid face contorted with anguish as she tried to control her emotions.

'Times have changed, Fran. We have changed. We're not in a position to help all these people. Your father's right. We have to look after ourselves now. That is the simple reality, Fran. That is the truth.' I felt myself being torn apart, pulled in different directions. Why should I surrender to this unbearable ugliness that had descended upon us, suffocating the sweetness of the past? Mamma seemed to have recovered.

'Come here, Fran. Come and sit on my knee.' She had not encouraged this for years, not since I had reached my seventh birthday. Now she enveloped me in her scrawny arms. 'Darling, war does terrible things. It causes anger and grief and terror. Its venom of bitterness bites into the very soul of man, to create this chaos and turmoil that you're feeling now. It has drowned all the sunlight of love and good but I promise it won't last for ever.'

'How long?'

'I don't know. It's like when you're ill, Fran. The doctor never knows how long the infection is going to last. Do you remember when you had that boil on your elbow? It grew and grew until it finally burst and then the pain was over.'

'But the doctor helped by giving me pills,' I pointed out. She stroked my head.

'Yes, he did,' she replied thoughtfully, 'and we have a doctor in Jesus and his pill is prayer.' Suddenly she clasped me so tightly, so passionately. 'Fran, whatever happens, you must promise you will never forget to pray to Jesus. Will you promise me that?' She pulled me away from her body and stared into my eyes. How strange, I thought. Only a few weeks ago, Assad and I were making promises to Allah, and now Mamma wants me to make a promise to pray to Jesus. In my fragility, I decided that the more promises I made the better.

'Mamma, I promise.' I reckoned that with both Allah and Jesus on my side I had less to worry about than most people, which cheered me up no end.

The next day the power station was shelled. The explosion vibrated through the mountains with a roar which brought all the villagers out of hiding in their cellars. I remembered once being on holiday on the coast in a fearful storm and hearing the sea crash against the rocks. The explosion had sounded just like that. We stood hypnotised, watching the billowing smoke creating its own monstrous black mountain that mushroomed into the sky. The women began to pray clutching their holy beads. Mamma made the sign of the cross and fell to her knees. Assad stood a few feet from me.

'Phew! It's like the atom bomb,' he whispered in awe. In school we had been taught that thousands had died in Japan. I began to cry.

'Why are you crying?' he asked.

'They might as well blow up the whole world for all I care,' I snivelled. Assad frowned.

'Really, Fran, you've got to toughen up or you won't survive the war.' I howled uncontrollably for now my only real friend seemed to be turning against me.

'I don't want to survive. I'd rather die than get caught up in this war,' I blurted out. Assad leapt in front of me and shook me by the shoulders.

'Don't you dare talk like that, Fran. You've got to survive to help me survive.' I stared at my dear, dear friend and felt deeply ashamed. Dadda was walking towards us.

'Sorry, Assad,' I muttered, 'I didn't mean it.' His eyes, like dark pools, softened as he gazed at me.

'It's all right Fran. I know you didn't mean it.' But Dadda had grasped my hand and was leading me firmly away from Assad.

From that moment we had no more electricity and moved full-time into the dark cellar. Now that she was unable to bake bread, Mamma spent much of her time praying. During the day, Dadda sat upstairs in the dark shuttered kitchen with his shot of home-made brew mixed into his tea and smoking his cigarettes. The coffee supplies had run out. Nobody spoke much. Now that we were no longer receiving information about the war through the media, there was a general lack of conversation. Twice a day Dadda produced the battery radio from under the floorboards and every night he disappeared into the village to pass on the latest news bulletins. Since the war had spread into our valley I noticed that Dadda was the first to take any risks. Now that the invisible war was manifesting itself, my father's self-imposed war against the Muslims was perhaps becoming as obsolete as our passports?

The city was being shelled. Although as the crow flies it was twenty-five miles away, we could nevertheless hear the shelling and in the shadowy twilight we could see the flickering lights of burning buildings reflected in the sky. On the second day after the shelling of the power station the water supply ran out. For me, this turned out to be a blessing in disguise, as we were now forced to trek down to the river for our ablutions. It was bitterly cold, but nevertheless preferable to remaining within the dark confines of the cellar, and would perhaps provide a chance to meet up with Assad and my friends. The men were working six-hour shifts as vigilantes, climbing the mountains with their guns to keep a lookout, whilst the women and children scrubbed the soiled clothes on the granite rocks.

The men had dug holes for toilets among the nearby trees and had made a large sewage pit into which families could empty their buckets. I came to hate those toilet holes. I would squat over one, my knickers round my ankles, shivering against the cold, praying that Assad would not appear and see me in my compromising situation. Often I found that I could not piss, the cold was too debilitating. I could always tell the temperature, according to whether or not the piss had frozen before it hit the hole. Sometimes I would spend so much time willing myself to piss that my legs would cramp up with cold and by the time I completed my task, I was unable to stand. I would have to rock forwards on to my knees and then struggle with my frozen knickers. It was like scraping ice up my bottom and then I would run and run and run till my body began to sting and warmth slithered like a glow-worm to the tips of my fingers and toes. But I hated having to piss outside.

Every morning, Mamma and I walked down to the river muffled in clothes piled upon clothes, those to be washed worn on the outside, so that our hands were free to carry the water containers and sewage buckets. If it had not been so cold, the visit to the river would have turned into a happy social occasion, with the women chattering and the children playing around them. As it was, communication was minimal. The women rhythmically scrubbed away in the freezing water, their hands purple with cold, whilst we children, holding our noses with numb fingers, would empty the sewage buckets and fill the water containers. On one such morning, Assad, Ben and myself were at the sewage pit when we heard frantic screaming from the women. It brought the men careering down the mountain and we dropped our buckets and raced to the river.

The women were bunched together, like sheep, clinging to

one another, the washing forgotten. They were pointing to the
river as the men appeared. At first I could see nothing but the
green, foaming waters. I heard Assad laugh in an almost carefree
way. But then he was feverishly twisting his fingers, his eyes
wide. 'Oh, no,' he cried out and he started to weep unrest-
rainedly. The shock of seeing Assad cry, for a moment diverted
my attention from the river. 'Don't look, Fran, don't look,' his
voice unfamiliar in its rising hysteria. That, of course, forced me
to turn my eyes towards the river and I saw them. Corpses, rising
and falling with the river currents, skimming along like racing
skiffs. We watched the bodies float by. Nobody ventured into
the freezing waters. There was not a living soul at that moment
who could have moved, even had they wanted to. Then the
river swallowed them up. The men stamped their feet, blew on
their fingers and silently returned to their lookout positions. Ben
put his arm around Assad and coaxed him towards the road
home. Without thinking, I wandered back to the sewage pit and
automatically gathered up all the stinking buckets. As I
squatted, stupefied, over the toilet hole later in the day, my
heart was as frozen as my piss. I was never able to cry like Assad.
After that, Mamma always boiled the water.

The cold was a terrible problem. However many clothes we
piled on during the day it made no difference. Dadda would
light the paraffin stove in the cellar for only one hour, so as to
conserve the fuel. We would sit shivering in our sleeping-bags
for hours, just waiting. When Mamma lit the camp stove, we
huddled close to it straining for heat, the steam from the pan of
tinned food bringing false hopes of warmth. Three times a day
Mamma brewed hot tea. Otherwise we had hot water spiked
with sugar and oats. Only when Mamma used the stove, did we
light a candle. Then we were forced back into the merciless
darkness to wait for the hours to tick by until we could fall into
a shallow, shivering sleep.

One morning Mr Ahmed came over shouting Dadda's name from outside the door. The house had been fortified and the shutters were kept permanently closed. Mr Ahmed knew that he would be unable to enter. Dadda edged up the cellar steps in the darkness and we could hear his footsteps crossing the airless rooms to the front door. It seemed like hours before he returned. Mr Ahmed's youngest son had apparently gone absent without leave from the front line and had turned up in the village the previous night, to tell his father that our lines were being pushed back and that enemy soldiers had set up barricades on all the mountain roads. Our village was cut off to the north and it would only be a few days until the invaders arrived. I couldn't see Dadda's face in the dark, but I smelt his fear. Dadda explained that some of the families had now decided to flee south to the city and were going to cross the mountain pass tonight by the old path. 'Is Assad going?' I asked.

'I don't know what they have decided,' he replied. I think Dadda must have been sitting on the bottom step for I heard him move over to Mamma and calmly ask: 'What do you want to do?' Voices magnify sound when one cannot see a face. I could hear them breathing in unison. Then Dadda's voice of authority. 'Mamma, I think you and Fran should go tonight. Idris is expecting you in the city as we had arranged in case we changed our minds about staying here.'

Mamma's voice, thin and whispering, asked: 'Will you come with us?'

'No,' Dadda replied decisively. 'I have lived here all my life and my father before me. I will not be forced to flee my home.' There was a long silence.

'Then we will stay with you,' said my mother.

CHAPTER FOUR

We sat in the darkness shivering, waiting in the abyss of silence. Our blindness isolating each one in a cocoon of self-absorption. The frightful sense of despair and hopelessness defied faith. There were no defences or pretences left. I ought to pray, but how could I pray to Jesus who is so holy, when I lived a life that was so unholy? Come to that, what was holy anyway? I felt remorse and deep contrition for my past sins whatever they might be. I heard myself promise Jesus that if we were not killed, I would become a nun and spend the rest of my life in His service. I would make the same promise to Allah if necessary. 'Oh please, Jesus, don't let us die,' I moaned. Dadda shuffled over to me in his sleeping-bag, took me in his arms and rocked me. With my head on his chest, I could hear his heart racing like an engine.

'Mamma, light a candle,' Dadda instructed. Mamma fumbled around in the dark and we heard the striking of a match and then that soothing flame appeared casting its shadow like a small white blister of sunlight.

'Mamma, make us some hot tea and find some home-made cake. We're going to celebrate.' Dadda extracted himself from his sleeping bag and lit the paraffin lamp. 'I know which tin the cake's in,' I told Mamma as I crawled across the mattresses onto the bare floorboards. 'Dadda, what are we celebrating?' I asked, putting my head into the gap between the concrete floor and the wood slats as I reached for the cake tin.

'Life', he replied, 'and all that's beautiful. You know, Fran, you can pray with your eyes and ears as well as with words. Have you not felt the joy of the exquisite scent of roses? Have you not listened to a piece of music which gathers momentum and sweeps you above all the world's distractions in one golden moment of harmony? Have you not read a poem that inflames the fire of your spirit and raises your mind and heart beyond the hesitations of reality? All these are intimate experiences which are beyond our grasp, but not beyond our reach so that we can know that there are still goodness and beauty and love to be praised.' And so we had a party by candlelight, hostages in our own basement.

Mamma and Dadda sat side by side, arm in arm, grasping large mugs of tea spiked with Dadda's special home-brew, warming our toes by the paraffin stove and keeping as far away as we could from the encroaching jaws of death. There are some moments one hopes never to forget. Dadda's defiance of death was one such moment.

For the first time, Dadda allowed the fire to stay in all night and we slept entwined in one another's arms embracing the warmth of our love. I hoped that I would never have to wake up, but at dawn I heard Dadda pick up his gun and slip up the cellar steps to walk up the mountain for his morning shift. I knew Mamma was awake by her trembling. 'Will he come back?' I whispered. She clasped me to her breast.

'Of course, darling. He'll be back for lunch. He's never missed a meal in his life.' Dadda returned, but not alone. 'We have company, Mamma,' he announced, supporting Nanna Azerbagic down the steps. Nanna's old bones had stiffened with age. 'Fran, come and help.' Between us, we lowered her minute frame onto the mattress and she lay there like a wounded crow, her flowing black skirts spread out like extended wings.

'Where did you find her?' Mamma asked, rubbing circulation back into Nanna's frail hands.

'She met me on the way back and asked me to visit her daughter and the children. The eldest two boys are on the front line and Leyla and Nanna are on their own. They have no heating, Mamma, they must come here.' The Azerbagics had already suffered greatly. Nanna's husband had been killed in a tractor accident before I was born. Leyla's husband Davor, Nanna's son-in-law, had fallen ill with terrible stomach pains some years afterwards and had died of peritonitis in the city hospital. The two eldest teenage boys became young men overnight and worked their father's vineyard, assiduously planting and hoeing in order to keep their nanna and mother out of debt. Every autumn, the village children gathered with their parents to spend a week picking the Azerbagic's grapes, for it was too much labour just for the two young lads. The younger daughter and son, Andela and Navid, attended school with Assad and me but they were older than us and we had had little to do with them. 'Of course the family must come here,' Mamma was saying. 'Is it safe outside?'

'For the moment,' replied Dadda.

'Then Fran can go down to their house and help them pack up. It will do her good to get out of here for a while. We didn't go down to the river this morning so she can get some water at the same time. Don't forget to take the bucket.'

'Mamma, I only have two hands,' I protested.

'Then your father will have to help you. I'll heat up some tinned soup in the meantime. Nanna, put this blanket over you.' Mamma loved looking after people.

'Come on, Fran, I'll collect the bucket and do the sewage pit and the river and meet you at Leyla's.' Dadda looked at the gun in his hand and reluctantly laid it down. He, also, had only two hands!

Nanna's daughter Leyla was a striking woman with high cheekbones. She was vivacious and incurably romantic. 'Fran, darling,' she kissed me on both cheeks as I went into her house. 'How lovely to see you,' she exclaimed as if we had not met for many months, though we had exchanged words only the day before.

'I've come to help,' I explained. 'What would you like me to do?'

'Will you help the kids sort out the food in the kitchen. Your father's a brick. I hope your Mamma doesn't mind us all coming over.'

'Of course not. She'll love the company,' I enthused in my delight at the prospect of having somebody closer to my own age to talk to. By the time Dadda arrived with the filled water containers and cleansed bucket, the hall was bursting with boxes of food and suitcases of clothes. Dadda looked aghast at the amount, but said nothing. But the youngest son, Navid, had noticed his reaction and said quickly:

'Mother, we don't need all this. We can come back each day and collect what we need.' Dadda nodded in agreement. But Leyla was not to be deterred.

'Darling, we must have a change of clothes and Nanna needs her shawls.' Navid threw Dadda a pleading look. My father said gently 'Leyla, our cellar is small and we will be very cramped as it is with seven of us in it. Can you not just bring your sleeping-bag and a box of food for tonight?'

Leyla agreed and our desolate little group locked up her home and walked the five hundred yards to our house. I was very tempted to ask Dadda if I could drop in to see Assad. I needed reassurance that he had not joined those crossing the mountains to the city the previous night, but I was heedful of

Dadda's feelings and did not want to create a scene in the presence of Leyla and her family.

Although the cellar had seemed quite spacious and bearable previously, it now became a nightmare of immobility, with the addition of Nanna and Leyla and Leyla's daughter and son. If anybody wanted to move, they had to clamber over bodies in order to do so. There was no more space for mattresses, so several of us squeezed ourselves into sitting positions on the three that were there for Mamma, Dadda and me. It was a relief when someone had to go upstairs to use the bucket, one almost felt one could allow oneself to breathe out. Dadda moved the camp stove upstairs into the cold so that Mamma could boil a pan of water. We would then form a relay, handing the mugs of steaming tea down into the cellar. Although we could hear gunfire and shelling reverberating across the mountains, we made no mention of it. The war seemed to be hastening onwards, suddenly becoming closer as we became overwhelmingly aware that we were soon to be part of it.

The next night, Dadda left the cellar door open for air. It was a disturbed night of coughing, moaning and the jarring of limbs if anyone stirred. It was impossible to avoid the sleeping bodies when making a visit upstairs. At dawn Dadda sloped off with his gun and Mamma busied herself upstairs in the bitter cold to make some kind of hot breakfast. Dadda returned unexpectedly. 'Fran, Navid, come to the kitchen,' he called. Leyla's son and I crawled from our sleeping-bags and joined my parents. Dadda was grey, unshaven and drawn, his breath short, his manner troubled, but his gaze was unswerving.

'We can see the movements of soldiers on the next mountain. They will be here by tonight.' Mamma stretched out her arm and Dadda took it. 'We're going to try and hold the bridge for as long as possible.' Indescribable fear gripped me. Slowly I came to a total awareness of what was about to happen. It was clear to me that we were going to die. We had been placed apart from the rest of the world. The chosen victims to be sacrificed. I no longer stood on this earth; I was weightless: free from earthly ties, burdens and fears. The soldiers could do nothing to me. Neither gun, nor sword could touch me. Evil thoughts and actions were far away. I felt my identity seeping away. My very self deserting me. There was no space for further pain. 'Fran. Fran.' Dadda was shaking me.

'It's OK. I understand.' My voice grated like broken glass. Mamma appeared serene but busy.

'Fran, Navid, you must lock the door of the cellar – no candles, no noise. With a bit of luck they won't find any of you and they'll move out in the morning. Mamma, you must leave the stove upstairs. You wouldn't be able to use it in the cellar in the dark and it would anyway be too dangerous. Navid, take the buckets downstairs. You will have to do your toiletry in the cellar, I'm afraid. There must be no movement. If they believe the house is empty,' he shrugged his shoulders, 'they'll move on. It's your only chance. Do you understand?' There was no emotion in Dadda's voice. He could have been giving us instructions on how to set up camp in the forest. Navid, who had remained silent throughout, now spoke to Dadda.

'I will deal with the buckets, but then I'm coming with you. Please, there is no discussion but I don't want my mother to know.' Mamma put her arms round his shoulders. Navid was fourteen years old and looked younger. Mamma talked quietly: 'Navid, your nanna, mother and sister need you.'

'My brothers are fighting for their home, their country, their family. I am old enough to follow in their footsteps.' He stretched his neck to make himself an inch taller. Dadda placed a hand on the boy's shoulder and agreed, almost conspiratorially.

'The boy is right. He's old enough to fight for what is his. Have you a gun?'

'Yes, back at the house.'

'Right. Go and get it and I'll meet you down at the bridge.' Navid hesitated. 'I must say goodbye to my family?' It was a question. Dadda lit a cigarette slowly, deliberately, playing for time.

'Not if you don't want to. You're old enough to fight for your country, you're old enough to make personal decisions, but I warn you – your mother will know.' Navid melted like wax in a torrent of tears. Before Mamma could reach him, I had him in my arms. I looked at my father; his face was dark. His glance was hard, almost absent as if he was far away. His large mouth was set firmly, but his hardly perceptible lips moved as if he was trying to say something. I heard nothing. Navid was gasping, taking large breaths in order to control himself. When he finally became calm again, I let him go. He smiled weakly, in both shame and gratitude. Choking back the tears he said 'Fran, will you tell Nanna, Mother and Andela?'

'Sure,' I answered. Navid wiped his nose on the sleeve of his coat and acknowledged my reply with a nod. Then without any further glance, coolly, almost with complete detachment, he swung out of the kitchen and through the front door. Mamma, Dadda and I were alone. I noticed Dadda's arms were thin and white above the line of his shirt cuffs. His large frame had shrunk, but he looked at us with the composure of a general addressing a staff meeting. 'Now, my sweet, wonderful ladies. One last thing.' He unbuckled his belt and handed it to Mamma. 'See the concealed zip in the leather? I've hidden 500 DM. You might need them. Keep the belt on you. Here, let me help.' He fumbled with the buckle before clipping it securely around Mamma's waist. He stood directly in front of his wife with his arms resting on her hips, as if studying some artistic masterpiece. Mamma was still as a stone, standing tall and proud, her blue eyes steady. I heard Dadda whisper two words: 'Thank you.' He kissed her and then, as if caught up in a tornado, he turned in one brisk movement, picked up his gloves and his gun, kissed my forehead without embracing me and was gone. I stared after him. He had not even hugged me. He had not said the word 'goodbye.' 'Dadda, Dadda,' I screamed after him, but before I could follow, Mamma was holding me, completely smothering my trembling body in her love and her desolation.

Mamma and I descended the cellar steps, achingly aware of our loss. Before we could speak, Leyla had noticed the absence of her beloved son. She opened her mouth to ask his where-abouts but realised it was unnecessary. She moaned, tearlessly clutching at Andela. I could just make out Mamma waiting with her hand upon her heart. I retreated into my sleeping-bag and curled up, blocking my ears with my fingers and shutting my eyes tightly. I must have fallen asleep for I woke in the darkness to the whispering voices of Mamma and Leyla.

'I could kick myself for not checking,' Leyla was saying.

'You weren't to know she didn't have them on her,' Mamma was replying soothingly. 'Do you know where they are?'

'Yes, they'll be in the cupboard in the bathroom. They weren't beside her bed or I would have seen them and packed them.' I deduced that Nanna was in need of some pills which had been overlooked when transporting their personal belong-ings over to our house yesterday. Leyla was squatting beside her mother whose breathing sounded shallow and erratic. I decided that she must have a heart condition. Suddenly there was a burst of gunfire which silenced us. Finally, Leyla said, 'I shall have to go and get them.' Andela began to screech like a parrot. 'Shush, shush,' Mamma soothed her, 'we must be very quiet. Leyla, you can't go. Perhaps tomorrow it will be safer.'

'I'm not sure if Nanna will be alive by tomorrow, if we don't get them today.'

The noise of gunfire from our valley grew nearer. It would be daylight outside and somewhere in the midst of all that thunder, my Dadda would be defending our right to freedom. 'Let me go, Mamma,' I heard myself say through the blackness. 'Mamma, I can't stay here any longer. Leyla, have you got the key?' There was a pause.

'Oh, Fran, Navid had the key! Wait a moment. Nanna, have you got your key on you?' I strained my ears but couldn't hear the reply. It was Leyla again.

'Yes,' in triumph. 'We have a back door key.'

I began to unmuffle myself from my bedding and cast around with my hands for my boots. Now it was Mamma who spoke:

'Fran, I don't want you to go. I know you feel you have to do something to help. I know it's claustrophobic in here, but it's very dangerous out there.'

To my knowledge, I had never deliberately disobeyed my mother, but then I never really had been without my father. I tied my laces.

'Mamma, don't worry; I'll be very careful and go via the orchard and across the paddocks so as to avoid the road. It's not very far, after all.'

'You know where the bathroom is?' Leyla was asking. 'It's off the hall. The back door will take you into the kitchen and then into the hall and the bathroom is the first on the right.' I was pulling on my coat and searching in the pockets for my gloves.

'I know, Leyla, and the cupboard is above the washbasin.' I was ready. Mamma's voice was very close.

'Fran, if your father was here, he wouldn't let you go.'

'If Dadda was here, I wouldn't have to go,' I replied sharply. I heard weeping, but from which of the women I could not tell. 'Remember, Mamma, what Dadda said: no noise. I'll be back soon.' I couldn't see her to give her a hug. Anyway, I wouldn't be more than an hour at the most. I heard Mamma's response as I climbed the steps to the kitchen: 'Fran, my darling, be careful and if you should see your Dadda, kiss him for me.'

From the light outside, I guessed that it must be late afternoon. The road was completely empty and I was almost tempted to walk the five hundred yards straight down it to Leyla's house; but I had told Mamma that I would go via the orchard and across the paddocks. The noise of gunfire was distant but constant. I bent low, running beside the hedges. Stopping frequently to look round. I felt no fear. If truth be told, it was exhilarating.

After crossing the third paddock I lay down flat in the ditch to draw breath. A blanket of low-hanging clouds fused into the grey mountain. More gunfire from the direction of the river. Once again I looked round for patrols. There was no one in sight, so I continued to run, keeping parallel to the bushes which shielded me from the houses and road. I was enjoying my freedom. Another hundred yards and I would have a good view of the bridge, before turning left towards the main road. I knelt in a hollow obscured by foliage. Beneath me the arabesque bridge stood out, pale in the dusk light, with its three yawning arches separating the green flowing waters. I could hear the gunfire and see the flashes. Well up the road, a line of tanks were crawling towards the bridge, their silent guns swinging like elephant trunks. I was in no doubt that they could destroy every house in the village with one burst of fire. What good would a machine gun be against tanks? I felt my mouth becoming dry and began to shake with fear. No one is free if they fear death as I feared it at that moment. I felt that I was watching history take its course.

Both sides were spraying bullets across the river. Each burst was followed by an almost religious stillness as the sound was swallowed up in the hollow of the mountain before the next burst cracked out. My eye was caught by a group of men attempting to retreat back to the village only to be struck by a shell. It whistled across the river and exploded among them throwing bodies and gravel into the air. There was a lull. Then the silence was suddenly transformed into a dull roar that tore at my eardrums. This second shell shattered the wall of the first house in the village, tearing at its very roots. Bricks, wood and debris whirling into the air, drawn upwards to the sky and colliding in mid-fall, pulverising the main road on landing. Hell had broken loose.

I came to with difficulty. I did not know how long I had been lying there, or even if I had been conscious. The world had been filled with noise and uproar. Now there was silence and I realised that I was at least alive. I crawled out of the hollow peering through the dark trying to assess the damage caused by the shelling but it was too dark to see anything. I started down the wet slope which suddenly grew steeper, found myself slipping and falling, rolling over and over, my face whipping through the wet grass until I came suddenly to a halt in a newly excavated dug-out. My traumatised body refused to continue and I could not argue with it. I rested in the dug-out, my mind stumbling to catch up with what had happened as I endeavoured to piece together the dreadful evening. I struggled and floundered as waves of nausea over-whelmed me. There could be nothing left of the village, no human could live through that shelling. I was entirely alone. My head was aching. There was a distant rumbling like a train exploding from a tunnel. I tried to sink into my frozen hole, my head pressed against the dark walls of mud. In my mind I was running, slithering, waving my arms through a swirling darkness of chasing shadows. I was escaping down a tunnel of acrid smoke, my nostrils pouring green snot, my throat burning and constricted.

I awoke and vomited, felt better and laid my head back to sift through the dreams that had begun in bitter reality. I felt contaminated by the mere fact of what I had observed and could not dissociate myself from death. I thought my mind was going to give out, a dam seemed to be bursting in my brain. In my half-dreaming state I must have shifted my feverish body, for I heard the scrape of boots and rapid speech: 'Shit! It's Fran.' I was being rolled over. 'What the hell is she doing here?'

'Is she alive?' I kept my eyes closed. I knew then that my nightmare was over, for I recognised the voice.

'Assad, they're dead. They are all dead. I saw it. They're dead.'

Assad was kneeling beside me. With his gloved hand he wiped the vomit from my chin. I could smell it. 'No, Fran, they're not all dead,' he reassured me. 'Drink this.' Assad was placing something between my lips and I gulped down water. There were two figures crouching behind him. I cried out in fear. 'Fran, it's OK. It's Ben and Mustafa.'

'They're all dead. I saw what happened on the bridge,' I insisted.

'No, Fran, you're wrong. Look at me.' Assad grabbed my head, our noses almost touching. 'We're alive. I know there are others hiding. Some of us have been captured and they're holding them in the village hall. Here, drink some more water.' My confusion was abating and I could feel my mind slowly coming to terms with what Assad was saying.

'Where are the tanks?'

'In the main street. They've blown the bridge,' Ben replied.

'What about our houses?'

'Some have been shelled,' said Assad. 'The ones nearest the river have been the worst hit. I think yours and mine are still standing, but the soldiers are systematically ransacking every house in the village, so it's not safe to go home.'

'But Mamma and Leyla . . .' I began as Assad put his finger to my lips.

'Shush, Fran. I'm sure they're all right. If they're found they'll be moved to the village hall with the others. There's nothing we can do till daylight.' Mustafa picked up a rifle and said that he was going to continue down the trench to make sure there were no patrols. 'Any chance of finding any food anywhere?' Ben asked. 'I'm absolutely starving.'

'Doubt it,' replied Mustafa. 'I've got some chewing gum. Here, Fran, you have some; it'll take away that dreadful taste in your mouth.' Mustafa pressed the chewing gum into my hand and disappeared into the blackness. Ben, picking up his rifle, departed in the opposite direction. 'You guys stay here. I'll see what I can do about some food. Fish and chips OK?'

'I want a McDonald's with tomato sauce,' Assad responded. 'And Fran would like a chocolate milkshake.' But Ben had slipped quietly away. Assad placed himself next to me, his knees under his chin.

'How are you feeling, Fran? Warm enough?' I had not noticed that I was cold. 'I'm numb,' I told him. In fact, I was exhausted and had no wish to talk, but Assad was feeling chirpy. It must have been reaction. 'How the hell did you get here?' he asked. I told him the story of Leyla moving in with us and how her nanna had left her pills behind.

'It was very brave of you to offer to fetch them.'

'Not really. I was desperate to get out. The air down there was suffocating.' I did not mention that I had hoped to see Dadda and that I had not said goodbye to him. But I had thought about it. I had not said goodbye to Mamma either. 'What about you?' I asked Assad. 'How do you come to be here?'

'I decided that I would fight beside my father.' I could hear the pride in his voice. 'But at the end of the day, they ordered me back to the trenches because they thought I was too young. The older ones were allowed to go down to the river with spare ammunition.' There was a note of regret.

I did not know how to ask the next question, and did not know whether I wanted to hear the answer.

'Do you know who's been killed?' Assad took my hand and played with my fingers.

'I'm not sure.' I knew he was lying. He knew that I knew it and neither of us pursued the point. Changing the subject was a relief.

'What are we going to do now?' I whispered.

'We'll wait for the others to get back and then we must find somewhere safe for the night. I don't think the soldiers have found the trenches yet, and I don't think they'll bother to do anything else tonight. They're all bedded down. Haven't you noticed the silence? – they'll wait for daylight now. But I don't think we should risk staying here.' I had been slow to realise that both the shelling and the shooting had ceased and that the noises of the day had been locked away by night. There was only the noise of emptiness. I curled into Assad and wondered how Mamma was coping. She must be so frightened for me. And where was Dadda? Could he have been one of those bodies I saw flying through the air after the shelling to crunch limply to the ground twisted and broken? I made a valiant effort not to be sick and choked back the bile.

'Do you want some more water?' Assad handed me his bottle. 'Poor Fran, it must have been hell on your own.' He cuddled closer. 'But from now on we'll look after each other.' He squeezed my arm as I lifted the bottle. The water misfired and dribbled down my chin. Eventually Mustafa returned. 'I went the whole way until I reached the north/south trench – not a living soul.'

'How many dead?' I asked quietly.

'Sorry, Fran, that was a figure of speech. There was nobody dead. Where's Ben?'

'He went to McDonald's to buy some hamburgers.' We giggled. Mustafa was fourteen, tall, handsome and skinny as a cat. He had captained the junior basketball team at school and because of his natural leadership and prowess at sport, had been well liked by all the students. In fact I had been told that many of the girls shared a certain sweetness for him. Personally I had always preferred Assad with his considerate nature. Mustafa was rather pleased with himself, which I found galling. At last Ben appeared through the darkness. We heard the scuffing of his boots long before we saw him. The exertion of running and ducking had left him breathless. 'They're all over the place down there,' he gasped. 'They've moved into one of the houses. They've barricaded both ends of the street. Here, I found these in Mr Ahmed's shed.' He emptied his pockets of apples and plums and potatoes.

'How do we eat the potatoes?' Mustafa asked the question in all our minds.

'We'll have to eat them raw.'

'Let's eat the fruit and keep the potatoes. We might find a way of cooking them tomorrow,' I suggested.

'In a saucepan, on a hob, with roast beef, I suppose. Get real, Fran.' Mustafa's sarcasm always made me wary of him. I was about to retort when I realised that the boys were stuffing fruit into their mouths and I was being left behind. I grabbed a share.

'Ben, we've got to get out of the trenches before daylight,' Assad insisted.

'I know. I've been thinking. If we go back away from the river and cross the road beyond their barricade, we can get to that copse up the hill behind Navid's garden. There's a brilliant view of the village from there and we can see what's going on.' It was agreed. We finished our fruit and then, ducking and bobbing we made our way along the trench under the stars, the night fragrant with the smell of cordite.

CHAPTER FIVE

We spent the night in the copse behind Navid's garden. When I had set off for his mother's house the previous day to collect Nanna's pills I had given little thought to what might lie in wait for me before I reached my destination. When I awoke in the copse, Mustafa's lanky limbs were spread-eagled above me. I edged from under them and he did not stir. Ben and Assad were missing, perhaps gone to the river to refill the water bottles. I looked down at our village. I had done this many times, always with a pride of belonging. Normally the chimneys would be smoking by now, the women bracing themselves against the cold as they tended the chickens, cows and ducks. The old men would be out in the fields leaning on their hoes, nurturing their vegetables. But today was different. I struggled to take in the strangeness. A strangeness that seemed to have nothing to do with me. The whole area stank of devastation and decay. No longer a picture postcard. The arabesque bridge had been hit and gaped like a wounded creature. The nearby houses had been shelled to rubble and there were mud craters instead of gardens. The trees were black. Charcoal and brickdust, wood and glass littered the labyrinth of pathways linking the houses.

There was still sporadic shooting. I watched and listened as echoes of intermittent gunfire bounced back from the mountain. The square was full of bomb craters and empty apart from enemy soldiers guarding the village hall. In the main street were stationery tanks alongside evacuated houses. There were quantities of potholes and mounds of broken glass. Right at the top of the road beyond the last building, a barricade had been erected and a group of soldiers were sitting on sandbags playing cards. I watched, unable to relate to what I was seeing and then decided to try and get closer without being seen. I had noticed the machine-guns on the opposite hill so I was going to have to wriggle snake-like through the undergrowth. As I moved forward I was muttering 'Bastards, bastards, bastards'. Dawn had broken and stinking soldiers appeared from their all-night revelry to open their trousers and fumble with their enfeebled cocks. They peed anywhere and everywhere. Some pulled their trousers down to crap, their white buttocks gleaming like jellyfish, polluting what was mine: contaminating the gentle harmony of my past. 'Bastards, bastards, bastards.' I wept. I turned away and sat with my back against a tree taking in great gulps of air and staring at my mud-clogged boots. Why did I feel so responsible, so ashamed when none of it belonged to me any more? A commotion forced me to look back. A group of twelve soldiers were herding some teenage girls towards the village hall. I recognised Nanna's granddaughter Andela as well as Jasmine, Zlata and all my older school chums. The girls seemed distraught rather than merely frightened. They were not wearing coats and the fronts of their dresses had been torn. I could see the pink bulges of their breasts. Then, I knew why they had been separated from the other captives. 'Fucking bastards, fucking bastards,' I moaned rocking myself backwards and forwards, forwards and backwards. 'The fucking bastards, fucking bastards.' I saw the haunted faces of my friends, their stumbling walk of shame, the sagging humiliation. 'Fucking bastards, fucking bastards,' the words became manna to my spirit.

Ben found me repeating obscenities under my breath. He sat beside me without saying a word, watching, listening and waiting. Hours must have passed by the time a convoy of open-backed trucks pulled up outside the village hall. A detachment of gun-toting soldiers jumped down with their Kalashnikovs and entered the building. There was a lot of screaming and then two solitary gun shots. Silence. The door opened and two corpses were thrown into the street. 'It's Mr Ahmed – the one on the left is Mr Ahmed,' Ben whispered. 'Can you see who the other one is?' I could see the body and I imagined that I could see the agony on the face, but I could see no face. My eyes were too blurred. I sat back with that sinking sensation of helplessness. Nothing was left. Nothing would ever touch me again. 'They're bringing them out, Fran,' I heard Ben's voice. Sure enough, the soldiers were assembling everyone in the market place.

'I can see my mother,' Ben said. 'I can see her, Fran. And there's poor Mrs Ahmed kneeling beside her husband. Oh, Fran, Fran. I can see your mother too.' Mamma? Mamma was there in the market place? No, no, Mamma was hiding in the cellar of our house. Ben was grabbing me and forcing my head up. 'Look, Fran. Down there. She's going over to Mrs Ahmed. She's alive, Fran. She's OK.' I searched the crowd of friends and neighbours, my eyes flickering frantically across each face. Then I saw Mamma kneeling beside the corpse of Mr Ahmed, her left arm round the shoulder of Mrs Ahmed. Catholic and Muslim were praying together. A soldier, realising what was happening, marched across to them and butted Mrs Ahmed with his rifle. Mamma screamed and I saw him smash his gun down on the back of her skull. Mamma was lying in a pool of blood whilst the others were lined up. They separated the men from the women and told them to return to the village hall. I averted my eyes from the motionless body of Mamma and looked along the lines of men. I was pretty certain Dadda was not amongst them. The women and children were being thrown into the backs of the trucks like bales of straw. There was much screaming and wailing. The men were at the windows shouting for their loved ones, arms banging on the glass. The soldiers outside pointing guns at their heads. Two of the soldiers picked up Mamma's limp body and manhandled her roughly onto the last truck.

The cacophony of screaming and wailing from suffering mothers and children was surely the deep pit of hell the priest had once told me about. The pit where the devil is trapped with all the lost souls. As the trucks were driven away, the lament subsided until you could hear nothing except the men banging on the windows: drumming their anguish. I shook my head from side to side. Each question harboured another: Was Mamma alive? I could hardly bring myself to think of her. My fear for her wanted to explode from my body. I did not know whether to choke with rage or tears as I crumpled to the ground. Why was this happening? Why had they separated the men and where were they taking the women and children? Where was this hatred coming from? Everything in me hurt. I could not account for this physical pain. I discarded my gloves and blew warm air into the hollow of my cupped hands, hoping to neutralise the cold threads of malice creeping into the very core of my being. Revenge lay heavy on my heart.

'Fran, they're bringing our fathers out,' Ben was saying. I crawled to his side. The men were being marched out single file in silence. They stood erect as if attending a funeral. Orders cracked through the air and a group of soldiers appeared with machine guns. One by one the men joined hands, some embraced. Each seemed to be helping his neighbour to stand upright. The shots rang out. I did not see their blood spilt because I had turned away at the first click of a bullet going into the breech. In my mind I saw my Dadda's profile: his forehead, his nose, his mouth, his chin, his neck and then the tears came and his image died with those slain in our valley that terrible morning.

The onslaught of fatigue was sudden and miraculous. I slept and through my dreams felt rivulets of my tears cascading down my body. I could smell my skin as blood streamed from every pore. The wet warm dampness between my legs finally woke me. The fear that I too had been shot was so great that it was minutes before I was able to put my hand down to check that what I could feel was only urine. I was wrapped in a timeless presence, astonished to discover that I was alive. I kept thinking of all that I owed but unable to clarify to whom the debt should be paid. The distraction of seeing Ben lying in the foetal position, his gun to his head finally brought me to my senses.

'No, Ben. Don't shoot. The noise will bring the soldiers up here and then we'll all be caught. Ben, please, give me the gun.' I had to take it from him. I sat back on my haunches holding the rifle. My legs rubbed together and I could smell my own urine. Ben lay there with his mouth open, as grey as pewter apart from his eyes which were pink and raw. I could see that he no longer wanted to know anything about this world – that his interest in it had finished the moment the guns had turned on the men. I touched Ben's forehead with my gloves and blotted up the sweat of fear. I pressed my lips to his open mouth but he was unable to return from where he was. I squatted behind his head holding it gently in my urine-soaked lap until he was ready to wake. Like a headstone I sat, locked into the beat of Ben's heart, waiting for him to open the door. Assad and Mustafa found me that afternoon. I had done nothing throughout those hours apart from wiping away the tears that would flow down Ben's face. I could not move. I so much wanted to lie down to drown in sleep but my homeless mind sorrowed with the beat of Ben's heart. Assad and Mustafa sagged beside me speechless, their red eyes screwed up with pain. The dark descended and the cold ate into our bones. Our world had emptied. We drifted into a merciful sleep.

It was the noise of tanks that woke us. They were heading south towards the city, lights snaking along the mountain road, the stick-like shadows of soldiers following behind them like dogs at the heels of their master. I was shivering. So were the boys. I could not feel my limbs and when I tried to stand, my legs crumpled beneath me. Mustafa crawled across and began to rub my legs energetically. Assad was doing the same for Ben. At last, I could stand but I felt weak and disorientated. It was Mustafa who told us to form a circle. With our arms round one another's waists, we stumbled first to the left and then to the right, lurching backwards and forwards until we had a rhythm and found that we were dancing in unison, the blood pounding through our veins as the army below us tramped out of our lives.

We finally sat down cross-legged, the guns at our sides. 'We've got to find food.'

'We must wait for daylight. They might have left soldiers in the village.'

'We must get water first.'

'We should do that now, under cover of darkness.'

'Let's split up and do a recce. Fran and Assad, go to the river and we'll go and see if the barricades are still up and try to find some food,' said Mustafa.

'Where shall we meet?'

'Back here's as good a place as any.'

'What if they've left patrols?'

'Avoid them, you idiot.'

'No, I don't mean that. But should we go into the village?'

'No, definitely not. Too risky. Wait for daylight.'

'Has anybody got a watch? What's the time now?'

'Ten past three. That gives us at least two hours.'

'Right then. Can I have your water-bottle?' asked Assad. 'Here, Fran, you take mine.'

'See you, guys. Take care and keep your heads down.'

Assad and I made our way down to the river bank, keeping low, mainly sliding, eyes darting to left and right. We took the rutted path that led us north of the village and then the short cut through the ravine; scratched and bruised, falling and picking ourselves up again, until we reached the flowing water. We rested behind a rock and watched and listened. It soon became clear that we were lone fugitives. 'Come on,' whispered Assad. We broke from cover and slipped down to the river, lying prostrate at the water's edge to gulp the cold water. When I had filled my belly, I took off my jeans and pulled off my soaking knickers. 'What are you doing?' Assad whispered.

'Washing my knickers,' I explained as I squeezed and rubbed them in the agonizingly cold water. I did not feel obliged to explain but did so and was glad that I had. I knew Assad would understand. I pulled up my trousers and hung the knickers round my neck, my head through the hole of one of the legs. It was then that we heard a thin hasty whisper from behind us. Assad gestured to me to crouch down. At first we saw nothing and then they appeared like ghosts out of the darkness. I was not sure whether or not they had seen us, crouching below the rock, but I guessed that we had been spotted because the whispered murmurs ceased and the shapes stood with their guns pointing at us. I wanted to live. I wanted more time; life suddenly seemed very short. I was not frightened, just resigned. Perhaps I had broken through the barrier of fear? Perhaps revenge and hatred had gobbled it up and vomited up blank resignation in its place. I heard my name spoken in a small

anxious voice and then Assad was rushing forward and clutching the first shape. I heard something and the shapes moved
towards me, their rifles lowered, swinging beside them, a
concatenation of voices that I could identify from the past.
Adjin, Mo and Gregor: three school friends. What a laugh!
Gleefully, we grabbed one another. Now we would be seven.

We were back on the brow of the hill, elated at the
improvement in our fortunes with the increase in our numbers,
swapping our amazing stories of survival. Ben and Mustafa had
returned with the news that the barricades were still up,
guarded by four soldiers and that there was activity in the
square, despite the tanks having moved on. Adjin, Mo and
Gregor explained that they had fled into the pine forest the
previous evening, before the soldiers crossed the bridge. They
had walked miles upriver, almost as far as the next village,
when they had found a rowing boat and crossed to our side.
When they met up with Assad and me they had been making
their way back to our village, hoping to find food. They had not
envisaged the possibility of soldiers remaining here and setting
up camp. Neither had we. Adjin, Mo and Gregor listened wide-
eyed and nodded incredulously when we told them of the
crimes perpetrated by the bastard soldiers. The stories over, our
voices dried up: hatred blistering into despair and the silence of
ocean-deep repulsion.

At the first touch of pink in the sky the seven dark, ragged
figures crawled half-way down the hillock to the shelter of the
copse, which gave us an eagle's eye view of the village. Our
hunger was a pain pulsating inside us like the engine of a ship. I
dreamed of food-laden tables, sweet and tender meat steaming
in its juices, of rosemary and garlic. I could smell freshly baked
bread dripping with melted butter and plastered with home-
made strawberry jam. My body craved nourishment and I
braced myself against the next wave of hunger. Why could

my brain not stop and think about something new? Why did I have to remember what food tasted like? 'I'm going to die of hunger,' I hissed through my teeth.

'No, Fran, you might well die, but not yet of hunger.' Mustafa was getting on my nerves because he was right!

'Why in hell didn't you find some food on your recce? That's what you were supposedly going to do,' I responded.

'Fuck you, you little bitch. We risked our lives to see if the soldiers were on the barricades. There was no way we could get to the houses.'

'Fuck you too, Mustafa!' I replied furiously. 'Why do you think you're better than everybody else? It wasn't any less dangerous going down to the river. At least we managed to get the water. We kept our side of the bargain.' It was Adjin, now the eldest in the group, who had also been the most senior boy left in the school, who interrupted.

'Shut up, both of you,' he rebuked sternly. I tried not to think of my hunger. We dozed fitfully. Anguish rolled down as the dawn yielded to day.

The soldiers spent the morning excavating a site behind the village hall where they unceremoniously threw the corpses of our dear ones. We watched them as they foraged through clothing. Watches were ripped from wrists; good leather boots clawed from legs, pockets emptied and the contents placed in the soldiers' pockets. Then, the final indignity, they used hatchets to cut off the fingers with rings on them. I lay back and looked at the sky, somehow suspended between the emptiness of life and the cruelty of death. My outrage was tempered by my lack of energy: anger muted by hunger. My sunken spirit felt dislocated and off-balance. I hoped that the soldiers would find us and kill us.

It was the sight of soldiers in the square making breakfast over a fire that galvanised us into action. As far as we could see they had all gathered there, apart from two left on the far barricade. Adjin took control.

'We must split up and find food whilst they're eating breakfast. Anybody who's got a home still standing, try there first. The rest, search the garden sheds for vegetables and fruit. Remember to stay low and keep quiet. Leave the guns here.'

'I'm not going without my gun,' Mustafa protested.

'You'd be a fool to take it,' Adjin reasoned. 'You can't move as fast if you are carrying a gun and if you're caught, they're more likely to shoot you if you have a weapon. But please yourself. Fran, one of us will go with you.'

'Just because I'm a girl doesn't mean I can't look after myself.'

'I'll go with her, my house is next door,' said Assad.

'OK. Everyone get back here as soon as possible. Remember, the soldiers won't be eating breakfast the whole morning. Get in as fast as you can, and get back even faster.'

Assad and I moved rapidly through the copse, keeping the trees between ourselves and the village. I was relieved to see that the machine-guns on the opposite hill had been removed. We reached the open paddocks where there wasn't any shelter.

'We have two options,' Assad reflected. 'We can either go up over the brow of the hill and round past the barricade, or else we can make a run for it from here and hope the soldiers on the barricade don't see us. What do you think?' I looked up the main road and saw the two men on the barricade wrapped in their coarse grey woollen coats. They were propped on their elbows, playing cards over an upturned box. They appeared to be oblivious to anything else. Not once did they raise their eyes from their gambling. We sat patiently watching them, tired out by the events of the last forty-eight hours and eagerly antici- pating food. I made a reckless suggestion. 'Let's sprint it. I can't face the hill.'

'OK. If we can get across those paddocks, there's a trench

close by. You see that walnut tree? Head for that. I'll be right behind you.' Suddenly my heart was hammering, my head swimming. I was terrified that I was going to be sick again.

'No, you go first and I'll follow.' Assad went. His fearlessness and his unexpected turn of speed dumbfounded me. Forgetting my fear of being sick, I clenched my teeth and set off like a bullet from a gun, running as I had never run before.

I reached the trench and sprawled into it choking for air. Assad was already peering over the edge. 'Well done, Fran, they didn't see us. Come on, let's keep going.' I stood up swaying.

'Keep down, Fran,' Assad urged. We walked on towards the square bent almost double to keep out of sight. Now we were in Dadda's orchard beside the woodpile and straining our ears for sound. 'I think it's safe. As soon as you've found the food get out and wait in the trench for me,' Assad directed and, wiping his sweating face, he bolted towards his own house. I looked at my home, pitted with shell marks. But the back patio was intact and the shutters undisturbed. I straightened my shoulders and consciously grew an inch as I walked steadily up the steps. I emptied the flower pot in which Mamma kept the keys and they rattled out onto the wooden verandah. As the key clicked into the back-door, I was overcome with a wild excitement. I was home. Nobody could touch me. This was my house, my security, my life, my world. All would be well. Within these walls were all my memories: my Mamma, my Dadda. The closed shutters had contained my far-reaching hopes.

I walked into the dark kitchen with just a streak of light cutting through from the opened door. But the floor of Mamma's tidy kitchen was covered with pots and pans, smashed plates, broken china and upturned chairs and table. The skirting-boards had been torn away from the walls and the sink was filled with excrement and with empty bottles. 'Oh, Mamma, I'm so glad you're not here to see this.' Tears filled my eyes. How I longed for Mamma. I picked her apron from the floor just to keep myself in touch with her. I held it to my lips, I missed her unbearably: could feel my heart breaking as I smothered my sobs. With tears pouring down my face I opened the door into the hall. It was full of smashed furniture and piled high with our clothes which had been turned out of the cupboards upstairs. I sensed that I was alone because anybody else in the house would surely have heard me by now. My tears ceased. The inner turmoil subsided. I started a methodical search for warm clothes, pulled off the knickers I was still wearing round my neck and clambered out of my jeans. I put on four pairs of clean knickers, jogging trousers over my jeans and so many T-shirts I lost count. Two more sweaters. Several pairs of different coloured socks. Finally I put my coat back on and laced up my boots. I reckoned I had been only a few minutes and returned to the kitchen. I noticed Dadda's lighter on the floor so picked it up. Its small flame was still working. The cellar door was open and I went down the steps. The cellar was wrecked; sleeping-bags torn into strips, mattresses ripped with a knife, but what joy I felt when I saw the floorboards undisturbed! I pulled them up and, using the flame of Dadda's lighter as my torch, filled my pockets with tins, grabbed the tin opener and a few candles. It was then that I saw it, pushed right into the corner of the space below the floor: invisible unless one knelt with one's face actually on the floorboards and shone the light right in: Dadda's leather belt, all coiled up. Mamma must have taken it from her waist before they caught her. She had hidden it, hoping I would return to find it.

I strapped the belt round my waist, my fingers fumbling at the buckle. It was far too long for me so I knotted it and fled up the stairs into the kitchen. With one last glance, I was out in the fresh air. I closed the door quietly, scoured the orchard for soldiers, moved hastily through the bare fruit trees and threw myself into the trench. I gulped air greedily and there was a pleasant haze in my head. I had felt like this once before when Dadda had given me a glass of slivovitz. At the same time I ached with weakness. At one point, I thought I heard voices, but when I listened hard all I could hear was my pumping heart. I peered over the trench. My home was still a friendly witness to the love and compassion of my parents, to my grandfather who had built it. Still surrounded by its plum trees beneath which I had played under the spring blossom and from whose shelter I had watched the geese fly south in autumn. A couple of magpies fluttered over my head looking for a place to settle, their feathers ruffled by the wind. Suddenly, I caught sight of movement and saw Assad darting low as he did when playing tag. The enchantment of those few moments was swept away as Assad landed beside me.

'Shit, they've been through my whole house. It's a bloody dump.' In his indignation he was forgetting how noise travels.

'Shush.' I put a finger to my lips. 'Mine's a mess, too. I don't know what they were looking for, but they've ripped open all the mattresses.' Assad was staring at me open-mouthed. 'What's the matter?'

'What on earth have you done to yourself?'

'Nothing. What do you mean?'

'You look like Michelin Man. You're twice the size you were when I left you.'

'I had a change of clothes, I was smelly.' He began to laugh hysterically.

'Quiet, Assad, someone will hear you. What's so funny?'

'Fran, you're so cool. Here we are surrounded by soldiers who'll kill us if they see us. We have no shelter, no food and you go into the house to change your clothes. Did you put your dirty ones in the washing machine?'

'Just you wait – I'll have the last laugh when you're stinking and haven't got anything to change into. I got the food as well.' I wondered whether to mention the belt, but held back.

Assad was slipping a small knapsack from his back. 'Here, put it all in this.' He held it open. I emptied my pockets. 'Come on, let's go,' and we began the trek back. But our good fortune was over. We could hear the soldiers marching up the main road towards the barricade long before we saw them.

The sentries were no longer playing cards, but standing to attention to hand over to their replacements. Orders were barked. The card-playing soldiers lowered their Kalashnikovs and sauntered down to the square. Assad whispered in my ear: 'We'll have to go round the back of the hill.' I nodded. These new men were fresh on duty and would be alert after a good night's sleep.

It took us over an hour to get completely out of sight of the village. I slumped to my knees in the grass, sweat streaking my face. 'Assad, I'm not going on till I've eaten.' Assad raised his head and surveyed the green landscape. I could see he was unhappy. 'I have to eat and so do you,' I persuaded. I felt exhausted and sick and lay down with my eyes closed. A brigade of terrorists would not have moved me.

'Fran, try and move. We're too exposed here.'

'Assad, I have to eat.' He walked round me as if circling a wounded prey.

'Sorry, I'll open a tin. Here's some water.' I peered at him dully – and fainted.

When I came to, Assad had taken off my outer layer of clothing and was slopping water over me. 'Eat this – but not too fast.' With my fingers, I scooped up the mackerel he had mixed into a tin of baked beans. It was cold and delicious but there wasn't enough. 'Any more, please.' I felt like Oliver Twist.

'No, Fran, not till we get back to the others.'

'Have you had some?'

'Yes. I had the other half while you had your unscheduled nap.'

'I feel better now.'

'Good. Then can we move on. I'll take some of these clothes in my knapsack. I think you were being suffocated by them.' As he pulled me to my feet I noticed the empty tins.

'We must bury the tins or the soldiers might find them and put two and two together.' Using our nails we scratched at the earth, buried the tins and placed a few stones over them. We then headed up the hill.

Assad and I were the last of the group to reach the copse. It was midday and the few remaining soldiers were strutting round the square, taking turns with spades to fill in the mass grave nearby. Our scavenging from the village had achieved more than we had dared hope for: between us we had collected tins of soup, corned beef, pickled herring, kidney beans and an abundance of fruit. There were several tin openers; each of us thinking that the others wouldn't remember! While we gorged ourselves, like babies gulping their mother's milk, the soldiers spread more earth over the mass grave. It was growing into a mound by the time the sun set.

'We've got to make decisions,' the speaker was Adjin.

'We could use the boat and go across the river and live in the pine forest,' suggested Gregor.

'We had a cow shed in the pine forest,' said Assad. 'Father and I built it, but I don't know if it's still there.'

'I think that's crazy. We should head for the city,' Mustafa volunteered.

'But we're safer here. The city's being shelled all the time.'

'There's no food here. Hell, what's that?' We ducked instinctively but there was no whistle of bullets passing over us, just a raucous crackle. Through the trees we could see bonfires blazing into life; lighting up the valley. The wooden buildings of our village were ablaze. The light and warmth played on our faces, our shadows dancing like huge gargoyles as the flames glowed beneath us.

'The scum are burning our houses,' cried someone. A sharp scudding breeze raised the flames into the sky and clouds of black soot obstructed our vision. I could take no more. Assad dug into his trouser pocket and produced his holy beads. Deprived of the power of speech, driven out of our minds by the horrors we had witnessed, we fell to our knees weeping in desolation, our prayer an uncompromising curse upon the world that would no longer help us.

CHAPTER SIX

Our flight across the mountains to the city seems like years ago. Looking back at the past bring unexpected spasms of revulsion. Not because of the destruction and cruelty brought about by man in a sophisticated world about to enter the millennium, but because the very sophistication of that world seems to paralyse the wellsprings of compassion. Luxuriating in their comfortable union of Western democracy and economy, Europe had adopted the badge of conscientious objector. In reality it was playing Pontius Pilate and had left our country to be crucified. The USA had placed an embargo on us. We were not allowed to buy weapons in order to defend ourselves. Who were these people making such decisions? None of us in our village had ever met an American. But despite the fact that the Americans were 5,000 miles away, with a decided lack of interest in our country, our industry or our welfare, they had nevertheless instructed the world that our country should not be provided with weapons. Who were these faceless people?

At school I remember being taught by Mrs Ahmed about the annihilation of the Jews by Hitler and the subsequent 'sin of omission', the guilt associated with those who knew but did nothing in the face of such evil. She told us that in 1936, Hitler had screamed out at Munich that 'the world must learn to hate, to hate and once again to hate'. And that at that point the Western world still refused to halt Hitler's evil march forward.

It is clear from my own experiences and from testimonies gathered from displaced persons arriving in the city that substantial violations of human rights, including executions, beatings and rape were daily events. As far as we were concerned, the world had become willing accomplices to genocide. Assad and I remembered a visit to the city to see Steven Spielberg's film, *Schindler's List*, portraying the Holocaust. Never in a million years did we believe that such barbarous inhumanity could come to our own city and that the so-called civilised world would watch this living nightmare while refusing to intervene. I remembered Mamma once saying that where there is the greatest danger, there is also the greatest need. She had been referring to the nightmare which was then taking place in Rwanda with the massacre of the Hutu and the Tutsi peoples or so I had believed at the time.

Tight-lipped and silent, we climbed the dirt track for the last time, never looking back at our stricken homes now reduced to ashes. Words would have been an unwelcome interruption to our thoughts about our past. Days and nights became indistinguishable as we journeyed. With the copper light of dawn, we sought cover, twisting beneath foliage, draping green veils of pine branches over one another to obscure the brutal daylight. We slept fitfully, released in imagination from our unendurable pain. When the evening glowed a distant salmon pink, we appeared from our lairs like cautious lizards, heads darting around, scouring the horizon for enemy soldiers. Then we would squat in silence, devouring tinned food with filthy fingers, before advancing further south across the mountain passes towards our disembowelled city.

It was on the third night that we found the cave. We heard the moaning long before we reached it and none of us was ever to forget the smell of decomposing flesh. In front, Adjin and Mustafa penetrated the darkness, rifles cocked, shouting 'We're friends from Zepen, our village across the mountain. We won't hurt anybody. We have food.' The whimpering ceased but we were now close enough to hear the sound of breathing. 'We have a candle, we're going to light it. We're not going to hurt anybody. We're refugees like you,' Adjin announced.

'Fran, bring me a candle from the knapsack.' The candle spluttered starlike and by its light we were able to see a group of huddled children, clinging to one another, victims of some unnameable shared tragedy. I stifled a cry as I stumbled over a dead body. Children were clawing at one another and recoiling from the thin flame of the candle.

'Oh, Jesus,' Adjin swore. I remember thinking it an amazing expletive for a Muslim, as I stared at lumps of humanity lying face downwards in the earth. It was difficult to know which ones were still breathing.

'Shit! Let's get out of here.' Assad was tugging at my elbow.

'We can't just leave them.' It was my voice, I think.

'Fran, is that you? Assad?' Tiny voices from among the group. Adjin walked forward and thrust the candle under the chins of three small children, their stomachs swollen with hunger. 'Aren't you the Jambrosic twins and who are you?'

The third girl, a child of no more than five years whispered 'Vedra'. We stared at one another, words failing us in the sheer horror and obscenity of this unexpected encounter. We had known the twins in the village. Vedra, I had never seen before. Emotion surfaced and with outstretched arms I ran to the twins and Vedra, hugging them, attempting to convey love in the only language I could still use. 'Adjin, they're starving. We must feed them.'

'Shut up, Fran,' Mustafa hissed. 'If we feed these three, we've got to feed the others and we haven't enough for everybody.'

'Who's everybody?' I gestured around wildly. 'Most of them are dead.' Adjin had lit a second candle and Assad was walking over bodies, stopping occasionally to feel a pulse. Adjin tore at the knapsack and began opening tins.

'Where's your mother?' I asked the Jambrosic twins, while holding firmly to little Vedra's hand. They pointed into the left hand corner of the cave and Gregor, with Assad, disappeared into the darkness. I remembered Dadda reading out the list of our neighbours who had decided to flee before the war came to our village. The Jambrosic mother and her twins had been amongst them. 'Where are you from?' I asked Vedra. Her hollow eyes stared from an emaciated face. 'Katztu.'

'But that's sixty miles north.' She simply nodded and then said to me, 'It was your mamma that gave us bread when we passed through your village.' I felt a deep shudder within me and held it back.

'But that was weeks ago. Where's your Mamma now?' Vedra wearily lifted her arm and pointed in the direction of Gregor and Assad.

'Bring them here, Fran,' said Adjin. 'All of you children come here. Eat very slowly, your stomachs aren't used to food. Chew it well.'

'What shall I eat with?' Vedra was staring at the sardines in oil.

'Your fingers.' Gregor and Assad reappeared from the depths of the cave, holding their noses and looking physically sick.

'Nine women and three more little ones,' Gregor said in a clipped voice.

'All . . .'

'Yes – the way they've placed themselves, it looks as if they went in there to die so that the children couldn't see them. The stink is desperate. How many kids are alive?' asked Assad.

'Eleven.'

'How did they die?' I asked him.

'There's no sign of violence – maybe starvation? Hypothermia? It's hard to tell with just the light from a candle.' The children were wolfing down the food, all the food we had.

'Slowly slowly. That's all there is,' I advised. 'Give them water, Ben.'

'But not too much – here – take the top of my water bottle so as to limit what they drink.' Mustafa passed his water bottle to Ben who had lined the children up. I gave little Vedra her water ration. I slumped to the floor and rocked her in my lap, like Mamma had rocked me when I had been five. It seemed so incredible that our group of seven aged between twelve and fifteen were now the adults responsible for eleven small orphans close to death. I suddenly remembered my promise to Mamma that I would pray to Jesus every day. Today my prayer would be bitter resentment. As far as I was concerned, Jesus had allowed all this to happen in the first place. The twins had fallen asleep. So had little Vedra. I wrapped her waiflike body in my coat and went over to the boys who were talking quietly.

'We can't leave them,' Gregor was saying.

'We can't take them with us,' replied Ben.

'What do you think, Adjin?' asked Assad. Adjin did not reply. He was sitting crosslegged, his rifle resting across his knees. He looked so young, so thin, so tired. I knew he was listening. Perhaps he was just listening to the noise of the shelling over the city, but none of us really noticed that any more. We were more likely to notice it when it ceased.

'We can't just leave them to die,' Gregor repeated.

'What do you suggest we do then, Gregor?' asked Mo, the quietest of all the boys. Mo was small and round-shouldered with lousy teeth. When he smiled, which was rare, the teeth showed mossy and cavernous. I had long felt the urge to plug them with putty and spray them with white paint.

'I don't know – I don't know any more than the rest of you,' Gregor replied almost with a hint of hysteria.

I felt I should have spoken up, but I could not think of anything to say that would be constructive. How could anyone think normally any more? Everybody sensed the hallucinatory quality of our authority. Each one withdrew into a silence that had become second nature. Eventually Adjin spoke.

'There are two courses of action. First we must carry the dead outside and bury them. The second thing we need to do is to send out a hunting party. I know it's risky because the soldiers could well hear our shots but we have to find food for everybody. One of us will have to backtrack to the last stream to collect water. It can't be more than a mile. Mustafa, will you come with me? After all you were the best shot in the school.'

'Of course, Adjin.'

'Ben, Assad and Mo, as soon as it's light, can you start shifting the bodies and looking for a fox hole where we can bury them? Gregor, would you be willing to fetch water?'

'No problem, Adjin – it won't take more than half an hour.'

'What about me? What can I do?' Adjin momentarily stared at me and then dropped his eyes. 'Dadda always told me that I was as good as the next man,' I said. Adjin put his rifle aside and lifted his hands. I sensed his compassion, his strong sense of humanity as he stared into his open palms, not wanting to meet my eyes.

'OK, Fran, I know you're strong and you will have to be strong for what I'm going to ask you to do.' He sighed and shifted his position. 'If it's not too much to ask, I want you to search every dead body.' My voice was distorted as I squeezed out a horrified 'No!' in my disbelief. All too clearly I remembered the soldiers outside the village hall going through the corpses of our menfolk. It was Ben who first realised what was in my mind.

'No, oh my God, no; Adjin, you can't make her do that. It makes us no better than the soldiers.' Adjin glanced from side to side, clearly understanding our trauma. He swept his hand through his hair.

'I'm sorry, it was wrong of me to ask you, Fran. But don't you see that it's got to be done. It might give us some clue as to who these people are. One day someone's going to be looking for them. If it was your mother or grandmother wouldn't you want news of them or would you prefer to think of them as just missing?'

'The children can surely identify them?' Gregor reasoned.

'I think that some of those women back there clutching their dead babies are nothing to do with these children,' said Assad.

'We should search them anyway. They might have something we need which could make the difference between life and death.' Mustafa was always clinical.

'Like what? A spare nappy in a bag for their dead kid?' Gregor was screaming.

'Lower your voices – you'll wake the little ones,' I begged. I was beginning to suspect that Adjin was right. However intolerable the duty, it was after all no worse than having to carry the bodies outside and then bury them, which was what the boys were going to have to do. This war was turning me into a monster, just like the soldiers.

'It's OK Adjin, I'll do it,' I said as calmly as I could.

'Look for rings, bracelets, neck chains – any form of identification. But first, ask the children to identify their own mothers if they are among the dead – and write down the names. Has anyone got a pen?' Assad silently handed me his.

'I've no paper.' We all looked blankly at one another.

'I've got a postcard of Zanzibar but there's no room on it,' said Mo.

'What about the back of the sardine tin labels?' Mustafa had his moments. We pulled the labels off and I put them in my pocket.

'I'm going to put out the candle,' said Adjin, and darkness enveloped us.

Mo's voice was the last thing I heard before I drifted into sleep. 'Hell, I'm so hungry. I would just love baked beans on toast.'

The boys had gone when I awoke next morning. The small children still lay clutching one another, their eyes closed, their breathing shallow, their uncertainty diminished by unconsciousness. I clung to the last thread of sleep, just to avoid facing the misery of that morning. Assad, Mo and Ben were first back with the information that there was a hollow just to the left of the cave, which could be used as a mass grave. They began the grim job of taking the bodies outside and laying them out in rows so that I could perform my grisly task. One by one the children filed along the line of bodies, their hollow eyes as dead as the figures on the ground. They had crossed the threshold of unendurable pain and were now anaesthetised by indifference, their capacity to feel completely drained. Apathetically, almost aloofly, they pointed out a mother, a sister, a grandmother whilst I wrote names on the back of the sardine tin labels. No one was capable of speech; pale and trembling the children voluntarily returned to the darkness of the cave which represented the deep shadow of their own spirits.

Affliction hung in the air, like the forewarning of a snowstorm, which immobilises life on the mountain. The boys, squatting by the hollow, watched my every movement, knowing that something truly unnatural was in process. I took off the first black lace shawl and began to place the belongings of the dead woman inside it. I made a point of focusing on the immediate clothing, never once looking at faces. They're like wax dummies, I told myself as I tore off a hand-embroidered blouse. Shoes, clanking bracelets, cardigans, underwear, keys, sewing kit, photos, cosmetics, were all thrown into the owner's shawl. As I left one body naked and moved along to the next, the boys, as if part of some macabre funeral cortege, moved forward as one and lifted the corpse into the communal grave. Gregor was back with water by the time I had completed my task.

'I need to wash. Can I have a bottle?'

'No way,' said Gregor, 'this is drinking water. It's precious. There's twenty of us here. If you want to wash, go down to the stream.'

'Fuck you!' I screamed. 'If you'd just done what I've done, you'd be demanding a fucking shower.'

'Fran, I only meant . . .'

'Go to hell.' All the stored up bile was unleashed. I began to run down the mountain towards the stream. I stripped off all my clothes and stood up straight as a broom handle in the middle of the icy water listening to a voice from my childhood. Mrs Ahmed was telling us the story of Dietrich Bonhoeffer, one of the few Christians in Germany who had dared to stand up to Hitler. Bonhoeffer's discipline had cost him his life. He was hanged with piano wire in one of the concentration camps. Over fifty years had passed and my country was in a similar situation. What of the cost of my own discipline? Supposing that I was martyred? Would someone in the future remember the price I had had to pay? And for what? I ducked my head under the water as if in baptism and blew bubbles. I emerged drawing in deep breaths, my short-cropped fringe sticking to my forehead.

Two eyes stared, looking in bewilderment at the phenomenon of a naked girl standing in a stream considering the possibility of martyrdom. We stared at each other mesmerised.

His ears were black and pointed, his nose snow white. His body was the shape of a mongoose, small and smooth. He was sandy coloured, with a stump of a tail. Ugly as hell, unsteady on his short stubby legs, but his eyes were two black pools of tenderness. As I drew nearer to him, unable to tear my eyes from his, I found his audacity irresistible. I reached out and touched him. He smelt my wet hand but did not venture into the water. 'Where did you come from?' I stepped onto the grass and tickled his neck. He had no collar. 'So what's your name?' I lay down under the watery sun to dry off, he lay down beside me quietly as if we were lifelong companions. The harshness of life and the imminence of death vanished in the glow of our encounter.

His short legs and malnourished body proved unequal to climbing up the mountain. So I carried him. As I reached the cave, Adjin and Mustafa were skinning rabbits.

'What have you got there?'

'A dog.'

'Where the hell did you find him?'

'Down at the stream.' The others had heard our voices and appeared from the hollow. 'He's one of us,' I said.

'What do you mean by that?'

'He's a refugee,' I replied, 'on the run like us.'

'Tonight's dinner, more like it.' Mo was prodding him. 'We could put him on the spit with the rabbits.' I swallowed my dismay.

'There's not much of him, but he'll feed a few mouths,' Ben agreed.

'Give him here Fran, I'll break his neck,' Adjin offered. I clasped the dog to my chest, breathing quickly. My fury erupted in a sob. 'You bastards, all you ever think about is food. I found him. He's mine and you're not going to eat him.' The children had appeared from the cave, roused by my screaming. The boys stared at me with unruffled calm. 'Fran, look around you – these kids are ravenous and you want to keep that dumb animal.' It was Assad this time.

'It's another bloody mouth to feed,' reasoned Mustafa. A circle of terror surrounded me. It was more powerful than my fatigue and hunger – it was like a fever. Holding the dog with my left hand I grabbed Adjin's rifle with my right. 'If any of you touch a hair of his head, I'll kill you.'

The boys had become rigid as I waved the rifle at them, their faces like granite. Assad moved as if to apprehend me. 'Don't you dare.' I placed my finger on the trigger. Terrorised and motionless, they stood waiting as if for some final calamity to overtake them. It was Mustafa who spoke first in a voice more husky than usual.

'Fran, calm down, we were only joking. Of course we won't kill your dog. Will you give me the gun? It's loaded, you know.'

'Not until you promise you won't hurt him.'

'We promise.' Adjin was very pale. They all nodded their agreement and I handed the gun to Mustafa who immediately uncocked it and retrieved the cartridges.

Mo shrugged his shoulders and said, 'He wouldn't have made much of a meal anyway, he's no bigger than a baked bean.'

Gregor took the opportunity to change the subject as I sat down with the dog, now relaxed in my arms. 'If we had one tin of baked beans here do you know how many each of us would have?'

'Depends on the size of the tin, doesn't it? Divided by twenty, I reckon we'd get five each.' Adjin and Mustafa had returned to skinning the rabbits. I opened my mouth to correct them to say that we were now twenty one to feed, but thought better of it.

'So what are you going to call him, Fran?' Gregor asked.

'I don't know – I haven't thought about it, really.'

101

'Well, he's always going to be Baked Bean to me – he's even the right colour,' said Mo. We gawped at the dog, sleeping in my arms. He was reddish and almost the same shape as a baked bean.

'You can't call a dog Baked Bean, don't be ridiculous,' I objected.

'Why not? We could call him B.B. for short.' And thus it was that my ugly friend with the tender whirlpool eyes joined us for a dinner of rabbit on a spit.

As we had not seen any soldiers for some days, our confidence was increasing. We moved around openly and spent the next few days covering over the mass grave. Even the children began to leave the cave and gouged out the earth with their bare hands to help to fill in the grave and they began searching for branches for our cooking fire. I decided to transfer the dead women's clothes and belongings from the shawls in which I had been keeping them. If I sewed up the shawls we could fill them with leaves and grass so as to make mattresses for the little ones.

Using laces from the women's shoes, the boys were able to set up a tripod over the fire, with a stick carved in the shape of an arrow for a roasting spit. We boiled water in the empty kidney bean tins, and I was able to make nettle soup. The boys had a difficult time finding enough meat for so many mouths but we managed. Every morning, Mo and I would take the children down to the stream where they could wash and play. Their eyes began to shine with a light I had not seen before. Baked Bean followed me everywhere with the fidelity of a lover. Never boisterous, never demanding, just being there. At night he would curve into my body. He kept me warm and soothed my spirit into sleep.

I had noticed that Mo frequently took out a postcard and focused on it as if charmed by it. There was something very intimate about the way he kept looking at it almost as if he was looking beyond it.

'Why do you keep reading that postcard?' I asked him one day.

'I don't read it. I know every word of it. I look at the picture. The blue sea, the white sands, palm trees – my brother is a teacher out in Zanzibar and he says it's quite beautiful and above all, peaceful. It's a kind of physical exercise I do. I place my heart in the picture to forget about all this suffering and hate. It makes a change from struggling against all this pain. It's like having a beautiful friend far away whom you love. It takes me away from here. Zanzibar is my sweetheart.'

CHAPTER SEVEN

It was B.B. who alerted us. He had been playing boisterously with the children in the stream and had suddenly grown still, staring up the mountain, his ears quivering. Mo grasped the situation long before I did and called the kids round him. 'Not a word from any of you – I think we have company. Go over to those rocks with Fran and keep absolutely still.' B.B. followed us as we merged into the rocks – it was the first time I had heard him growl. Mo had climbed up the willow tree above us from where he could get a better view. 'Everybody lie down,' I hissed. 'B.B. come here.' With unswerving loyalty B.B. bounded over and sat at my feet. He might not have a noble pedigree, but he was unquestionably the smartest dog in the universe. Mo, who was now on the first branch of the tree, put up his hand, showing three fingers, and pointed up the mountain. I could neither hear nor see anyone. I glanced around and realised that we were in a fairly secluded spot and unless the three intruders actually came downhill to the rocks, they could not see us. B.B. gave a long low growl and I yanked him into my arms. Then I saw them. They were in army uniform with Kalashnikovs slung over their shoulders. Their heads were shaven and they were carrying their caps in their hands. They looked no more than eighteen. I wondered if they might be deserters. It was impossible to tell whether they were the enemy or some of ours – in army fatigues everyone looked the same. One of them pointed to the stream and they began to descend. 'Oh, Jesus, please, please' I begged. I buried my face into B.B. and promised God the most outrageous things if he would only make them change direction. If they reached the rocks, they could not miss us. I could hear their conversation.

'You've got to shoot the bastards to show them we have power.'

'Surely, we can prove that to them without having to murder them.'

'It's not murder. They're saboteurs, traitors, terrorists. They're fucking up the world with their fucking subversive acts.'

'Fucking dirty Muslims.' They had passed under Mo's willow tree and were heading directly towards the rocks where we were hiding. One of the soldiers stopped and put on his cap before lighting a cigarette. As he offered the other two the packet, there was a commotion behind them as Mo dropped from his branch and began to run up the mountain.

'Fuck it – get him,' shouted the soldier with the cigarette. The other two chased after Mo, grabbing their Kalashnikovs from their shoulders. The third soldier threw away his cigarette and careered after them. The guns fired, as Mo zig-zagged up the mountain. I watched the pursuit dry eyed. I was too accustomed to pain. The guns fired again and Mo dropped like a stone. There was silence. I stroked B.B. and thought of the blue sea, the white sands and palm trees of Mo's beloved Zanzibar.

We buried Mo that night. Swallowed up by the violence of war, only the wind to carry his name across the mountain tops. None of us spoke. We all knew that he had saved our lives. His extraordinary heroism only fermented a grief that ebbed and flowed deep within me. I kept Mo's postcard and promised myself that I would write to his brother in Zanzibar one day. I desperately wanted the world to know the courage of a fourteen-year-old Muslim boy, who had a sweetheart off the coast of Africa. As in all great anguish, human solidarity was the balm that soothed our shared desolation. During the following days, our spirits revived and once again I began to take the children down to the stream to wash and play.

One afternoon I was using coarse grass to clean little Vedra's teeth when I noticed the boys huddled together arguing.

I put the grass into Vedra's hand. 'Here, you do it.' And I joined the adult group.

'What's going on?' I asked. They all looked at one another.

'We'd better tell her,' Assad said.

'Tell me what?' As usual it was Adjin who took the lead.

'We've got to move to the city.'

'But why, we're doing fine here.'

'Fran, by tomorrow we'll have run out of ammunition.'

'So? We'll find berries and I'll make more nettle soup.'

Gregor was playing with stones he had gathered from the stream.

'Fran, it won't be enough. There are too many of us.'

'Let's shoot one of the children and eat her,' I burst out. I bowed my head, confused. The hellish vision of what I had said absorbed us all for a moment. Gregor broke the silence.

'Adjin and Mustafa want to go and do a reconnaissance and see if we can get through the front line. We think the city might be surrounded.'

'Then why move from here?' In the few short days, the cave had become my security. I was scared of change. I stood looking at my fine friends with uncertainty. The look on each of their faces seemed to be saying 'Don't create division.' What a motley crowd we were. I became newly aware of all that I had conveniently forgotten: the suppressed horror; the shame of being free and undamaged when so many were being trapped or destroyed. The suggestion that we move on brought all my old terrors to the surface. I clenched my teeth and retorted, 'Do what you like. I don't care.' I picked up B.B. and walked away.

Mustafa and Adjin were away for three nights but it seemed like weeks. We hadn't eaten meat for three days and I was concerned for B.B. who resisted my nettle soup. On the fourth day, while the children were all in the cave, the two boys arrived back, hesitating before they approached as if they felt themselves to be strangers. They looked desperately thin and weary. Their faces suddenly seemed older and more experienced. Gone were the childlike expressions of bold and innocent daring. We clustered round, newly animated by their return and eager for news. Adjin sat down gravely and from his pockets pulled two loaves of bread. We gasped and stared at the loaves mesmerised. They were beautiful, almost seductive.

Adjin opened his penknife and sliced. The renewed lust for food was reflected in every face. 'OK, two slices each to start with.' Nobody moved. Adjin laughed. 'Go on, they're not poison.' I gave him a grateful glance and took the first slice. Each mouthful was better than the last – it was an orgy. 'We'll save the second loaf for the children. Now sit down and I'll tell you what Mustafa and I have found out.' Adjin and Mustafa had walked about fifteen miles when they had seen enemy soldiers flanking the mountain north of the city. The soldiers had appeared to be well equipped and highly organised. 'So what did you do then?' Ben asked.

'We backtracked, crossed the river and approached the city from the west across Mount Tabor – we followed the old mule trail – it was full of refugees with our soldiers bringing in ammunition and rifles on donkeys. Our soldiers told us that this was virtually the only way into the city and that the enemy are going to make a push for it during the next few days. So it's vital that we all leave immediately.'

'Did you get into the city yourselves?'

'No, we didn't try. We thought we'd better get back to you. Our soldiers told us that there was no problem getting into the city at the moment, but not to wait too long. They gave us their bread; sorry it's a bit stale by now.'

'What about the main roads?'

'Impassable. Enemy checkpoints every two miles.'

'And shelling?'

'They say the city has been damaged considerably. The good thing is that the enemy haven't yet realised that our soldiers are using the route over Mount Tabor, so they're not shelling there although they are apparently going to make a push to take it. But there's a very dangerous area as you enter the city called Sniper's Alley. Our main problem with the little ones is going to be time. There are only ten hours of darkness to get across the river, over the mountain and through Sniper's Alley.

'We should save the children's bread for tonight,' I remarked.

'You better tell them about the other problem,' Mustafa encouraged Adjin.

'Yes, well, they've mined the whole area we've got to cross to get to the mule trail across Mount Tabor.'

'Can't we see the minefields?'

'Not at night, you can't.'

'Shit! You mean we've got to lead the kids across minefields in the dark?' said Assad.

'That's about it. We have no option. Doing it in daylight would be suicidal.'

'Surely there's another way?' I said hopefully.

'Well,' Adjin hesitated. 'There might be a route from the south but our soldiers told us that there's a front line there too and anyway it would be at least another forty miles for the kids to walk. It's too far, Fran, in their condition.' B.B. nosed me and I tickled his neck.

'So we leave tonight?' Gregor sounded excited.

'No, we leave this afternoon as a group and cover the first twelve miles in daylight. It's fairly safe till we get to the mountain overlooking the city. Then I think we should cross the river and split into three groups. If we can send the children down to the stream this morning and pick up white pebbles, I will lead the first group across the minefields leaving the pebbles as markers for the rest of you to follow.' Adjin's words were measured, restrained and unemotional. Bold words for one so young. He continued more sharply. 'It's going to be hard on the kids, but they will die here if we don't move to the city, so we have no choice.'

We all sat dumbfounded, each of us, no doubt, desperately seeking another way out. But war does not bring choices, only the choice of survival or extinction. With heavy hearts, we began to prepare for our expedition.

I had never realised how slow and tedious it could be to walk with small children. Adjin was forced to cut the pace as the little ones soon flagged. At the beginning, Mustafa in the rear was encouraging us to move faster but he had now given up and lapsed into silence. Between us adults we tried to carry the smallest ones, but we were so drained of strength ourselves that we frequently had to rest. We had left the cave around midday and according to the sun we had covered only ten miles by late afternoon. There could only be two hours of daylight left at most.

'We must stop. The children are exhausted,' I implored, but Adjin insisted we must reach the river, so we staggered on, time and distance losing all meaning as our pitiful procession surged forward in stops and starts. With the final gleam of dusk we reached the river and gave the children their bread. Despite their insatiable hunger, the little ones could hardly lift the food to their mouths. I soaked one of the shawls and washed their faces. We let them drink as much as they wanted and then took off their shoes and placed their raw and blistered feet in the river. It all seemed so hopeless. How in the devil's name were we going to cross minefields and then another mountain? I attacked Adjin and Mustafa.

'Look at them. They can't continue,' I harangued. 'Even if you do get them across the minefields, they won't be able to climb the mountain.' Dirty, dusty and in rags, Adjin and Mustafa could scarcely conceal their exhaustion, and I knew that beneath their show of obstinacy, they realised that I was right. For both men, failure had once had no meaning. They had always been winners regardless of consequence or price. Now with neither food nor fire in their bellies they were experiencing for the first time what it was to be beaten.

I looked at the dark mountains that encircled us and then along the narrow fertile land by the stony river bank. I could just make out a narrow track leading to some poplar trees and then I glimpsed the shape of a building looming behind the trees. 'Quick before the light goes – follow me.' The effort to put on their shoes was too great, so the little ones staggered barefoot after me, whilst the boys struggled behind fighting their exhaustion. By the time we reached the building, the night was pitch black and the temperature was dropping rapidly. Hidden by the poplars and a moonless night, we circumnavigated the building. It appeared to be a semi-ruined barn riddled with dry rot. The planks had deteriorated and straddled the ground leaving yawning gaps. 'How do we know there aren't soldiers in there?' whispered Assad.

'We don't,' I replied.

'We can't risk taking the kids in there – suppose they have guns?'

'If we don't take risks we'll die.'

'You could get us all shot with that attitude,' Assad replied.

'Shut up you two,' Gregor interrupted. 'I've got a better idea. Let's send in B.B., then we'll know if it's occupied.' The conversation was about to degenerate into an open fight as I protested, when Adjin intervened.

'Fran, Gregor is right. It's common sense. You're usually quick to see that.'

'Suppose they shoot B.B.?'

'They have to see him first,' said Ben. I wanted to block my ears. I loved B.B.

'Truly Fran, it'll be all right. B.B.'s a survivor and he's quick. If they're in there they won't catch him,' Assad persuaded. So it was I slipped B.B. under my arm and tiptoed to the edge of the barn.

'You're the smartest dog on earth B.B. – now prove it,' I whispered in his ear, thrusting him through a small hole. Almost immediately I heard him growling which turned into prolonged barking. Before we could decide the next move, a shot was fired from within. I uttered a piteous sob, screwing up my eyes to see further than the wall of darkness. I hurled myself through another, larger hole screaming 'B.B. come here. Don't shoot him, he's only a dog. B.B. come here.' I felt the familiar wet nose against my face as I lay in the straw. I gathered him to me and crouched down trying to decide where the shot had come from. I was too tired to play the games of war. I stood up and said: 'Thank you for not shooting my dog. There is a group of children outside who have just walked fifteen miles. They're cold and they're exhausted, so we're coming in here for the night. We'll try not to disturb you,' and with that I leant through the hole and shouted to Assad to bring them all in. It was then that I felt the gun against my head and a voice said 'How many of you?'

'Seventeen.' I stood very still, 'and of course the dog you didn't shoot.'

There was a small chuckle from the darkness to the right of the gunman behind me. 'Kristoff, put down the gun. I know that voice – it's Fran.' A body came forward and clasped me, squeezing B.B. into my chest. It was Navid, Nanna's grandson, Navid, who had left our house so suddenly in order to join up when the rest of his family had come to take refuge. 'You really had me scared,' Navid was crying with laughter, thumping me on the back. I was crying with relief that I was alive, that Navid was alive, that B.B. was alive. Then the boys were there and they were all crying. Kristoff, the gunman, kept murmuring 'Please, noise travels in these hills. Quieten down. Do stop crying. Please everybody stop crying.' But we continued to cry happily till we could cry no more. Sleep finally embraced us with the sweetness of a kiss.

I woke to B.B. licking my face. 'I can wash myself, thank you.' I pushed him away and then, remembering the previous night, opened my eyes. The sun had risen and the horizon was clear. I checked the little ones who were still fast asleep. 'They're OK', said Kristoff. 'Sorry I put the gun to your head last night but we weren't to know.' I turned to Kristoff. He was exceptionally small with strong cheekbones and sad drooping eyes.

'Don't worry. But I would have killed you if you had shot B.B.,' I replied, looking him straight in the face. 'Where's Navid and the others?'

'Gone for supplies. We weren't expecting so many for Bed and Breakfast' Kristoff replied good-humouredly. 'They'll be back soon.'

'How long have you been here?'

'About three days.'

'With Navid?'

'Yes, we met up when crossing that mountain.' Kristoff pointed to the mountain we had walked across the previous day. 'I gather you all come from the same village.'

'Yes, at least quite a lot of us do.' I tried to remember our village but it all seemed like a dream.

'What happened?' Kristoff's questions disturbed me. I resented having to answer them and wanted to lead him astray. I certainly had no inclination to share our misfortune with a stranger.

'It's a long story. I don't want to talk about it.' Why couldn't I remember our village? I could hardly remember what Mamma and Dadda looked like. I plunged into the corridors of memory and could discover nothing. It was as if a new skin had developed encasing all recollection.

'You OK? asked Kristoff. 'You've gone as white as a sheet. Sorry, I didn't mean to probe.'

'For God's sake, stop saying sorry – I'm going outside, I need some air. Come on B.B.' I thrust past Kristoff rudely with B.B. dancing round my ankles. We scrambled down the slope to the river's edge where Assad lay cushioning his head on his hands, the water bottles heaped beside him. B.B. lapped up some water, carefully ensuring that his paws didn't get wet. I lay beside Assad and eventually rolled over on to my elbow and looked at him. 'Can you remember the past?'

'What do you mean by the past?'

'Well, can you remember your home? Your parents?' There was a pause.

'I suppose so.' Assad thought for a moment. 'Yes, it's a bit fragmented though. Why?' Suddenly I was furious with myself for bringing it up.

'Doesn't matter – just wondered.' Assad got up and began filling the water bottles.

'What's the matter, Fran? We've always shared things together.'

I could not bring myself to tell him that the past was obliterated under a new-grown skin and, worse still, that I could not envisage any kind of future. It was the final straw that I no longer felt able to confide in my oldest friend. We walked back to the barn in silence, but as we were about to climb through the gap, Assad took my hand. 'Fran, we have to live each day as it comes. Just concentrate on the present. When all this is over and order comes back to our lives, so will the past. Don't worry about it.'

'I don't want to forget – well, that's not altogether true either.'

'Just keep to the present,' he repeated, 'and we'll survive.'

A feast was taking place in the barn: bread, tomatoes and tinned fish.

'Come and join the finger-meal,' Kristoff hailed us.

'Where did you find all this?' Navid wiped the remainder of the fish from round his mouth and grinned spectacularly.

'Bartered for it on the mule trail a couple of nights ago.'

'With what?' asked Assad.

'My watch – but then Adjin and I had to find fresh bread this morning.'

'So there's a pâtisserie near here?' I asked naïvely and everybody laughed. I looked round the barn at their smiling faces.

'No, Fran – we pinched the bread from the front line,' Navid explained.

'Navid, in his uniform, looks like the enemy and he just strolls into the kitchens and helps himself' Adjin enlightened me. 'Here, have some more – on the house!' Everybody cheered.

Navid and the boys had been discussing our plans and it had

been agreed that Navid and Kristoff would join our group. Navid knew the terrain and he now began to brief us with an icy authority.

'We go tonight as soon as it's dark, leaving in groups of four or five, fifteen minutes apart. Kristoff will row each group across the river and I will take the first group across the minefields, leaving the trail of white pebbles for you to follow. We need some rope for the children to hang on to, so they can follow exactly in our footsteps, crossing the minefields. Once we hit the old mule trail, we're safe and we'll meet there. Now what are we going to do about rope?'

'We could tie the shawls together,' I suggested.

'Have you got eight?' I nodded, 'OK, two tied together for each group. You must make it absolutely clear to the little ones that they must follow exactly in your footsteps. Fran, you'll have to carry B.B. If you have a spare shawl, you can make a sling for him. Right, anybody any questions?' Navid looked at each of us.

'Are we likely to meet any soldiers? Or be sniped at?'

'No, they don't bother to patrol the minefields, so we should be safe enough. The guns are directly above us on that mountain but hopefully they're pointing towards the city and not at us.'

'If that's the case, surely we could cross it in daylight which would be so much safer for all of us?' I suggested.

'It's a hell of a risk for even one person to cross the minefields in daylight, as they can see us from the mountain. I don't think we'd have a hope in hell with so many of us. OK, everybody get some rest. It's going to be a long night.'

We slept as well as we could and when the time came we all hugged Navid and wished him luck. He left with Kristoff and three of the little ones. Kristoff had left his watch with us. Fifteen minutes later, Adjin and Gregor and their three little ones rose together and once again we exchanged the silent ritual of farewell, the repeated words of encouragement. For the next fifteen minutes, my head hammered. It concerned me deeply that I could not remember the past and that time seemed so strange. It made me feel a captive and that therefore my freedom must be an illusion. How much was a figment of my imagination? Was I playing with fire? What were these chains that fettered my mind?

'Time, Fran,' Assad whispered as he handed Kristoff's watch to Mustafa. Once again in the darkness of the barn shadows, we all hugged. I held little Vedra's tiny hand and with my right arm supported B.B., sleeping like a baby in his sling. The Jambrosic twins, with their hair tied in tails, trotted beside Assad, like small ponies.

The noise of the distant battle rang in our ears. There was little wind and it was a clear moonless night. The madness had begun again and they were shelling the city under cover of darkness, but for us the darkness breathed compassion embracing the past. Mindlessly, I followed Assad. I suppose we had walked for half an hour along the river towards the boat when Assad beckoned us to join him and told us to sit down. 'Why isn't Kristoff here?' I whispered.

'He is – over there, just coming in to the jetty.' I could just make out a figure sculling across the river, slipping through the smooth water to his mooring.

'Come on,' Assad ordered and one by one Kristoff helped us into the rowing boat. There were tarpaulin sheets which we snuggled beneath as Kristoff skilfully cleared a mooring buoy and began rowing rhythmically towards the further bank. As I stared at the stars, twinkling like daisies, I could feel B.B.'s heart pumping in unison with my own. Kristoff shipped his oars and we gently slid alongside the jetty and he motioned us to disembark. Kristoff gave Assad a long stick, 'You might need it to prod the ground in front of you. See that scarf, follow the trail from there. Good luck. See you later,' and he was gone, swallowed up by the silent river. I took the shawls from round my neck and began to tie them together into our rope. 'Remember, we must keep very close and concentrate on where you put your feet,' said Assad. 'Try to follow exactly in the footsteps of the person in front of you.'

'Like Good King Wenceslaus,' murmured little Vedra, clinging to her piece of shawl rope behind the twins. As the night was not pitch black we could see the white pebbles with ease. Our progress was nevertheless extremely slow because Assad insisted on prodding the ground in front at every step. One pace, two paces, three paces. I fixed my mind on the step ahead and when I reached a hundred, I started again at one pace, two paces, three paces. After a couple of hours I was in a daze, my head and shoulders aching with tension.

The explosion came suddenly: short and sharp, it must have been about half a mile ahead. We stopped in our tracks as the eerie silence descended again. My mind was still counting paces when I realised the significance of the explosion. 'Adjin,' I screamed and I was about to break the line myself when Assad's steely voice reached me choking with emotion, 'Fran, don't move.'

Little Vedra began to cry. 'What's happened – what was that noise?' I thought I was going to be sick. B.B. was struggling to free himself from the sling. Assad's voice again: 'Everybody kneel down where you are. Don't move.' I dropped the shawl rope and clung to B.B., who was now agitated. I could see over the heads of the children. Assad's shoulders were shaking as he mourned his friend.

'It's all right Vedra. We're just resting.' But Vedra had stopped crying. She looked over her shoulder at me. 'Was that Adjin and Gregor and the others?'

I felt my back arch beneath the terrible burden. My heart burst with the memory of Adjin, of his boldness and compassion. Adjin who had had the heart of a lion and the gentleness of a lamb. Sensing that he must be close while knowing that he had gone, I stretched out my arm to touch him and clawed thin air. Any hope of safety evaporated as terror turned to meet me.

CHAPTER EIGHT

We passed the place of death and our hearts melted at the hollow darkness of that huge hole in which was buried the valiance of youth. We walked round it knowing that flesh had scorched the earth and that we must never look back. We arrived at the mule trail almost blinded. We did not see the thin bent shoulders of the refugee women staggering up the track, nor the lost children in rags upon rags, limping at their sides. We did not see the shadows of our soldiers, laden with guns, enticing their donkeys forward as the animals staggered beneath their huge loads of cartridges, shells and machine guns. Reality had been fragmented by the shedding of innocent blood. Slowly and silently we joined the caravan of human hopelessness rolling as one exhausted torso across the mountain pass.

In Sniper's Alley the guns were waiting for us.

Nobody ran. We just tightened our hold on the children and surrendered our lives to the spluttering flashes. The war was over for Mo, Adjin and Gregor. The dead were still, the dead made no noise. In Sniper's Alley the wounded moaned; some screamed as they fell. One or two writhed, their outstretched arms pleading for help as we tripped over their dying bodies. One man grabbed at my ankles, bones like ivory sticks jutting out from bleeding flesh. We kicked to free ourselves, sometimes tripping in their blood, picking ourselves up, floundering, lurching, holding tight to one another. All the time I clasped B.B. to my chest and that was the last thing I remember.

The trembling had started again – my head was a muddle. I could hear Mamma but could not see her. Her voice came from way down inside. Mamma was washing my face, wiping away my tears. I opened my eyes and B.B. was gently licking my ears. Little Vedra, in her torn print dress, shyly slipped a finger into my clenched hand. 'Are you better?' she asked. I was lying on the makeshift seat of a burnt-out bus which was full of tangled wreckage. The sun reflected against the broken windows. There was no noise until, suddenly, a high-pitched whistle. It was Assad and little Vedra laughed with delight. She flew down the aisle of the bus followed by B.B. 'Assad, Fran's better,' I heard her shout. Assad and the twins crowded round me. Assad was so pale with black welts beneath his eyes. 'Oh, Fran, I thought you were going to die.'

'Why? Am I hurt?' I stared down at my body.

'Not physically,' was all he said. He kissed me on my forehead like Dadda had always done. 'Come, kids, we're going to celebrate now that Fran has come back to us.' They dispersed, leaving B.B. lying on the floor of the bus, his clear eyes looking up at me. I sat up and in one leap B.B. had landed in my lap, light as a butterfly. He curled himself into my stomach and released himself into sleep, totally at peace now that he knew I was well.

The little ones returned with bread and raisins.

'Where did you get that from?' I asked amazed.

'They gave it to us at the soup kitchen,' Vedra replied. 'And we've got something special for you, Fran.' The twins opened their hands and on each palm were four immaculate feathers.

'How lovely. Where did you find them?'

'Down by the river.'

'But you mustn't go down . . .'

'It's OK, Fran,' Assad interrupted. 'We were very careful. They've stopped shelling. Now you must eat and here's some water.' I ate slowly, devouring every morsel, not dropping a crumb. They watched me as if I was performing some miraculous ritual.

'What happened, Assad?' I had finished the last raisin.

'You tell me,' he smiled. 'What do you last remember?'

'Sniper's Alley.'

'Nothing after that?'

I shook my head.

'We were walking out of it when some of our soldiers appeared. They picked up the little ones and brought us all to safety. They let us sleep in this bombed-out building and then told us to go to the Karatz area for safety. But you insisted we should go to Idris's house – your father's friend – so we walked down to the river. Don't you remember?'

'No.'

'When we got to the river, the whole of Idris's road had been shelled, so we made our way here a few streets away and found this wreck. You've been sleeping ever since.'

'How long ago was that?'

'Yesterday. I tried to wake you a couple of times but you didn't respond. I was scared you'd given up.' Tears blurred his eyes.

'Oh, Assad, I'm sorry,' I mumbled. Suddenly I remembered the others. 'Ben? Mustafa? Did they get through?'

'I don't know, Fran. Navid's alive. He was with the soldiers who took you to safety. He said he would wait for Ben and Mustafa and the other children at the end of Sniper's Alley and send them on to Karatz. Navid reckoned Kristoff would come with them as they were the last boat-load he would be bringing across the river and he would stay with them and help them through.'

'It's a not matter of help. It's a bloody lottery out there.' I burst into tears. 'I wish I had died with Gregor and Adjin,' I whimpered. My head crashed back as Assad's hand struck my face. He bent over me, his eyes quite neutral, no anger, no tenderness. 'Fran,' he hissed. 'We've come this far. I'm not going to let those bastards beat us and nor are you. This is part of the promise of friendship we made when we were in the prayer room at my house. But now, while it's quiet, we've got to find food and a more permanent residence. I'll take the twins if you will keep Vedra.' I was sitting with food in my belly, unhurt and alive. But my head was spinning as I tried to absorb this new landscape of change and take in all that Assad had told me.

As soon as I stepped out of the bus, I could smell the cordite. We were in a side-road with the stumps of trees which would once have formed an avenue but had now been salvaged for firewood by the locals. Ahead and behind us were burnt-out cars in which I could see shadowy figures – presumably in hiding from unknown antagonists. The buildings on either side of the road were mounds of rubble. A new sound came from the city centre as the mortars fell. I felt small and fearful as I scavenged in the trash, listening intently to the rumble of the heavy Howitzer shells falling on the outskirts of the city. Everything around us seemed dark. Everything had been damaged by the shells. Some children with sticks raised over their shoulders were standing by some guttering. They had killed a rat and were squabbling over their raw dinner like a pack of wolves. Then B.B. pranced forward. They saw him and for a moment were overcome with astonishment. Then, shouting and waving their sticks, they pursued him across the wasteland.

'Go back to the bus, Vedra. I'll be along as soon as I've found B.B.,' I ordered. But I was too weak to run for long. Thoughts whirled in my head as I gasped for breath. Surely they wouldn't catch him? Even if they did, there was hardly enough flesh on him for a single mouthful. B.B. was too smart for street urchins! Surely they would see that the rats were bigger than he was? Time crept by with mortal slowness. Surely, they wouldn't catch him? Try as I might to think of something else, my thoughts continually reverted to the image of B.B. savagely beaten to death to stay their hunger.

I turned into a main road and found myself face to face with a convoy of white trucks. There were five or six young men dressed in shorts and grubby T-shirts, wearing baseball caps back to front. On their feet, they wore boots with steel caps over heavy woollen socks. They were unarmed. I was so agitated by the loss of B.B. that caution was abandoned. I approached the nearest unshaven man, who was tearing at the cardboard boxes on the back of his lorry. 'Excuse me, Sir, did a small brown dog pass this way?' The man ceased his work and blinked at me in perplexity.

'Have you seen a small brown dog?' The man took off his cap and wiped the sweat from his face. He was flushed, his eyes bloodshot from too little sleep and probably too much drink. Only then did I realise he was neither one of us, nor the enemy, and he certainly wasn't familiar with our mother tongue. The man waved me to the next truck where a giant figure, with hair falling to his shoulders from his baseball cap, stood with his back to me supervising a chain of men unpacking the rows of boxes banked neatly one on top of the other.

'Excuse me, Sir, have you seen my dog? He's small and oval and he's called Baked Bean . . .' I would have rambled on in my misery if the huge man hadn't turned. Suddenly, I remembered. This was 'god', whom I had met on the ski slopes all those years ago. 'God', who had picked me out of the snow and given me chocolate. The same dishevelled beard below the downtrodden horseshoe moustache, the same stunning blue eyes staring out of his tanned face. The man stood in the centre of his open truck like a bronze sculpture of Achilles, one foot resting on a box. His formidable physique was no less impressive than when I had seen him five years earlier. He tilted his head slightly and in our language said, 'That's a strange name for a dog.' I nodded breathlessly as the man crouched before me just as he had done when I was seven. With his lithe arm he pulled at my nose as I dared to whisper 'God! You've come back.' The man lifted me up onto the back of the truck as if I was still a small child. He gazed at me in bewilderment. Five years was a long time and I had changed. Would he remember me? Then I saw light beginning to dawn! The man smiled at me bewitchingly. 'You always were a strange little kid,' he said. 'Can you ski now without falling over? Mind you, you're so thin I think I could probably blow you over.' He shouted to one of his drivers who came across and they exchanged a few words. 'Well, my little lady, when you're a bit older we'll celebrate with champagne but for the moment it's like old times. Have some chocolate?'

I stayed and helped god unpack the boxes. They were full of flour, oil, salt, pasta and sugar. He told me that when the war had broken out here, he had decided to become an aid worker and had joined a non-governmental organisation called Comfort Aid, who were sending convoys of food out from England every six weeks. This was his fourth trip.

'But how do you get past the checkpoints?'

'We have a UN card which will work as long as they let the UN in here, but I've heard rumours that the city is going to be blockaded so I don't know what will happen after that.'

'I hate the UN'

'Why's that?'

'Dadda told me they were coming here to protect us. We all thought they would look after us but they don't. They stand and watch us die and don't lift a finger.'

God came and sat beside me in the truck and gave me a hard, challenging stare. He hitched up his left knee and placed an arm across my shoulders. 'Fran, their hands are tied. Their mandate is to deter aggression, not to defend your people.'

'They could have stopped all this suffering.'

'Their policy is to alleviate suffering where they can, but they are not allowed to use force to stop it.'

'Dadda told me that the UN charter was for the benefit of people – that it had been set up after the atrocities of the last world war. Dadda said that now it is governed by politicians who have their own agendas. He said it had moved away from being a UN of the people and for the people to being a UN of the politicians for the policies of the member countries. He said UN bureaucracy comes before reality.' I found it comforting that I could remember my father's words, despite having no clear picture of what he looked like.

'Are you going to defend the UN?' I challenged. God laughed at me.

'I didn't think you'd be one to get interested in politics,' he chuckled.

'I'm not, but Assad says only the politicians can stop all this. So what do you reckon to the UN?' God rubbed his beard thoughtfully, staring at his boots.

'I just don't know. It seems that the UN has failed to stand against aggression. They failed to implement UN Security Council resolutions and therefore failed to provide the necessary resources to defeat the aggressors. I guess what should have been a clear policy of arming your people and assisting them with immediate air-strikes on military targets, has been reduced to a peace-keeping and humanitarian venture.'

'So policy now is just to feed us . . .' I replied bitterly.

'Hold on, Fran. You're not being quite fair. If the UN hadn't moved in, this war would have escalated and could well have spread to other countries. They're also a great asset to us non-governmental organisations. If their sappers – the engineers – weren't here to replace the bombed bridges with Bailey bridges, our trucks would never reach cities like this one and you'd all starve to death.' Once again he rubbed his beard thoughtfully and then continued. 'You know, in a way the UN are in a hostage situation themselves. They're not an army – well, not in the aggressive sense – they're a peace-keeping force caught here between warring factions with deep religious and ethnic differences. But they have to remain impartial themselves. It's a cocktail for disaster. Now I must get back to work. Look at all these children waiting for us to give out supplies. I'd better go and organise my other drivers – back in a tick.'

He jumped down from the back of the truck and waded through the growing mass of people lingering for hand-outs. It was then that I remembered B.B., but decided to wait for god to return. I began to scavenge through the boxes and found some preserved fruit and nuts. Hiding behind other columns of cartons, I gave in to temptation, eating delicious handfuls, whilst those in the street patiently awaited their turn. I desperately needed to pee, so I pulled down my jeans and crouched down watching the urine dribble down the sides of the boxes turning the cardboard a dark brown as the liquid spread. Having eaten all I could manage, I filled my pockets with more. I would tell god when he returned. I must have dozed off for I was jerked into life when the truck shuddered as god jumped into the back. 'Fran, where are you?' I peered out from behind the boxes. 'Good, I thought you might have gone.

Sorry I was so long, but we had to unload the other trucks – I've sent them back to base, so would you like to help me?' I nodded as he handed me a box. 'Give one box to each person in the queue.' It took us an hour before the truck was empty, although people were still standing around hoping for more. God was standing in the road talking to some of the children, whilst I was sitting on the back swinging my legs, wondering whether he would help me look for B.B.

A small girl tugged at my foot. She was a wisp of a child with dark curly hair, hardly older than the war. I patted her on the head like I would B.B. and told her that all the food had been given out. She looked hungry, but no hungrier than all the other children in the city. She persisted in standing in front of me, alone.

'What do you want?' I barked. 'I've told you, there's no food left. Go on, hop it.' I had to tell god about the food I had stolen and I had to find B.B. I had no time for some wretched street kid whose mother let her wander about in a city full of soldiers. She moaned so quietly that I barely heard her.

'Bugger off.' I pushed her away with my foot. The child just stood there with two tears on either cheek. I said nothing and looked straight over her head. If Mamma had been here her eyes would have filled with tears for this infant. If Mamma had been here, she would have wept to see the darkness of my spirit. I remembered the words she had taught us at Sunday School, out in the paddock, one summer morning, as we were making daisy chains: 'When I was hungry, you fed me. When I was thirsty, you gave me drink. When I was a stranger, you took me into your home. I tell you this – anything you did for one of my brothers here, however humble, you did for me. This is my Commandment: love one another, as I have loved you.' Mamma had been a good woman, I thought. Like a sharp sword piercing my heart, I realised that I had used the past tense. My guilt towered higher than my head. Mamma was probably dead and I was still alive though I didn't deserve to be.

'Come here, little one. What do you want to tell me?' Without a word, she took one step forward and pointed at her feet. She was barefoot.

'You need some shoes?' She bit her lip and nodded. I knew there were none in the truck, so I shouted over to god. 'This child has no shoes. I suppose you haven't got any back at your base?' He walked over to the truck followed by children like bees round a honeypot.

'I really don't know, but I have some lace-ups in the cabin.' He threw me the keys. I had had no idea how high off the ground the driver's cab would be, and only after three efforts was I able to scramble in. The white running shoes were in a plastic bag under the passenger seat along with some bottled water. I lay across the seats and guzzled half the water. The lace-ups were huge, I reflected, as I drank some more. Still, they were better than nothing. I climbed out and returned the keys to god, who appeared to be making a list of the children's requirements.

'Here you are,' I said triumphantly. The child and I stared at the vast white canoes which could have been made for a polar bear. She stood quietly, her arms at her sides, making no effort to take possession of the shoes. 'I know they're huge, but your feet will grow,' I said feebly. Suddenly she looked up, as if shocked out of sleep and sighed deeply.

'What's the matter now?' I expected a small murmur of a reply and was quite shocked at the plummy dismissive voice in which she responded: 'They're no good. You don't understand. When Mummy and Daddy were killed, they hadn't taught me to tie my laces.' I was not prepared for such an explanation and stood speechless. We stared wide-eyed at one another: two fighters assessing each other's strength. With great gravity I bent down, picked up her minute body. I walked across the road away from the truck.

'I will teach you how to tie your laces.'

'When?'

'Now.' I sat her next to me on the kerb. And then it happened as I was bending over to put on her shoes. The volley of gunshots whistled past, raking the cobblestones, echoing on down the street and bouncing off the buildings. Havoc broke out as some children ran for cover whilst others threw themselves to the ground throwing their arms over their heads for protection. I remember the screaming, as I flung myself over my infant, grimly thinking that Mamma could be proud of me now. The noise ceased as suddenly as it had started. 'You all right?' I asked and without waiting for a reply I rose on one knee and surveyed the chaos across the road. Children were lying by the truck which had also been hit. Petrol was pouring from its belly. I saw god's massive body cloaking a couple of little ones by the rear wheel on the driver's side. The screaming was over and I could hear suppressed weeping. I was on my feet. I stared at the wounded children lying by the truck. A tiny barefoot waif, who could not tie her laces, had saved my life. Only a minute previously, I had been sitting in the direct line of fire.

I ran across the road and stared at the carnage. My escape had been miraculous. Adults were now on the scene. I heard someone say that the last ambulance in the city had been blown up during the previous week, but one fire engine was left and the fire station was two streets down. Three kids had been badly shot. Five were walking wounded.

Someone arrived with a car and the unconscious children were unceremoniously lifted into it and driven away at high speed. I looked round for god; perhaps I could help him! I noticed a crowd at the rear of the truck and then understanding exploded in my head. I struggled through the mob of spectators, all giving advice at the tops of their voices until they heard my wail.

'God!' Complete silence as I threw myself down beside him. Someone was holding god's wrist. I was mesmerised by the hole in his leg. 'He's alive!' said one spectator. 'Anybody got a car?' The one and only car had gone. 'What about the fire engine?'

'It's the other side of town dealing with the library which has just been shelled.'

'How far's the hospital?' a stranger asked. 'Could we carry him there?'

'No stretcher.'

'You can have my wheelbarrow if it's of help.'

'Better than nothing,' somebody said. Hands grasped me and pulled me away from god, so that he could be loaded into the barrow. A woman stuffed a scarf into the hole in his leg, which now hung limply over the side. Two men took the handles, whilst another supported god's head, and wheeled him down the centre of the road. Trembling, I followed, at a distance.

The hospital had been shelled and from the ground up-wards it was useless. But in the basement, it was business as usual. Little was left of the roof and the walls were pitted with shell holes. Sandbags blocked all the windows. It was a carcass. But the long basement corridors, with their decrepit pipes belonging to the ancient central heating system, were a subterranean hive of activity. Scrubbed kitchen tables were being used for operations whilst the patients lay on blown-out doors and on planks of wood along the unlit passageways. The doctors were obviously working night and day by candlelight with little or no equipment. I came to realise that as there was no electricity in the city, there were no fridges or freezers for plasma and no form of sterilisation. It was well known that major wounds in either legs or arms often had to be dealt with by amputation. And there was a severe shortage of anaesthetics and antibiotics.

I sat beside god for hours in the darkness of the corridor, longing for a cry of pain, a small sigh, a movement, any acknowledgment that there was life in that powerful body. He remained unconscious.

Grief stalked the pavements.

CHAPTER NINE

God was operated on twelve hours after his arrival in that cheerless basement corridor. For twelve hours I had sat beside him in the dark, listening to the groans and screams of the acute surgical cases. The stony-eyed nurse agreed that I could see him for a few moments after the operation. God was in a cubicle, curtained off from the confusion in the passage, lying in a bed without any coverings. I gazed at his leg in tremulous silence. His shorts had been cut and the leg was thickly bandaged.

'Time you went.' Stony-Eyes was palpably hostile.

'Why hasn't he woken up?'

'See those bruises on his head – that's why. He's had a hell of a knock and the doctor reckons there's bruising round the brain – maybe more damage than that but we haven't an X-ray machine down here, so who knows. Personally I'd be more worried about his leg. With no antibiotics, we find that gangrene sets in very quickly and then of course we have to amputate. Is he your brother?' I was about to deny it, but instinctively heard myself say 'yes'.

'Well, young lady, if you want to help him, the best thing you can do is find him some antibiotics.'

'How do I do that?' Stony-Eyes flared her nostrils and glared at me.

'There are ways,' she replied.

'What ways?' I insisted.

She lowered her voice. 'Black market.' I was mystified.

'Forget it, you wouldn't have the money anyway.' I was intuitively reluctant to admit to having a belt of ready cash around my waist.

'I could get money.'

'Could you, now.' I knew she was playing with me.

'Yes. If you help me, I'll help you.' We stared at each other.

'That sounds neighbourly,' said Stony-Eyes. 'Come with me. We can't talk here.'

Mechanically, I followed her up the steps to the street where there was a momentary lull in the shelling.

'What's the deal?' I asked, trying to give my voice a professional intonation.

'There are plenty of antibiotics at the UN hospital in the Gazda suburb – distribution is from the warehouse at the UN centre there. I have a contact name but he won't do business over the phone.'

'So how do I get hold of him?'

'He works and lives in the UN compound.'

'So, what you're saying is I have to somehow get into the compound which is no doubt guarded and make contact with him there.'

'You've got it in one.' Stony-Eyes' iciness made me feel sick.

'How much do you want?'

'FiftyDMs. Cheap at the price for saving your brother's leg.' I stood for a moment weighing up whether or not I was about to become a victim of Stony-Eyes' underworld connections. Then I had a mental picture of god with only one leg, unable to ski.

'OK, it's a deal. I'll bring you the money in the morning.' I walked away into the black night, almost lighthearted. Part of it was sheer exhaustion, part was my resolution that I was going to save god's leg. But that vital sense of conquest vanished when I realised that I was totally lost. I became panic stricken. I had not even checked the name of the road where our bus was parked, let alone the area. Fatigue, despair and intolerable tension seized me: my eyeballs pricked and I found myself starting to cry. I heard someone shout 'Get off the bloody street. Don't you know there's a curfew,' but whether or not it was directed towards me, I neither knew nor cared. All I knew was that I had to flee this kingdom of death. For so long I had seen nothing but the dirt, wounds and blood of mangled and dying men. I was marooned in this broken world of warfare, in which atonement seemed to lie in the death of the innocent.

I opened my tear-filled eyes and stared at the dull dawn with an aching bitterness. Hunger forced me to move. As I stretched my stiff limbs I felt something shift from my stomach. I froze. The last thing I needed was to be chewed by a rat, and then the nose nuzzled my face. It was B.B. My misery dissolved as I embraced him.

'You found me. You're the greatest dog on earth.' I squeezed him, stroked him and squeezed him again. I was delirious with joy. He was the most beautiful and gifted animal ever created. I swear he looked at me out of those sombre brown eyes with a gleam of amusement. All my vigour and optimism had returned. I rose and brushed the bomb-site dirt off my jeans.

'OK, light of my life, take me home,' and my sweet friend did just that.

When I got back to the bus, I found Assad, Vedra and the twins sitting on the floor. I regaled them with the events of the previous twenty-four hours and when I looked into Assad's eyes I could see his admiration. Little Vedra had scooped up B.B. and was feeding him the remains of the bread ration from the soup kitchen, whilst the twins sat listening intently as if I was telling them a fairy tale.

'So, Fran, how are you going to get into the UN compound?' Assad asked drily.

'We've got to create a diversion.' They looked at me blankly. Assad clicked his tongue. 'You're too clever by half, Fran.' I could see he was rejecting the idea.

'It can't be that difficult. Apparently there's only one man on the gate.'

'What about stealing a UN card?' one of the twins asked.

'No, that's out of the question. Everyone has their photo on their card.'

'Why can't you just go to the UN compound and ask the guard to phone this man and tell him to come to the gate?' asked Assad reasonably.

'Because no UN official dealing in the black market is going to publicly expose himself by coming to meet a contact at the gate in front of the guard.' There was a long silence in the bus. I licked my lips wishing I had not mentioned the problem of the antibiotics.

'OK, a diversion it will have to be.' Assad was struggling to sound detached.

'We could set fire to the guard house.' The second twin covered her mouth to smother a shriek of mirth. Assad tossed the twins a reproachful glance.

'Why don't you kids take B.B. for a walk?' he snapped.

'I can do it,' Little Vedra's chin trembled.

'Do what?'

'Make a diversion.' She flushed. We all looked shocked. Vedra was a pretty five-year-old with honey-coloured skin and hair the shade of autumn beech leaves. Her dark velvet eyes shone with a deep and fierce love that reminded me of B.B. Assad's ill-temper had blown away like a puff of wind.

'And how would you make a diversion?'

'Just because I'm little, doesn't mean I don't know things,' she replied mischievously.

'What do you mean, Vedra?' Assad's calm voice did not betray any impatience. 'Do you know what she's talking about, Fran?'

'Haven't a clue.' I realised the little minx was enjoying the attention. 'Come on, spit it out,' I encouraged.

'I'll go up to the guard and pretend he's touched me and make a big noise.'

I was not quite sure that I was understanding her. Neither was Assad.

'What do you mean, Vedra?' he asked somewhat stiffly.

'You're thick, Assad. I'll pretend he's touched me down there.' She pointed to her crotch. Assad turned a deep red.

'Vedra!' I tried to sound shocked but was unable to suppress a burst of laughter. 'But it's brilliant.' The twins erupted into helpless giggles.

Assad sat po-faced with disapproval and a sheepish self-consciousness.

'How does she know about that at her age?' he snorted. But little Vedra just beamed and said 'My mummy told me that if any man touched me there, he was wicked and I must tell her immediately. I know about the birds and the bees so I put two and two together. I had five older sisters you know!' I gazed down at this cherubic child.

'Fran, you can't let her do that,' Assad said gruffly.

'Do what?' The twins and I broke into gales of laughter.

'You know what I mean.'

'Come off it Assad, there's no harm. She's only going to pretend he's abused her and make a scene, a big scene, so as to divert all the attention. It's simple.'

'Fran, it's not right to let Vedra do that. She's only a small child.'

'She might be small, but she's older than you are giving her credit for.'

'I think we should go outside and discuss it without the little ones.'

There were passionate objections and one of the twins, grinning in triumph, said 'We're the ones to discuss it with, if we're going to be the actors.' Their faces were flushed with excitement.

'Hold it. You can't pretend he's touched all three of you – that's a bit over the top,' I said discouragingly.

'It was my idea,' Vedra said firmly.

'Yes. It was her idea,' I repeated. Assad was obviously very much against it. 'Come on, Assad, you're being a prude.'

'What's a prude?' the twins asked in unison.

'Never you mind. It's not good for you to know so much when you're so little. I'm going back to the hospital to see god and to get the name of the contact from the nurse. Perhaps Assad you could help prepare Vedra for her Oscar-winning performance,' I chuckled. Assad shook his head in disbelief. 'B.B., you stay here. I won't be long.'

It took me some time to reach the hospital again what with avoiding the bomb damage and the UN checkpoints. Stony-Eyes informed me that god had regained consciousness, before she asked whether we were still in business. As I was about to hand over the money she whispered 'Not here. I'll bring the dressings into your brother's cubicle,' as she pushed me towards his bed. God was asleep. His wounded leg stretched out and the bandages stiff with blood, obviously not having been changed since the operation. I perched myself on his bed and held his limp hand in mine. His eyes flickered and opened. He was staring at me. 'How are you doing, god?' At which point Stony-Eyes appeared with a dressing tray.

'Is he awake?' I said that he was and without further ado

Stony-Eyes uncovered the suppurating wound – it was scarlet, the bone laid bare. For a moment, I thought I was going to faint, but faced with her calm efficiency, I confidently held the basin for the bloody swabs. As Stony-Eyes was leaving I handed over the money and she pointed to an unused dressing. 'My contact's name is on the back of that.' God was moaning with pain.

'Can you give him some morphine?' I asked.

She laughed at me. 'We haven't had any morphine in this hospital for months. You can try the UN,' and she departed. I picked up the dressing and without looking at the name, put it in my pocket. I stroked god's head and promised him that one day he would walk, swim and run with two good legs. A couple of times he smiled at me, but I could see that the excruciating pain was draining his energy. At one point he screamed, 'Don't touch me,' and then sagged back, his face twitching violently.

'God, I'm here. I won't let you lose a leg. It'll be all right,' I sobbed, pressing my lips against his fevered cheek. I was so overwhelmed with grief that I found it impossible to speak and just lay beside him comforting his pain-racked body, my puny arms as far round his massive shoulders as they would stretch. I do not know how long I stayed, but I thought of the curfew and asked a passing orderly how long I had. He looked at his watch and told me that curfew started in forty-five minutes. I squeezed god's hand.

'I'll be in tomorrow.' I fled down the dark corridors, fled from the stench of decomposition and the screaming of the wounded, and climbed the steps into fresh air.

Once outside, I looked at the dressing Stony-Eyes had given me. The name written on it was André Pauchon. I memorised it.

The next morning Vedra, the twins and I started to put our plan into operation with Assad's reluctant agreement.

'OK, everybody. It's a good seven miles to the UN compound, so let's go to the soup kitchen first and eat. The kitchen is on our way.' I put the shawl round my neck to make a sling to hide B.B. It was also useful as a spare larder; we could slip food in there unnoticed.

The soup kitchen had been a shop in one of the main streets of the market-place. It was pitted with shell marks but still standing. I was taken aback by the queue of refugees – there must have been over five hundred of us and the day had hardly begun. There were six soup kitchens in the city, run by the locals and apparently supplied from the main UN warehouse. I could not help but reflect that should the enemy soldiers wish to score against us, the soup kitchens would be the places to shell since so many of us were all in one place.

My thoughts were disturbed by a commotion behind us. 'Fran, Assad!' It was Ben and Mustafa and their little ones shouting, and throwing themselves into our arms. Our joy was great and noisy, as we clapped one another on the back laughing and praising each other in our delight at having survived. The refugees, who had been silently queuing in front of the soup kitchen, broke into cheers, shaking us by the hands and congratulating us on our reunion. There was a festive spirit, everybody talking at once.

'Did you meet up with Navid?'

'Did you hear about Adjin and Gregor?'

'Did Kristoff come with you?'

'Where are you living?'

We told Ben and Mustafa about the bus in Karatz but that we were looking for somewhere safer. Whether it was the cheerful noise or just a kind gesture, the refugees in front waved us past and we found ourselves at the front of the queue being given soup and bread.

'You must come and see where we're staying,' Ben said enthusiastically.

'We can't today, we're on our way to the UN compound,' and Assad told them about god and how we had to infiltrate the black market to secure the drugs he needed. Time was passing and I was anxious to start walking as our time was limited because of the curfew. I heard Mustafa say, 'You can't be serious.'

'Well, have you a better idea?'

'Indeed I have. It's a question of who you know.'

'Well, do you know somebody? Can you help us?'

'No problem. I'll get the drugs for you. Have you got the money?'

I was reticent, not because I did not trust Mustafa, but we were in a public place and walls had ears. I gave Assad a knowing look. He understood.

'Finish your soup, kids, and let's go back to the bus,' was all he said. We made our way back, glad to be together again and pleased to be able to show Ben, Mustafa and the other children our new domain.

Ben and Assad took the little ones to fill up the water bottles from the nearest standpipe. I was alone with Mustafa.

'You're a devious one,' his eyes twinkled.

'How do you mean?'

'Well, you never told us that you had all that money on you when we were in the cave.'

'Actually, I had forgotten,' I replied truthfully.

'I believe you, but some wouldn't. Do you all sleep here?'

'Yes, it's quite comfortable but cold at night.'

'I can get you some blankets. What else do you need?'

'Nothing really.' My mind had gone blank. We were used to having nothing.

'You're not very organised, are you?'

'We've only been here for forty-eight hours.'

'There are agencies like UNPROFOR and UNHCR who provide relief items for refugees like us. By the way, what have you done with the list of names of the dead from the cave?'

'It's in my shoe.' Why did Mustafa make me feel so inferior I wondered, or was I aggrieved with him because I was getting the impression that he was trying to act as our leader, now that Adjin was dead. Perhaps it was simpler. I just did not like Mustafa telling me what to do. How odd, I mused. If it had been god questioning me I would have thought it was magic. 'Are you sure you can get the drugs?' I asked him, changing the subject.

'Trust me. I'll get them for you. Where's the money?' I pulled up my shirt, unstrapped Dadda's belt and pulled out a 200DM note.

'It's all I've got,' I lied.

'I don't know what the price is on the black market, but that should buy enough for a couple of weeks.'

'I need morphine and antibiotics.'

'Fran, I'll get what I can with the money you've given me.'

I hesitated and then asked, 'How do you know the people involved in the black market?' Mustafa was very still, his face strangely immobile.

'Less you know, the better, but my Dad knows the right people.'

'Is he alive then? Here in the city?' Never by word or deed had Mustafa ever shown emotion, so I was surprised when his eyes filled with tears. 'No, I think he was shot with the men at the village hall. But I know all his friends here in the city,' he added and changed the subject.

'When are the others coming back with the water?'

'The queues are about an hour long for the standpipe. Where is Navid?'

'He and Kristoff went to the front line to join our soldiers. I'd better be going. I'll bring you the drugs after dark.'

'But there's a curfew.'

'So what? I won't be able to manage it before, as the black marketeers only hand over the merchandise at night. Tell Ben and the little ones I'll meet them back at our base.'

'Do be careful, Mustafa,' but he had gone before I had completed the sentence. I picked up Dadda's belt with three notes left, and buckled it round my waist, I sat stroking B.B. with a mixture of relief and anxiety, unable to shrug off the notion that perhaps we should never have informed Mustafa of our plans to get black-market drugs. But I was relieved that Vedra was missing her performance of a lifetime, though I would never admit it to Assad. And I had lost fiftyDMs to Stony-Eyes for the name of her contact.

True to his word, Mustafa visited us after dark with two envelopes of pills. 'The large ones are penicillin tablets and the little ones are painkillers.'

'How often do I give them to him?'

'Three times a day – there's enough there for two weeks, which should see him through the worst. Tomorrow I'll bring the blankets.'

'Did you use all the money?'

'Yes.' I couldn't see Mustafa's face, but I wondered if he had taken a cut like Stony-Eyes and was then filled with remorse. After all he had kept his word and saved us all kinds of problems at the UN compound if we had had to go there with Vedra. Forgetting my doubts, I hugged him. 'Mustafa, I owe you. Thanks a lot.'

'It was nothing,' Mustafa protested.

'No, you're wrong. You might well have saved god's leg.'

Mustafa laughed. 'I'll tell you what. I'd like to meet this god of yours.'

'You will when he's better – that's a promise.' Mustafa squeezed my hand and disappeared into the darkness.

As the days passed, we began to settle into a routine. Assad and I, between us, made three trips a day to the hospital to give god his tablets, always taking him a bottle of water. Although this was time-consuming and difficult with shelling and the curfew, we felt unable to trust the orderlies with the drugs in case they decided to sell them on and I didn't feel inclined to hand them over to Stony-Eyes. God drifted between consciousness and unconsciousness and certainly wouldn't have been able to tell us whether or not he had been given his pills, so we played safe. The little ones started the day at the soup kitchen and then spent the morning queuing at the standpipe to fill all our water-bottles. Either Assad or I would take them down to the river in the afternoon to bathe and wash their clothes.

Mustafa indulged us with all kinds of unnecessary extras. Dolls for the twins, a pack of cards for Vedra and one time he even arrived with a ball for B.B. We had blankets now, which we used as cushions during the day. Ben, for some unspoken reason, decided to move in with us and cleared the tangled wreckage out of the bus while Mustafa and their little ones stayed where they were. Ben also found a wooden box for our meagre food rations which he pierced to make air holes. With the shawls, we curtained off one end of the bus and Assad and Ben spent a day creating a toilet hole in the floor. Our life was not ruled by time, but by the vagaries of shelling. Although Karatz was not a frequent target, it was within range of the guns in the mountains. Nowhere in the city was safe and we were all afraid. Waiting to be shelled was nerve-racking. We dared not think of the past; it was never mentioned. Equally we dared not look towards a future which seemed empty. We were condemned to the dull ache of the present, living under the shadow of mistrust, apprehension and hate. War had not only stolen our loved ones, but the optimism of youth that generates hope.

Within the week, god's fever had ebbed and his condition had become stable. Whether the pain had receded I never knew, as he never complained. But I could read in his eyes a blind and unfathomable rage at his illness. On my way to the hospital a few days later I suddenly realised that there were many more trucks and UN vehicles on the move. There was almost a traffic jam. 'What's going on?' I asked an old man standing on the sidewalk. 'Heavy fighting over Mount Tabor,' he told me. 'The enemy have pushed our front line back; by tomorrow night we'll be surrounded and under siege.'

But what about the UN? Surely they were not going to allow our city to be besieged. Over 100,000 refugees, helpless women and children? The old man, his eyes sunken into their sockets, shrugged his shoulders and stared into the middle distance.

I found god propped up in bed, pale, drawn and brusque with it. 'Fran, I've heard the news. I want you to go to the Comfort Aid office and tell them to come and pick me up.' I was horrified.

'You're not well enough to move.'

'Just do as you are told. The address is 21 Jedinsava. Do you know where it is?'

'No, but I can ask,' I replied glumly, handing him his two tablets. 'Here's a fresh water-bottle for you. I don't think . . .'

'I don't care what you think – just go,' he interrupted rudely. I swept the curtain aside and departed without a word. It took me most of the day to find 21 Jedinsava. It was a long walk from the hospital and the headlights of the UN trucks were switched on by the time I arrived. I knocked at the closed door. A small man answered. Somehow he looked as if he should have died

147

years previously. I presumed that he was the janitor. 'I'm looking for the Comfort Aid Charity,' I explained.

'Their office is on the first floor.' I walked in and as I started up the marble staircase he continued: 'Won't do you much good – they all moved out today before the blockade.' I walked on and fumbled at the handle of an office door. The office had obviously been abandoned in a hurry. All the paperwork had been shredded and files removed. On the wall was a map of the city with coloured pins and I saw photographs of the Comfort Aid workers on the opposite wall, with their dates of birth and their position in the charity. There was a stunning picture of god. I caught my breath. Underneath I read his name and details:

FATHER PATRICK KENNEDY,
D.O.B. 20.12.72,
Field Co-ordinator.

Chapter Ten

There is no privacy in a bus. I wanted to go to my room and close the door. When Vedra tried to talk to me, I told her to shut up. They all wanted to know why I had come home in such a mood. I could not stand their probing. I needed space. A snow-white muzzle commiserated with me in my corner where I sat cross-legged in the dark. There is a certain finality about being told things that one does not want to deal with. Why was I so angry to discover that god was a Catholic priest? I felt that he had deceived me – Mamma had always explained that priests were chosen and committed to the highest of Sovereigns whilst the rest of us were sinners. I had thought that god was one of us.

I was bitterly cold and huddled close to B.B. I knew that I must never let god know that I had found out the truth, no matter how hard I might find it to keep my own counsel. Nobody else must know either. I must forget about it. After all, it made no difference. But I knew that it did make a difference. Somehow in that moment, looking at his name on the office wall, god the man had become god the priest. I had a long talk with B.B. As always, he understood, and I knew that if he could have spoken, his words would have been wise and compassionate. B.B.'s conversation wasn't up to much, but he was a very good listener. He had this amazing quality of not quite participating, of always standing outside and watching us with his deep brown eyes.

Next day we braced ourselves for an onslaught of shelling. We obviously had no idea that this was to continue for the next six months. As usual, I walked the empty streets to reach the hospital two miles away. God was asleep, so I sat and waited. When he awoke he smiled. His incredible blue eyes were riveted on me, trying to read my expression.

'What happened at the office then?'

'They'd gone. They'd packed up and gone.'

'Nobody there at all?'

'Only the janitor.' God's face fell. I touched his hand and he quickly withdrew it.

'I can't believe they've just left me here.' I was afraid to say anything.

'They must have known I was here, mustn't they?'

'Not necessarily. For all they know you could be dead. They probably found the truck with all the bullet holes and assumed the worst.'

'But they would have checked with the hospitals, surely?'

'There are four hospitals in this city. Perhaps there wasn't time.'

'But if they've gone back to England, they'll tell my family and well . . . friends that I'm dead.' He looked shocked. I grunted non-committally.

'Here, take your tablets.' I held out my hand with the two pills. God stared at them. I could hear the thundery rumble of shelling above us. Too close.

'Shit! They've buggered off and left me to die in this hell-hole. Bastards!' I wanted to tell him that I would look after him, but I could not make my mouth move. God suddenly burst into violent, uncontrollable sobs. Instinctively, I threw my arms around him. He grabbed my wrists and threw me angrily across the cubicle. I heard him wail 'Oh, my God!' just before I hit the ground and cracked my head on the floor.

I was not really hurt. The pain was in my heart, not my head. I got up slowly. God had covered his face with his massive hands. His beard was wet with tears. I stood there, small and fragile, wondering where his Jesus was now, but not daring to mention His name. Should I tell god that I knew who he was? The shelling must have been almost directly above us now. The rumbling suddenly became a roar, the corridor trembled and plaster began to fall. I dived under god's bed as the candles flickered out. Where was the sweet fragrant Jesus that Mamma had believed in totally? The Jesus whom god had vowed to follow as his disciple. Jesus had deserted us just like the UN. And if Jesus had also cast god aside when he had been his priest, what hope was there for the rest of us? There was a commotion as the orderlies started running through the corridors and cubicles, relighting candles, checking on the patients. Someone screamed, 'We need a doctor here.' 'No, we need a Jesus here, not a fucking doctor,' I thought.

I heard the voice of Stony-Eyes. 'Everybody all right here?'

I crawled out from under the bed and nodded to her. God was lying back staring at the ceiling having recovered his composure. 'That was a bit too close for comfort,' I said brushing down my jeans. 'Bastards, targeting the hospital.' God didn't move. I sat on the floor and waited. I understood god's anger and sense of loss. The feeling that something is slipping through one's fingers and one can't do anything about it. His friends had left and his life had changed completely. It was what we had all experienced months previously.

'Fran, I'm sorry I hit you.'

'You didn't hit me. You threw me.'

'Oh! Whatever. I'm sorry.' I stood up and went to his bedside.

151

'I don't know where your pills are now.'

'Forget the bloody pills. I'm not taking any more.'

'Can I get you anything before I go? The shelling's stopped. I ought to move.'

'No, you go.' He waved me away with a small gesture.

'I'll see you tonight, then.'

'No, don't bother. It's a long way to walk and I don't need the pills now.'

I left him, but returned in the evening with his medication, hoping that he would have returned to his amiable self. But his disposition seemed to be much the same.

'What are you doing here?' he asked me. I noticed that his leg had been freshly dressed.

'I brought your tablets.'

'I told you, I don't want any more pills.'

'You sound like a spoilt brat. What do you want me to do? Crush them up and put them in a spoon with strawberry jam? Mamma used to do that when I was a small child. Trouble is we have no jam.' God remained truculent.

'I didn't ask you to come. In fact I told you not to bother.'

'Well I did come and I wish I hadn't. It's bloody miles and now it's bloody dangerous. They're launching flares, and shooting indiscriminately.'

'Well, Fran, I'm not encouraging you to be a martyr, so please don't come again.'

'If you feel like that I won't.'

'Probably best all round.'

'It certainly is if you're going to take it out on me each time I visit.'

'Don't be so pathetic,' he muttered.

'At least I'm not drowning in self-pity.' I was mad with him.

'Get out of here. What do you know? You're just a stupid

kid.' I grabbed his arm and struck him with the back of my hand, I was surprised at my own strength.

'And you call yourself a pr . . .' I caught myself just in time.

'I'm sorry, god. I shouldn't have hit you.'

'Don't you call me god, you bitch.' He was raging.

'Then what's your name? What should I call you?' I provoked.

'Get out, just get out and don't ever come back.' I went. Out into the relative quiet of the war outside.

Over the next few weeks, the ceaseless barrage of shelling trapped us in the bus. Assad and Ben did their best to keep our spirits up but the situation took its toll. Vedra and the twins found little to giggle about now that we had exhausted charades and all the other games we could think of. I sat playing patience, contributing little to community life. The boys risked their lives daily to queue for bread and water. God had been right. This was a hell-hole. When hunger did not leave us lethargic and indifferent, our boredom aggravated petty squabbles. Not a day passed without my thinking of god in the hospital. One morning Ben and Assad approached me purposefully.

'We need to talk,' Assad said gently.

'Do we? What about?'

'The future.'

I surprised myself by laughing. 'What pleasures have you in store for me?'

'Fran, dearest Fran, you're not helping,' and before I could pursue my sarcasm Assad continued: 'The snow will be here soon. We've got to find somewhere proper to live or we won't survive the winter.'

'Who wants to survive?' I asked bitterly.

'I do.' Ben was quick in his defiance. 'So do the little ones.' I looked at the small group playing ball with B.B. under the seats of the bus.

'OK! What do you want me to do?'

'We've got to risk the snipers and shelling and start looking for somewhere else.'

'It's a waste of time. There are over a hundred thousand extra refugees crammed into this city. Every basement, cellar, crypt, every building that's still standing is occupied and not with one family either – there are four or five families sharing every room.'

'We've got to try,' Assad persisted.

'We'd probably have a better chance if we split up. We could place the little ones individually – someone would take them in,' I volunteered.

'What – split up the twins?' Ben looked horrified.

'No.' Assad was firm. 'Absolutely not. We stay together as a family. We need each other.' I did not appreciate the wisdom of his words until later.

'Well, Fran, you can stay here and play cards. Ben and I are going out to find a place to live. We owe that to the little ones. You know, Fran, you've changed. Since you met god, you've changed and I don't like what I see.'

As they were leaving I shouted after them: 'Find Mustafa, he'll know of somewhere.'

I felt desperate and humiliated. I was bleeding from my own self-inflicted wounds. I was punishing god, I was punishing my devoted friends but above all I was punishing myself. B.B. crossed the aisle with the ball in his mouth. It was almost as big as his head. He dropped it, looked into my eyes and stood there quivering. As I looked at him, I saw Mamma's expression clearly reflected in his eyes. It was the way she looked when she wagged her finger at me. I could hear her voice reminding me: 'We are in difficulties on all sides, but never cornered. We see no answer to our problems, but we never despair. We have been persecuted but never deserted.' B.B. rolled over, his short stubby legs waving in the air waiting to be tickled. 'Let's go for a walk.' There was nothing else to do. There was nothing else to be said. Mamma had said it all. I could dream again, but this time with my eyes open to reality.

As we went outside, I heard the familiar thunder of distant shelling. We had learned to ignore it, as one ignores a train which regularly goes past the end of one's garden. Nobody was on the street, as a further six-hour curfew had been ordered during daylight in order to save lives. The fresh air combined with lack of food made me dizzy. My head felt hollow and I seemed to be walking on feathers. B.B. was trotting beside me and I was taking little notice of the direction, when I saw her in the park. At least that was what the open space had been called during my childhood. Now it was covered with simple hand-made crosses as far as the eye could see. She was about my own age with golden hair and sad dark eyes. Everything about her was soft. Her complexion was almost translucent and her pink lips gave an impression of delicate fragility. I almost expected her to break in half in the slight breeze. B.B. and I approached her tentatively.

'Hello, do you have someone buried here?' she enquired with an open smile.

'No, but I used to play here as a small child – on the swings over there.'

We looked to where the swings had been and could see only graves.

'Me too' she agreed. 'I guess every child in the city came to play in the park at some time.'

'Do you remember the clock golf?'

'Oh yes. My brother always beat me.' She said it so quietly that I could hardly hear her.

She was standing in front of a grave. I read the name carved on the cross: 'Dino – 1985–1995.' 'I'm sorry,' I said as her eyes brimmed with tears. She glided to the next grave and said in a steady voice 'My mother and father are here, close beside him.'

'Do you have another brother?'

'Yes – Boro. He's the eldest. He's on the front line somewhere.'

She pointed to the next cross which was now disintegrating. 'That's my grandparents' grave.' I noticed that all the graves gave the same date.

'Were they all killed together?'

'Yes. I'd gone out to the bread queue and our house got a direct hit. They were all together.'

'Where do you live now?' I asked.

She pointed to the hill beyond the park. 'In the tomb by that derelict church. It's very convenient. I can come and talk to them as often as I want.' She looked at B.B. with a smile.

'Is he yours?'

'Yes, well that's to say he's ours. There are six of us. Three kids, myself and the boys, Ben and Assad.' She laughed.

'Aren't you and I still kids?'

'I suppose we are. But real kids are little.' There was a splutter of machine-gun fire over the city. 'I suppose we should take cover,' I said.

'I suppose so. Do you want to come back to my place?' I was immediately apprehensive.

I had liked her the minute I saw her. She had pulled me out of my emptiness and had made me forget the jibes of the others. She was different. She wasn't full of hate and vengeance. But when she had suggested that I come back to her place I trembled without knowing what had frightened me. My own hate perhaps? Deep down I acknowledged my anger and my desire for revenge. This girl had brought me out of it. She took my arm. 'If we stand here much longer you might

156

not get to see where I live.' So to a chorus of gunfire we strolled across to the tomb.

'It's quite gloomy.' She stated the obvious as we descended the steps under the mound. She opened a heavy door. 'Hold on, I've got a torch. We'll light the candles.' I could feel B.B. shivering against my leg. I picked him up and tucked him under my arm. 'There,' she said. 'What do you think?' In the dim light I could just make out a small arched stone chamber. 'It's not the Taj Mahal, but it's as good as.'

'How old is it?'

'Haven't a clue. But it hasn't got any blocks of stone with carved figures lying full length, so I don't think it can be Christian.'

'It's amazing and it isn't really cold.'

'Don't be too sure of that. I haven't had a winter here yet.'

'How did you find it?'

'Came across it one day when I was looking for wild flowers to put on the graves. As there are no buildings round here apart from the derelict church, I don't suppose there's any reason for people to come up here. Especially now they've cut down all the trees for fuel. It's a bit exposed walking down the hill to the park, but I can't see any reason why they'd bother to shell here. That's the advantage. The disadvantage is that we're not near any standpipes and the river is miles away.'

'What do you do about food?'

'I go into town before dawn and catch rats.'

'How do you cook them?' Once again she laughed.

'I don't. I eat them raw. I skin them and take out the bladder and the innards. I don't eat the head either.'

'Jesus, I couldn't do that.' I was in awe.

'You could, if you had nothing else. What do you live on yourselves?'

'We used to go to the soup kitchen but since the blockade

stopped any food supplies coming in, we're buying bread from families that are able to bake and we steal what we can, when we can.'

'You buy bread? Or do you barter for it?'

'We buy it. I still have a little money left. It won't last long, as bread has trebled in price over the last few weeks – and there are seven mouths to feed with B.B.'

'Who's B.B.?' I extracted my dog from under my coat.

'This is Baked Bean. He's the smartest thing on four legs.' We both burst out laughing as B.B. tried to wag his stump of a tail.

'I guess I'd better get back,' I said reluctantly. 'What's your name?'

'Edwina. What's yours?'

'Fran.'

'Oh, please don't go, Fran, not yet, I've really enjoyed having someone to talk to.' I could not find the words for what I wanted to suggest to her. I believed that this meeting was more than a stroke of luck. Rather it was an act of providence and I recollected Mamma's words. 'We are in difficulties on all sides but never cornered. We see no answer to our problems but we never despair. We have been persecuted but never deserted.'

I could not turn my back on what seemed to be a providential solution to our problems but at the same time, my suggestion was going to seem impudent.

'Edwina, can I put a proposition to you? It's just a thought. We're looking for somewhere to live and you need food. If you give us a roof over our heads, we'll provide the food.'

We moved into the tomb the following day. Between us we carried all our possessions across the city. Assad needed some persuading because it would be so far to go to find food and water, but Ben won him over pointing out that it was probably

one of the safest areas in the city. Edwina looked radiant. While
there was more space in the tomb than in the bus I found the
constant darkness oppressive. I often spent the morning in the
cemetery with Edwina. Each morning there were new graves.
Burials took place in the middle of the night, as there was a
better chance of survival for the mourners. Any candles left at
the graveside by the funeral cortege were quickly appropriated
for use in the tomb. B.B. enjoyed the freedom of the park-cum-
cemetery as we could let him out there on his own. God
remained on my mind and I wondered desperately whether
or not his leg had healed. Eventually, I confided his story to
Edwina and described the difficult situation I now found myself
in because god no longer wanted me to go to the hospital. I
omitted the fact that I had discovered he was a priest.

'I'm sure it must be a misunderstanding.' Edwina reminded
me of Mamma.

'No, he said I was never to go back. He was really angry.'

'Fran, we all say things we don't mean when we're upset.'

'Yes, I know.'

'When he is better, what will happen to him? He can't get
out of the city whilst we're under siege. Where will he go?'

'I don't know whether he has any friends here.'

'I think you should make contact with him again. Look at
you, you're quite miserable about him.'

'I wish the telephones were working, then I could just ring
up the hospital, get the low-down and decide what to do.'

'Fran, go and see him.'

'I don't think Assad will like it.'

'Why not?'

'He blames god for me being so miserable. I think he was
jealous when I was going to the hospital so frequently. Perhaps
Assad thought I was paying god too much attention, but we
had to go regularly to make sure he got his pills.'

'I think you should go and see god and Assad doesn't have to know.'

'You're right. I won't be at peace till I know how he is and what's happening to him.' The decision was made and early that afternoon I walked to the hospital, accompanied by Edwina. It was five miles – a good deal further than when we were living in the bus.

I was unprepared for what was awaiting us. The hospital was in chaos. The injured were lying on the steps down to the basement and the corridors were clogged with mutilated and dying human beings. Exhausted orderlies toiled from one ghost-like figure to the next bringing dressings and any words of comfort that they could dredge up. We groped our way towards god's cubicle by the light of the flickering candle lanterns suspended from the ceiling. God was sitting on the edge of his bed holding a pair of crutches. I noticed that his shorts were stiff with dried blood. Remorseful, and still feeling horribly guilty because he was wounded and ill and I was fit and well, I began my prepared speech. 'God, I know you didn't want to see me but . . . Oh, you've shaved off your beard.' God looked quite different. His thick hair was neatly cropped and his moustache and beard had gone. He looked much younger. I had never noticed the brown eyebrows spaced well apart, nor his aquiline nose. 'I'm delighted to see you, Fran. I hoped you'd come.' God leant over me and kissed me on the cheek. My guilt and trepidation vanished. God appeared to have returned to his amiable self.

'This is my friend Edwina.' They clasped hands.

'I'm very glad to meet you, Edwina.' I realised she was overwhelmed by his size.

'How have you been?' I asked.

'They say I've made a remarkable recovery considering the bone was smashed, but I shall be on these crutches for some time yet. I'm quite adept at getting round though. What's been happening with you?'

'We've moved in with Edwina up near the old park.'

'You've left your bus?'

'Yes, Assad felt it wouldn't give us any protection with the winter coming. And it was a bit of a sitting target being in the road.' I realised that neither god nor I were intending to mention the past. Stony-Eyes walked in. She looked so haggard that I felt sorry for her.

'Ah, you've come to see your brother at last. He was getting quite worried about you.'

'It's been difficult what with the curfew and the shelling,' I muttered.

'You don't need to tell me! Our cases have doubled in the last few weeks. We need the space so we're discharging all non-urgent cases from tomorrow.' She turned to god. 'That's what I came in to tell you. We need your bed as soon as possible, like yesterday.' God was as pale as marble and I could see the fear in his eyes beneath the long black lashes.

'Yes, of course.' His reply was almost inaudible.

'I'm glad it all worked out and didn't turn into an amputation,' said Stony-Eyes. She gave me a knowing look and scuttled away down the corridor. Edwina broke the silence.

'Shall we help you pack?' God seemed to have recovered.

'There's only my wash things, which actually belong to the hospital. But I can't leave wearing these shorts.' They were the same pair he had been wearing when he was shot.

'I'll go and see if I can find you a pair of trousers,' I volunteered. An orderly showed me into a corridor which was curtained off by blankets. It was the morgue. 'Help yourself to the trousers you want.' The dead were stacked in rows feet to head, head to feet waiting for the darkness and their final journey to a burial place. I picked out a body which seemed to

161

be the same size as god. I guessed the man had died of natural causes as there did not seem to be a mark on him. I managed to get his trousers off and also took his sweater and shoes. When I returned, god and Edwina were sitting on the bed deep in conversation. Edwina said excitedly, 'Fran, god's coming back with us.' I was taken aback.

'Well, that is, if Fran agrees,' god quickly intervened.

'He's got nowhere else to go. Of course, you must come to us,' Edwina insisted.

I didn't know why I felt so unwilling but objections welled up within me. Was I frightened of what Assad would say? Did I think that god wouldn't fit into the group, or was I frightened for myself in some way? I never knew, but there was no doubt that my reluctance went a lot deeper than mere concern at there being another mouth to feed, another person to care for.

CHAPTER ELEVEN

As our city crumbled under the continuous bombardment, god slumped into a gloom which affected us all. He never left the tomb to help the boys find food or to take his turn queuing for water. Assad was quick to suggest that this was because he was scared. Ben had found a discarded boiler which we attached to a child's buggy Vedra had picked up from a bombed-out house. This provided us with a mobile water tank. It was, nevertheless, quite difficult to manoeuvre the buggy through the shelled masonry and along roads littered with craters, twisted wire and broken sewer pipes. When the boiler was full, it needed two of us to pull the buggy up the hill to the tomb. God invariably used his leg as an excuse not to help even though he was now able to walk without crutches. The crutches were being used to hold up the rope washing-line. My money had run out and food was becoming our major problem. There was no flour left in the city so no bread; no cats or dogs left to eat. I would only allow B.B. out at night for fear of losing him.

The sun wilted behind the mountains as winter hurled her first flurry of snow at the city to cloak it in white. As far as clothes were concerned, I used the hospital mortuary in the same way that the rest of the world uses second-hand clothes shops except that I never paid for what I took. There was no longer a black market as there was nothing to buy or sell. Assad and Ben had joined the civil defence network and would disappear for days to help on the forward first-aid stations near the front line. They would return glassy-eyed with exhaustion, their clothes stiff with frozen mud and stained with blood from the injured victims. They were so numb with cold that they were unable to undress themselves. They would lie down so that Vedra and the twins could pull off their pitifully baggy trousers. I would wash their scraggy limbs with cold water as they shivered and twitched like fish caught on a line. With clean clothes hanging slack over their fleshless hips, I would force them to eat their rations before allowing them to succumb to exhaustion, curled up under the grey trench coats I had stolen from the mortuary. Thus weeks passed in the darkness of our tomb. We only ventured out at night to catch the rats that had now become our staple diet. But our suffering and the fact that we were together made us strong. The instinct to survive was greater than the suffering.

One afternoon, when I was on my way to catch rats, a shell whistled past me and exploded some distance away, splintering a roof. Fragments came flying through the air, and I ducked down the steps of a cellar. There was a door and I tried the handle. It was open. I entered and found myself in a large bare L-shaped room: no carpet and no furniture. I was not alone. In the centre of the room sitting cross-legged on the floor was a wizened old man. Beside him lay three books. 'I'm so sorry intruding like this, but the shelling . . .' I began.

'Please, please don't apologise. You're most welcome. Come in, come in. I'm afraid we haven't any furniture left for you to sit on. We've used it all for firewood.' He hesitated and rolled his head from side to side. I knelt down beside him. The man wore a threadbare sports jacket over a couple of sweaters and an open-necked shirt. His hollow eyes in the bony withered face were kind and alert. 'Forgive me, I still use the royal "we". It's a habit after fifty odd years.' He smiled to himself. 'My wife died last week and my sons were killed on the front line last year. There is only me now.' I took his hand. The long thin fingers felt cold and dry. The war, so close outside, seemed suddenly remote.

'We have lived in this house for thirty years. My wife collected porcelain and I collected books. We had over five thousand books in the library upstairs. It was my work. I taught American literature at the university.' The old man hunched up as memories flooded back. His thick white hair was a beacon in the darkness. 'But my dear, what has happened to my manners. I have a tea-bag, you must have a cup of tea with me,' he insisted.

'Thank you, I would love one.'

He stared at his three books and then whispered to me, 'Would you like your tea with the Koran, the Bible or Dickens?' I was still holding his hand and I stared at him in bewilderment. The old man blinked and withdrew his hand. I had not understood his question. Without waiting for any reply, however, he bent forward and picked up one of the books, cradling it fondly before opening the leather cover. Slowly and meticulously he began to tear out one page after the other. He piled the pages one upon another and took a small pan and a bottle of water from the floor beside him. He poured water into the pan and then, taking a cigarette lighter from his pocket, he set light to the pile of pages. As the flames hissed into life, the old man held the pan of water above them. The destruction of his precious books felt to me like a desecration or perhaps the final spilling of his blood. And all to make a cup of tea for a stranger, who had disturbed his privacy.

'There is a certain amount of evidence to suggest that our genetic inheritance can predetermine the ways in which we are going to think and behave,' said the old man. 'Such evidence fits neatly with the modern idea of the "victim" society in which none of us has real control over his actions and therefore needs to admit no real responsibility for them. Lawyers in the USA and Britain are already invoking the science of genetics in order to claim that a whole range of "irresistible impulses" account for disordered behaviour. Such arguments can produce remarkable results.'

He paused to remove the boiling water from the flames which were already dying into nothing. Taking two cracked china mugs, he poured the water into them, carefully lifting the single, elderly tea-bag from one to the other. With great ceremony he handed me my mug.

'What sort of remarkable results?' I asked as I sipped my tea.

'In 1978 a man walked into the office of the mayor of San Francisco and shot him dead. At the trial, the killer's lawyers argued that the man had eaten a lot of sugar cakes for breakfast that morning which had distorted the impulse control in his brain. The jury accepted that argument and decided on a verdict of manslaughter rather than murder!

'But, of course, there is another side. There's the view that violence is a highly complex dynamic which cannot be treated as a single entity with a precise encoding in our genes. You cannot lump together everything from slapping a naughty child to shooting the mayor of San Francisco into a single char-acteristic called violence. This view, unlike the first one, does not deny the importance of both nature and nurture, our genetic disposition and our upbringing. Tell me, what do you think?' I had had difficulty in following this intellectual monologue but, not wanting to appear foolish, I replied 'I do believe that upbringing has an enormous influence on people. What we watched on TV and cinema screens before the war must have influenced us. Dadda used to say that it was poverty and greed that created wars.'

'Yes, indeed, the media has much to answer for.' This was, of course, a highly fashionable view of the war but I was glad to find it so authoritatively endorsed.

The old man continued his tutorial. 'Do you remember the shootings at the Jonesboro school in Arkansas by two boys? The State Governor declared them to be the result of a national culture of violence fuelled by television and film. I remember reading a comment by a professor at Arkansas State University declaring that just as soldiers are trained to respond automatically to targets, so children react to Hollywood films, videos and visual stimuli such as video games. In video arcades they learn to shoot and to kill. They watch as the bodies twist and the brains fly out. And we have the audacity to ask how they have learnt to kill and why they like killing, when we taught them how to do it in the first place. I find myself completely unable to accept the bland assurances of the sociologists that media violence has no effect on the young.'

'But that's not the reason for this war,' I said tentatively. I had finished my tea and felt out of my depth with this academic. The old man smiled.

'No, my dear, your father was right about poverty and greed creating wars. This war is about moving maps. It's about power and greed.' He closed his eyes and shook his head.

'One of the major difficulties in society is that problems seem so huge and so complex that we, as ordinary people, make this an excuse to do nothing. We believe that we are merely spectators of a developing situation which we feel helpless to influence and then we convince ourselves that only outside governments possess the power and resources to deal with our own problems. And yet it is self-evident that governments can only get away with what we, the people, allow them to get away with – that is if you're in a democratic country. I think the idea of people power will certainly re-emerge as an expression of

167

anger. I'm not advocating it, but there is, after all, a kind of anger which the Bible calls "righteous anger" and the psychologists call "justified anger". Until the world feels anger at the pangs of the hungry, the indignation of the poor, the alienation of ethnic cleansing, they are not likely to act effectively.' I could hear him breathing heavily.

'So what will happen to us?' I whispered. The old man put down his empty mug and his eyes filled. Outside we could hear the thumping of the guns.

'My dear, there was a great British statesman, Edmund Burke, who once said "As long as good men do nothing, evil will triumph" and we are at the heart of such evil at the moment. People power needs leadership, and there is a grave lack of leadership in this contemporary world. We need someone with vision.'

'What do you mean by vision?'

'Vision is an act of seeing, of course, but it embraces both insight and foresight. In the sense in which I'm using the word, vision is compounded of a deep dissatisfaction with what *is*, and a clear grasp of what *could be*. It begins with indignation over the status quo, and grows into a serious quest for an alternative. There is a great need today for indignation against the things that are wrong in our society. But indignation is sterile if it does not provoke us into positive action. Apathy is the acceptance of the unacceptable. Leadership begins with the refusal to accept the unacceptable.' I must have looked bewildered for he suddenly leaned forward and took both my hands.

'My dear, forgive an old man's ramblings. I haven't had the privilege of speaking to anybody for weeks. My wife was hit by a sniper's bullet and was in a coma for over a month.' Despite the tragedy of his wife's illness and death, the old man's face lit up when he mentioned her.

'It's a pity you didn't go into politics,' I said. 'Then perhaps we would have had a leader.' The old man squeezed my hands and then let them go, laughing raucously.

'You flatter me, young lady. But now it's time for me to sleep. Would you like to stay the night? You can have my wife's mattress.' The offer of actual bedding was almost irresistible, but I knew that Edwina and the others would be anxious for my return and as yet I had failed to catch the night's food.

'Thank you, but I must get back, or my friends will worry.'

'Quite, quite.'

'Can I come and see you again?' My request appeared to please him.

'Indeed you can but these are unpredictable times. One can never tell where one will be from day to day. I want to give you some food. My wife was a good woman of great foresight and she stockpiled tins in readiness – please take as much as you want, I won't be needing it.' I clapped my hands in speechless delight as the old man picked up a straw basket and piled it full of tins.

'What do you mean you won't be needing it?'

'I also have the gift of foresight.' He handed the heavy basket to me and I swung it over my shoulder. I was so excited that I wasn't listening.

'I promise I'll come and see you again.' I shook his hand vigorously. 'And thanks for the tea.'

'Au revoir,' was all I heard him say as he locked the door behind me.

'Au revoir, my dear young friend.'

I lumbered uphill to the tomb with the shawl covering my treasure, thinking about the delight on my friends' faces when I produced my basket. I struggled across the park avoiding the three burials taking place. Nobody noticed me and when I got to the tomb – they were all asleep.

The following morning's rejoicing revived our drooping

spirits. We feasted with restraint knowing that there would be more for the morrow. Since god's arrival we had hardly spoken to one another beyond what was essential. Now it was as if an ice-floe was suddenly beginning to melt, as our words spilled out. Laughter swallowed up some of the horrors and for a moment we glowed with love for one another as we enjoyed our feast before setting about our daily routines. The next day everything changed.

Edwina and the twins were out collecting the water, whilst Vedra and I had ignored the shelling and gone down to the river to scrub the clothes. The boys were working in one of the forward first-aid stations near the front line. On our return B.B. greeted Vedra and me as if we were long lost friends and we let him out of the tomb whilst we hung up the washing.

Despite the cold, we always left the door open because we needed that sliver of light. God was in the corner under his blanket, where he often spent the day sunk in his habitual gloom. It was only when I walked past the basket in which our precious tins were stored that I noticed the shawl which had been covering them lying on the ground. My heart missed a beat: that oppressive unbearable aching feeling in the chest that swells into the throat and lodges there so that one cannot swallow. I hardly dared to glance into the basket but I had to know. The basket was empty. I looked wildly round the room, not really expecting to see a pile of tins but in my anxiety hoping beyond hope that one of the children might have wanted to play with them. I went over to god, trying to remain calm, but my voice betrayed me.

'The food's gone.' God was lying with his face to the wall. He did not move.

'God, I'm talking to you. Where's the food?' I screamed so loud that B.B. and Vedra bolted in from outside. In my head there was a disjointed mixture of disbelief and despair.

'God, it was here when we left this morning.' Vedra picked up the trembling B.B. 'You bastard. You bastard. How could you? – did you eat it all?' I was crying, screeching hysterically as I flung myself upon god with the impetuous anger of a child, thumping his back with my small white fists. He made no attempt to defend himself, but continued to lie there, neither stirring nor confronting me when Assad and Ben walked in and I felt their arms pulling me back.

'I'll kill him. I'll kill him.' I was choking, my chest heaving.

'What the hell's he done now?' Assad stormed.

'The food's gone,' I whimpered, wiping my nose on my sleeve. The room seemed to freeze, except for the haunted eyes that turned towards god, staring at him in agony, the silence lengthening. Our shock was total. We were reduced to immobility. Vedra's control broke first. She buried her face in B.B. and began to sob. Ben moved across to her.

'Hold it, Fran, how do you know that it was god?' Assad was always sensible.

'Well B.B. can't use a tin opener,' I hissed.

'What about the others?'

'We all left together this morning and I checked that the food was covered by the shawl in case anybody came snooping around. I tell you it was there,' I screamed.

'OK, OK, Fran, calm down.' Assad strode over to god and hauled off his blanket. 'Well, what have you got to say?' God's bad leg twitched but apart from that he did not move. Assad kicked the twitching leg and god let out a howl.

'Damn it, you yellow belly. I'm talking to you.' God heaved himself on to his elbows and turned over onto his back. He had been weeping. His damp hair stuck to his forehead and there were wet streaks down his face. From outside we could hear the twins and Edwina arriving back from the standpipe.

171

They came into the tomb. 'What's going on?' Edwina looked at us in turn.

'That piece of sodding flesh that calls himself a man has eaten all our stock of food,' Assad was shouting.

'Oh no, you must be mistaken. God, what happened?' asked Edwina. God looked wretched. Despite eating all our food, he looked so emaciated and vulnerable. Even my anger was receding.

'It's as they say. I've eaten all the food,' he admitted.

'How could you be so self-centred? How could you bring yourself to take the food from the mouths of the little ones?' Edwina protested, staring at him in disbelief.

'I'm sorry. I'm so sorry. I couldn't help it. I didn't mean to.'

'You couldn't help it,' repeated Assad sarcastically. 'You miserable, selfish bugger. I hope you rot in hell.'

'I've been rotting in hell these last few months, so don't concern yourself on that score.' God still had some fight left in him.

'And what do you think we've been going through?' Edwina was shouting through her tears of disillusion. 'Do you think you have a monopoly on hell?' God shook his head. He bent over in shame. We all felt so defeated and hopeless.

'Well, what are we going to do now?' asked Assad.

'There's nothing we can do – the food's gone, so we'll have to go out tonight for some more rats,' Ben replied.

'Wait a moment. There's more to it than that. What about bloody god?' Our eyes were now riveted on Assad.

'Well, what about bloody god?' I demanded.

'What are we going to do with him?'

'I'm not sure I'm following you.' My anger was receding.

'He's got to be punished. He can't get away with stealing all our food.'

'What do you want us to do, crucify him?' I asked sarcastically. Assad stared at me blankly.

'We could hang him,' one of the twins mumbled.

'For crying out loud, you can't be serious about killing him!' Ben paced the room.

'I'm deadly serious about doing something.' Assad's voice was clipped. He stood resolute and I wondered what was lurking at the back of his mind. God lay down again, silent tears pouring down his face. Ben shrugged his shoulders and said calmly, 'I don't see there's anything we can do.'

'Oh yes, there is.' Assad was seething.

'Such as?' Ben asked.

'Well, in the first place he can't stay here any longer. Who's going to trust him?'

'But where can he go – he doesn't know anybody.' Edwina's anger was receding too.

'I don't bloody care where he goes.'

'You can't just turf him out on the street, he'll get killed,' I pointed out.

'Best thing for the bastard. I never wanted him here in the first place. I knew he'd be trouble.'

'Assad, that's not fair.' Edwina was snivelling.

'Fair? What's fair? He's done nothing to help since he arrived – we've watered him, fed him and clothed him and in his gratitude he's now stolen all our food. He's scum.' Assad spat the word out. Although in my heart I agreed with Assad, somehow I could not go along with the idea of throwing god out. My brain was whirling.

'What if he gets food for us for the next week?' Ben suggested.

'No, I don't trust him. He's got to go,' insisted Assad.

'If he's killed because we've chucked him out, will you be able to live with that?' Edwina asked. She had pulled herself together.

'I'll live with it.' Assad threw himself under a grey

trenchcoat. We looked at each other in desperation. Vedra lowered B.B. to the ground, walked over to me, took my hand and squeezed it. I ignored her.

'We could take a vote on it,' Ben suggested.

'No vote,' said Assad, not attempting to disguise his bitterness. 'Either he goes or I go.' I turned and gazed at him. I remembered the past, the good times before the war. How Assad had always protected me, how before dawn we would leap the rocks playing tag by the river. How loving and supportive he had always been. We had lain in the cornfields listening to the birds, the deep heartbeat in our fidelity to one another eclipsing the hardness of the earth. I could not imagine a life without Assad. It would be like extinguishing the light of my life. Assad who had always been resilient, cheerful and sensible. Our eyes met. Assad's eyes had always sparkled. Now they were bitter with hatred. He glared at me.

'Fran, what do you say? God's your friend.' Ben brought me back from the past.

'You're right, god must go.' I was agreeing with Assad. The others exclaimed in surprise. I looked over at god. Tiny B.B. was consoling him. He looked like a bird resting in the palm of god's massive hand, offering help and comfort to this broken man. God lifted his head and met my eyes. He clenched his arms about his head trying to fend off his trembling as B.B. climbed up his body and curled up under his armpit.

'Fran, you can't mean that?' Edwina pleaded.

'Assad's right. He's got to go. How will we ever trust him again?' I was remembering the first time god and I had met all those years ago. It had been St Nicholas's Day. Dadda had bought me a pair of skis and I had thought that this man was God. Suddenly, I felt sick.

'I'm sorry god, I really do mean it.' God acknowledged my words by raising his hand. He slowly rose to his knees and then to his feet. B.B. jumped to the floor. God's wasted body was like a runner bean. No longer the gigantic man who had seemed so formidable when I had first met him on the mountain. God bent down, picked up B.B. and kissed him. Slowly he limped over to me and handed me my dog.

'I'm sorry I let you down, Fran,' he looked round the room, 'I've let you all down. You who gave me everything. It will be no consolation, but I want you to know that I had failed both my God and myself long before I met any of you. In your kindness and unconditional love, you have been sheltering a loser all this time.' God put on his overcoat. He cupped my chin in his hands and kissed me lightly on the lips. He turned on his good leg and limped away.

Chapter Twelve

The months passed and nobody mentioned god's name. The shadow of shame within us was a testimony to our guilt. It had been wrong to expel god. Assad's anger burned like fire until one morning he returned from his work at the forward first-aid station with the news that the UN had negotiated a ceasefire between the warring armies.

'Does that mean the war's over?' asked Vedra.

'No. But it will mean that convoys can get through with food.' But the date of the ceasefire came and went bringing no major change in our lives. Although the shelling of the city had lessened, we continued to live in fear. The international convoys were unable to get through and we settled back into our own routine of taking the 'water buggy' to the standpipe, going to the river and hunting for rats to eat. The soup kitchens had been closed for many months because there was no more food to hand out. Illness stalked the city, no doubt compounded by dehydration and malnutrition. Winter had taken its toll of the front line too so there were fewer soldiers to fight in the mountains. We were given another date for a ceasefire, another promise of humanitarian aid. Nothing happened. However, by spring, the shelling had become intermittent although indiscriminate sniping continued in the streets. With the warmer weather and fewer mortars about, we started to

venture out in daylight. It was the first chance I had had to visit
my old academic again. I took Vedra with me and we descended the steps to find his door locked. I shouted and
hammered on the door.

'Do you think he's dead?' Vedra's disarming frankness took
me aback.

'Why should he be?'

'It's just that I remember you saying that he had told you that
he wouldn't be needing the food any longer and that was why
he was giving it to you.' We debated the feasibility of breaking
down the door. Vedra picked up an iron bar from the gutter.
With infinite care she wedged it between the door and the
lock. Astonishingly, the door split open.

'Supposing he's just gone out and he comes back and finds
his basement door bashed in?' I asked her.

'So what, he can mend it or find a new lock.' Vedra was
turning into a no-nonsense young lady. We peered inside and
called out but there was no response. With the door wide open
we could see that the room was just as I had found it on my first
visit – except that my friend was no longer there. His books had
gone too. We walked into the room. Vedra picked up an
envelope and began to open it. I protested. She went back to
stand in the light of the doorway whilst I browsed in the far
corner. I chuckled. The remains of the stockpile of tins was
undisturbed.

'Fran, I think this is for you.' I joined her in the doorway and
read the paper she handed me: 'My dear young friend, I believe
you will visit again and I hope you will find this letter. My
situation is intolerable without my wife and there seems to be
no solution and no sign of peace. Nobody is asking for
forgiveness and nobody is offering it. Therefore, I have decided
to opt out. I have the necessary pills. I will be leaving here
tonight. My wife and I would like you to have the room – the

remains of the food and the two mattresses against the wall. The room is blocked off from our house upstairs which is full of refugees. It has been an oasis of peace for us – but no longer. With reference to our conversation about the need for leader-ship, I would like to add that a leader recognises the extent of his task and the strength of the opposition. He knows, too, that his own contribution may be small in the overall scheme of things. But he remembers the words of the wise statesman who said: "Nobody made a greater mistake than he who did nothing, because he could do only a little." Au revoir my dear.' I was sad to think that I would not see my elderly friend again. But I somehow knew that he was at peace – and thanks to his generosity we would be moving upmarket.

We moved on the day the ceasefire was implemented. The rejoicing on the streets was loud and for the first time in many months we heard the drone of heavy trucks as the UN convoys crawled through our ravaged city leaving a plume of dust in their wake. Relief and exhilaration swept through every heart. Tears of pleasure are far removed from tears of grief and hopelessness. The few remaining church bells tolled in triumph and the chanting from the bombed-out mosques flowed har-moniously across the plucked wastelands. From our cellar steps, we could see the heads of hundreds of refugees bobbing along the road, clutching one another, embracing in ecstasy, now that the terror was behind them – or so they hoped. I looked up at the mountains and saw the first UN Hercules curl and dip towards the makeshift aerodrome. We were delighted with our new home in the basement. Assad, Ben and the twins were busy opening tins for a feast. I walked across the room and placed Mo's postcard of Zanzibar on the marble mantelpiece. I thought about Mo, Gregor and Adjin: our friends who could never share our good fortune.

We never believed that the ceasefire would be permanent, but to our surprise it lasted for a week during which deliveries of food supplies arrived constantly in the convoys. Two main warehouses were set up and from there supplies were taken to the six soup kitchens in the city and queues once again became a sign of normality. The UNHCR set up offices and organised the medical evacuation of the seriously wounded, but we later heard that the UNHCR had been considerably hampered by the enemy authorities who were refusing access to doctors and nurses. Few actions could have been more callous.

There was the constant intimidating presence of the tanks and guns on the mountains and one was never safe from sniper bullets since the front line overlooked the city. As Government leaders, the United Nations and NATO debated political solutions, we heard stories of atrocities against our people in detention camps: their forced removal and an inhuman disregard on the part of the enemy for the needs of the sick, the old and the vulnerable. At one point the enemy authorities decided to levy taxes on all aid convoys crossing the mountains into the city. Aid deliveries were halted once more until the UNHCR and its convoys were finally declared exempt from tolls. Nevertheless convoys were repeatedly denied access on any pretext whatsoever. On one occasion it was the demand that all enemy prisoners be released. On another the authorities refused to allow petrol lorries to leave the airport, which successfully brought all aid transport to a halt. The harassment and intimidation of aid workers became the norm, particularly at military and police checkpoints. Obstruction of the international relief effort provided a major security problem for the UN and a grave diplomatic dilemma for participating governments. For our city it was a matter of life or death.

And yet Assad, Ben, Edwina, the twins, Vedra, B.B. and I had never been so rich. We collected regular food supplies from the soup kitchen. There was a standpipe for water in the next road and the two mattresses in the old man's basement never seemed to attract the cold or damp. The boys were now working at the warehouse, which was less stressful than the forward first-aid station, and though there was no money in the city to pay them, they were given special rations as a perk. For the first time ever, it was safe to leave our door open when we ventured outside. We always left one person behind with B.B. to guard our basement. B.B. wasn't much help at the soup kitchen or the standpipe and I was reluctant anyway to take him out often, as I was still afraid that hungry people might see him as a tasty morsel.

Every other day, half-hearted shelling blasted parts of the city. It was as if the enemy were just reminding us of their dominant presence. But the improved conditions had raised people's spirits. Death-dealing shelling was of less significance than the fact that flour, oil, coffee and pasta were to be had for the asking.

The loyalties of youth die hard. My relationship with Assad had been restored with the departure of god and we delighted in taking responsibility for the others. One morning Assad reminded me that I still had the names of the dead women we had found in the cave during our flight across the mountains. All this time I had been carrying the list inside my shoe written on the labels from the sardine tins.

'What should I do with them?' I asked him.

'I think we should take them to the UNHCR office.' It was a twenty-minute walk to the office but all was peaceful. We crossed the craters of one street and came into a semi-bombed side road. The road sign Jedinsava reminded me of my visit to the Comfort Aid office when god had asked me to go and find his friends to ask them to pick him up. The street sign was pitted with bullet holes but still attached to the roofless corner house which had housed the offices of the charity. Without really thinking about what I was saying I blurted out:

'This was where god's old offices used to be.' Realising what I had said, I glanced nervously at Assad. God had never been his favourite person.

'The offices are in the main street now,' Assad replied. I stopped dead.

'How do you know that?' Assad blushed and pulled at my sleeve to continue our walk. We went a few paces in silence before he replied.

'I happen to know.' His reticence was irritating.

'Well, how do you happen to know? As far as I was aware you didn't even know which aid charity he worked for!'

'He must have told me, or you did.' Assad was being evasive.

'No, I never told you and I don't believe he told you when he was living with us. Assad, why are you lying to me?'

'Sorry, Fran,' he muttered. I grabbed Assad by the shoulder and swung him round, so that he had to face me.

'Why are you lying?' He gave me a baleful glance and dropped his eyes. 'I'm not walking a step further till you tell me the truth,' I insisted.

'I can't.'

'Why not?'

'I made a promise.'

'To whom?' Assad's eyes were pleading.

'You wouldn't break a promise, Fran, so don't expect me to. Come on, we're wasting time.' He began to walk on. I decided to bide my time. It was not until we were sitting in the waiting room of the UNHCR office that I decided to try again.

'You made a promise to god, didn't you?'

'Please, Fran, drop it.'

'I can't. God was my friend and I let him down.'

182

'No, no. It was god who let us down.' But there was no resentment in Assad's voice.

I was surprised. 'Have you forgiven god?' I asked hesitantly.

'Yes . . . Have you?'

'Yes, but it was easier for me. I knew him better and I understood him.'

'True. I realised that there was something special between you.'

'Were you jealous?'

'I think so. You see, there seemed to be a secret between you and I felt left out. Was there a secret? Can you tell me about it?' Now it was my turn to feel uncomfortable. I had never told anybody about god being a priest. Was I going to have to give his secret away as the price of Assad's secret?

I decided to change the subject. 'Let's get back to where we started. How do you know about the new offices of Comfort Aid and what have you promised god?'

Assad chuckled. 'You devious little woman.'

'Nothing for nothing, Assad.' There are those who can be deflected and those that can't. I wasn't going to give up on this.

'OK, Fran, you win. For some months, god has been working at the forward first-aid post on the front line. Ben and I were working with him before we moved to the warehouse.' My mouth dropped open in my surprise. I was speechless. I had somehow presumed that if god had escaped death when he left the tomb, he would have taken the first possible transport out of the city, when the ceasefire started.

'Your turn.' Assad nudged me.

'I never promised god anything, but if I tell you my secret you will have to promise not to tell anybody at all. Even god doesn't know that I know.'

'What are you saying?'

'Just promise that you won't tell anybody,' I insisted.

'OK. I promise.'

I took a deep breath. 'God's a priest . . . or perhaps an ex-priest.' Assad whistled.

'Bloody hell! And he doesn't know that you know? How did you find out?' I explained my visit to the Comfort Aid office in Jedinsava before the siege at god's request and how I'd seen his name and his picture up on the wall.

'Now I understand . . .' Assad was saying, when the door opened and we were ushered into the small UNHCR office. The female bureaucrat behind the desk seemed amazed at our story of the dead bodies we had found in the cave and the small children we had brought with us to the city. She asked endless questions, writing down Assad's answers meticulously.

'Go on Fran, give her the list,' Assad finished. I jumped up, untied the lace of my right shoe and extracted the neatly folded somewhat damp sardine tin labels. 'Sorry, they probably smell a bit and it won't be of sardines!' But the woman was humourless. 'Wait here,' she snapped and walked out of the room. Assad and I looked at each other and burst out laughing. The woman returned accompanied by a man who gave us an unpleasant grin and asked us to repeat our story. Further notes were taken. Finally, satisfied that he had all the necessary details, the man asked us where we were all living. I was prepared to tell him but Assad was quick to intervene.

'It's a basement – the street has no name,' he lied.

'What part of the city? Off a main road?'

'We don't know the city very well. We've just moved into this basement where we've been holed up ever since. Now we've got to go.' Assad stood up. I stood too, confused now.

'Wait a moment, young man. Have you heard of Operation reUNite?'

Assad hesitated.

'It's a consultation point where parents can register and

search for their children on the CD-Rom database that contains details and photos of those registered. Save the Children UK will set up a database in the city as soon as we've got electricity. Why don't you pay them a visit and fill in a registration form?'

'Thank you, we'll do that – where's their office?'

'Down by the river, Hebranca 5. Good luck!' Assad grabbed my arm and dragged me out of the office before I could ask the man how we could get photos taken of ourselves, Ben, Edwina, the twins and Vedra. 'Why did you lie to him about our address?' I asked as we headed for the river.

'I think that they were really talking about unaccompanied minors. I don't want them nosing in and taking Vedra and the twins away.'

'They wouldn't dare.'

'Oh, Fran, you're so naïve. Part of the job of the UNHCR is to place kids in refugee camps – or at least in a place of safety.'

By now we had reached the river. It was beautiful with its backdrop of mountains, peak upon peak stretching away to the horizon. The current was swift and light, singing its lullaby. Women knelt on the rocks, a little further along, their sleeves rolled up, pounding the washing. The memory of Mamma making bread flashed across my mind. I clasped Assad's hand. He gripped my fingers with such tenderness. I knew with absolute certainty that we were one in faith, one in spirit.

Out of the corner of my eye, I caught the flash half-way up the hillside across the river. I threw myself to the ground. We heard a scream as the sniper fired a second time. Assad gasped 'The women have been hit. Stay here, Fran.' Zig-zagging, bending low, he reached the rocks. I could see the wounded women, their blood flowing into the river like red wine. Assad had just reached them when there was another shot. Assad jerked upright before plunging forward, his arms outstretched.

My support, my protector, my childhood love fell forward onto his face.

War cancels out any desire for glory. In fact it eliminates the desire to prolong anybody's life apart from one's own – except in those who are heroically brave. Assad was one such. My support, my protector, my childhood love had gone from me. Somehow his radiant spirit touched mine before anguish severed us. I heard myself cry 'No. Dear God, no. Please don't let him leave me.'

I do not remember stumbling to reach Assad's prostrate body. Suddenly I had him in my arms embracing a lifetime's pilgrimage. People were converging. Safe hands lifting us together, bearing us away from the bloody river of shame. So swift, so terrible was my torment that I couldn't even whisper Assad's name, though it pulsated through me piercing my heart with agony. We were taken to shelter and gently lowered onto a sofa. Someone was trying to unclasp my hand from Assad's shoulder, but I clung to him as a mother clings to her child. No-one would ever separate us. We could never be parted. A mug of warm tea was thrust between my lips and I was begged to drink. I drank, still clasping my friend. We had shared peace and war, we had grown up together, we had grown old together in our childhood. We had taken the counsel of our gods together and shared our secrets with one another. I could not leave Assad to his immortal destiny, to rot in the fathom-less depths of some dark domain. I could not submit to the destruction of this precious life. It would be a betrayal.

'Fran, Fran, it's me.' It was god. He was stroking Assad's head.

'Take your fucking hands off him, you chicken-livered bastard,' I screamed, shocked at hearing my own voice at last.

'Don't you touch him. He was too good for you.' I began to cry.

'I know. I do know. Let me take him next door and wash him.' I wanted to wash Assad myself, he was mine to wash. But whatever life-giving strength I had possessed, had died with Assad's final breath. I could no longer even cling to him. My fingers uncurled and my arms fell to my side. I felt god lift Assad from me. I struggled to rise through the murmur of kindly voices I could hear around me but sleep claimed me.

I don't know how long I was unconscious, but I awoke to strange faces except for god who was kneeling beside me washing my face and hands. Slowly he took off my shoes, then my socks and washed my feet. Seeing that I was awake, he sat back on his haunches and gave me his dazzling smile. At least I was not alone.

'How are you feeling?' The words hardly audible but so tender. I licked my lips. 'Here, have some tea.' God put his fingers in the mug and placed them in my mouth for me to suck. When he withdrew them, I felt able to speak. 'Where's Assad?'

'In the next room.'

'Don't leave him alone,' I whispered.

'No, he isn't alone. I promise.'

'I want to see him.'

'Of course you do. You will, but later. Rest a little first.'

I wondered how god came to be there. 'Where were you when it happened?'

'At the first-aid post.'

'Assad told me you were working there. He didn't mean to break his promise to you about not telling anybody. He couldn't help it. I made him.'

'I knew you'd get it out of him. In fact I prayed that you would.'

'Why?' God smiled to himself.

'Childish ego. I wanted you to know that I was doing something worthwhile.'

'Assad forgave you.'

'Yes, I know. Do you forgive me?'

'Yes.' God's eyes were moist and he pulled at my nose as he had that first day he met me on the mountain all those years ago.

'I always knew you were something special, Fran.'

'It was Assad who was special, not me.' The tears began to pour down my face and waves of uncontrollable despair heaved in my chest as I wailed with the passion of a woman in grief. I plummeted into an abyss of self-pity, so remote from anything I had previously experienced that its fire burnt deep into my soul.

'Fran, don't do this to yourself.' God was holding me.

'Assad wouldn't want you to grieve like this.'

'I didn't want him to die but he did.'

'Assad sacrificed his life for others. It was a noble death, Fran.' I felt too frail to explain that I saw nothing noble in sacrificing oneself for unknown others. If he had only stayed with me. If we had gone straight home after the UNHCR . . . Why had this happened? Why wasn't it somebody else?

'Why wasn't it you?' I groaned to god. He pushed me away, holding my shoulders firmly and looked me steadily in the eye.

'I've asked that question of myself, Fran. At one point I wished it had been me and not Assad, but then I realised that if it had been me it would have been too easy. Assad was killed instantly. He didn't suffer, he felt no pain.'

'You're going to tell me it's a blessing next,' I whimpered.

'No, I'm not going to tell you that. But Assad is at peace.'

'I don't know how you have the nerve to say that he's at peace when you don't even believe in God any longer.' His face was quite calm, too calm.

'Now what makes you say that?' I wanted to put my tongue in chains.

'Go on, get it off your chest.' Whether it was my fragile state or sheer malice I will never know.

'You're a priest, aren't you?' God looked around the room to see if anyone else had heard. Although he gave me his dazzling smile, there was something in his look which would not have encouraged a stranger to persevere. But I was different.

'Well, are you or aren't you?'

'Yes, I am. When did you find out?'

'Ages ago – when I went round to the Comfort Aid offices.'

'Do any of the others know?'

'No. I told Assad this morning.'

'I see. Can you keep it to yourself for the moment?'

'Sure. It's none of my business.'

'That's right. It certainly isn't.' God hesitated, 'I'm glad you told Assad before . . .' He put on my socks and shoes and tied the laces. 'Are you feeling stronger now?' I nodded and swung my legs off the sofa.

'Would you like me to say some prayers over him?'

'He was a Muslim, not a Catholic.'

'Makes no difference to me,' God replied.

'I think you're a bloody hypocrite, Father Patrick.' I was never to call him god again.

Chapter Thirteen

We buried Assad in the park. For once I was glad of the night as I entwined my fingers in his for the last time. I slipped his holy beads from over his head, the watch from around his wrist. The darkness lengthened and the weeping continued. I said good-bye. Patrick said some prayers, the children battled stoically against their tears, and B.B. scampered round our feet. I kissed Assad but all I saw was death.

The following weeks passed in a confused haze of memory. Sometimes it was Mamma in the kitchen, Dadda working in the orchard or Assad swimming at the waterfall. Sometimes I would sob in my sleep and Patrick always seemed to be there caressing me, rocking me back to a sleep from which the despised sun would awaken me to the reality of my loss. B.B. shared my inconsolable grief by snuggling into me and licking my tears away. Assad had never belonged to me in life, as he did now in death.

The bleeding wound of my heart began to heal. And one morning I was aware that hope was returning as a drawn blind allows the light to enter. Edwina brought me some food.

'You look better. We've all been so worried about you.'

'I'm sorry. There was nothing I could do about it.'

'I know. We all understand, Fran. Please don't think you're alone.' Edwina suddenly threw her arms around me.

'Have you been managing all right?' I enquired.

'Yes. Patrick's been staying. We couldn't have managed without him. What with Ben being at work at the warehouse, and getting the water and the food from the soup kitchen, we needed the extra pair of hands. Someone had to stay with you and Ben decided to invite Patrick back. I hope you don't mind?'

'No. I'm sure it was a sensible move. Where is he now?'

'Ben or Patrick?'

'Patrick.'

'He's at the Comfort Aid offices this morning. They're preparing a major trip to some enclave which the enemy have captured west of here. Patrick says that the soldiers are expelling Muslim women and children from the towns as well as the elderly. Draft age males are being kept back, but thousands of them are unaccounted for.'

'Where are Vedra and the twins?'

'Outside, playing.' Words I had never thought to hear again. The delirium of the past weeks was over if the little ones could play outside. The front door was open and sun streamed across the room. Edwina seemed to guess my thoughts.

'Yes, they're behaving like children.' We laughed, recognising that our own maturity was so much greater than our years. Arm in arm and with B.B. prancing beside us, we went outside to watch the kids at play.

Later on when the children were preoccupied with a card game and Ben was helping Edwina to put the bedding down, Patrick took me aside.

'It would do you good to get away for a few days, Fran. I'm going to be leading a convoy which is taking aid into Brnka. I'd be really pleased if you could consider coming with us. We can organise the paperwork and put you down as an interpreter.' I was sceptical.

'What about my age?'

'You could pass as sixteen and you've picked up a little English which is important because all the drivers are English.'

'But Patrick, you speak our language fluently.'

'True, but I'm the only one who does and that will be a problem if the trucks get separated. I really do need you, Fran. Think about it, will you?'

'What about the kids here?'

'I've spoken to Ben and Edwina – they're quite happy to hold the fort, and with you and me out of the way there are only the twins and Vedra to worry about.'

'Can we take B.B.?' Patrick paused.

'No, I'm sorry, he would have to stay here.' I hesitated.

'How long will the trip take?'

'About three to four days if we don't get held up by shelling.' He explained that there had been a mass exodus of refugees expelled from their towns in the west who had arrived at the town of Brnka, which had fallen to enemy soldiers. As a result, thousands of displaced women and children were being held in Brnka as prisoners without food or medical supplies. UNPRO-FOR had negotiated with the enemy authorities for convoys of supplies to be taken in for civilian use only.

'Please, Fran, say yes. I'll be leading the convoy and you can be in the second truck.' I wanted a change and it would be good to see the back of the city, even if it was just a matter of exchanging one pillaged town for another.

'OK. If Ben and Edwina really agree, I'll come.'

Considering the anarchy and chaos of the last few years, I was amazed at the amount of bureaucracy that seemed to be necessary for trucks carrying essential life-saving aid to get into Brnka. Papers specifying every pasta shell and every toilet roll had to be signed and stamped by the Ministry of Works and then by the UN. More papers with the registration numbers of trucks, the names of drivers and interpreters. I had to go to the office to have my photograph taken so that it could be stamped and fixed to my identification badge. Edwina insisted on washing and cutting my hair for the photograph. The twins had found a broken mirror some time before and I stared into it. My newly cropped hair made me look very young – perhaps even the age I was.

'I won't pass for sixteen.' Vedra obviously agreed. She slipped out.

'Do you have to be over sixteen?' Edwina was trying to pull my flattened hair into fashionable spikes.

'I don't really know, but it'll look suspicious if the convoy is carrying a kid, even if the paperwork is correct.'

'I'm sure Patrick wouldn't take you if there was any danger.'

'I'll probably be safer in a truck out there, than walking down the street here.' Vedra returned. She marched over to us and handed me a lipstick.

'Put that on and you'll look ravishing.' There was such sincerity in her little voice that we broke into giggles.

'Where the hell did you get this from?'

'Mrs Markovic upstairs.' Vedra knew most people in the blocked-off upstairs part of the house, and everybody knew Vedra.

'How do you put it on?' I had never used make-up before.

'Oh, Fran, you are hopeless,' said Vedra impatiently. 'Here, give it to me. I'll put it on for you this time,' and with the deftness of a portrait painter, she began to outline my lips. Edwina was shocked.

'How do you know how to do that at your age?'

'I used to watch my older sisters and when we were play-acting, we always put on make-up.' Vedra never ceased to amaze us.

'Stretch your lips like this, Fran. Good, and now rub them

together.' One of the twins came and looked over my shoulder into the mirror.

'Wow, you look like a tart, Fran.'

'Shut up,' said Vedra. 'She doesn't. Now let's do her eyes.'

'Have you got mascara as well?'

'No, black boot polish.'

'That's it. Enough, Vedra. I am not putting boot polish on my eyes.' Vedra looked vexed, so I added, 'You're a great make-up artist.'

We left the city at 5 a.m. in a convoy of six trucks, two of them belonging to Comfort Aid. We had all been provided with UN flak jackets and helmets. Patrick led the convoy with David and myself directly behind. David was an Englishman in his mid-twenties and I discovered that he had graduated from university with a double first in classics. David was small and pale with wavy blond hair and would not have looked out of place singing in a cathedral choir. As it was, his legs could hardly reach the pedals of the truck and, without power steering, he frequently had difficulty in turning the steering wheel. But David's lack of inches was compensated for by his enthusiasm. While he spoke little of our language he made a valiant attempt to pick it up during the first few hours. He seemed to be a natural linguist and I began to teach him sentences that might come in useful, such as: 'We have had a blow-out. Could you direct me to the nearest garage?'

However, when he informed me that the convoy was carrying twelve spare tyres, I realised that blow-outs were unlikely to require outside help and decided that it was going to be more useful to teach him to say: 'Please can I have two glasses of slivovitz. Could you please bring me the menu.' And David quickly picked up our words for every sort of meat and vegetable.

Progress was desperately slow, partly because half the time we were going uphill, but chiefly because we were heavily laden. It took an hour for the convoy to cross a Bailey bridge as it could take only one truck at a time. It was a revelation to see that the countryside was so undisturbed. Larks were singing in the morning breeze and I watched the sun slipping in and out of the clouds as if trying to catch a glimpse of our newly peaceful countryside. We came upon deserted villages redolent of the war. Any building which had escaped the shelling had been burnt to the ground.

We arrived at our first checkpoint within an hour of leaving the city. As we ground to a halt, with hardly an inch to spare between one lorry and the next, David told me that the secret of driving in a convoy is to keep as close as possible to the vehicle in front. When I asked the reason, speaking in our language, he pretended not to understand. I wondered why until I realised that the last thing the English drivers wanted to do was to give the soldiers the idea that they were familiar with their language. The stupider they could appear, the more chance they had of getting through safely. Then followed dreary wasted hours of showing papers to soldiers, who showed them to their officers, who disappeared into a temporary wooden hut. There was much waving of arms and dashing about, much picking up and putting down of Kalashnikovs, a good deal of shouting at patrols and general commotion.

At one point an officer accompanied by two soldiers marched up to the cabin of our truck, guns at the ready, and ordered us out. They were rude, hostile and stank of drink as they demanded to see our papers. I could see Patrick in the truck ahead of us watching proceedings in his wing mirror. According to the officer our papers were not in order. We were told to unbutton the canvas covering the back of the truck and take out every single box. I remonstrated until the officer angrily pulled out his gun, at which point I gave in. Everything that the aid workers had taken hours to load the previous night was now lying at the side of the road. I could not but wonder what would have happened to it all if it had been pouring with rain. The soldiers ordered us to open some of the boxes and they slit open a fifty-kilo sack of rice, leaving it to dribble onto the ground until the sack was empty. They had suspected that it might contain hidden guns. I pointed out that we were aid workers and carried no weapons. As if in retaliation they then pulled all our personal gear out of the cabin: food, water and sleeping-bags. They strutted around us making jokes about the English, intimidating the drivers with their time-wasting orders and demanding paperwork they did not need. It was a demonstration of power in order to humiliate the international aid agencies. All too frequently it succeeded.

We were forced to go through seven of these checkpoints as we crossed the front line. It was a dreary protracted ordeal requiring both patience and tact. David instructed me to 'Keep the buggers happy, then they might let us through.' The relief when we were finally allowed through each checkpoint was short-lived as we were only going to find another round the next bend. At some of the barriers, the enemy soldiers had set up what appeared to be life-size figures of Muslims – their bodies riddled with shot. I sincerely hoped that they were only puppets.

As night descended Patrick halted the convoy as we drove down a widening mountain road just across a pass. Camping stoves were brought out and hot meals prepared, while the drivers checked their vehicles for oil and water and filled them with diesel from the ten-litre tanks strapped to the trucks. I was stirring a large saucepan of tinned baked beans and sausages, having laid out six sliced loaves, when Patrick came over to me, beer in hand.

'Well done, Fran, standing up to those bastards at the first checkpoint. One has to be quite careful with them. They're an excitable lot and when they're drunk, they can get trigger happy.' I was about to answer him when two UN Land-Rovers appeared. The soldiers in their blue berets were hailed as old friends and given beers. I noticed the Canadian flag on their shirt sleeves. My English wasn't very good but I could understand more than I spoke. To my amazement, Patrick seemed to be talking to them about birds. But I eventually realised that different routes across the mountains were being referred to as 'raven', 'eagle', etc. When they had gone, Patrick sat down beside me on a boulder wolfing down his food. 'That was Canbat,' he explained.

'What's Canbat?'

'Sorry, Fran. Canadian Battalion. They're keeping the peace in this area. Tomorrow we'll be moving into the area of Norbat, that's Norwegian Battalion peace-keeping troops. Apparently the Raven route is closed because of shelling, so Canbat have advised us to go by the Eagle route into Brnka, which is a long way round. It's another half-day's drive, so let's get some sleep.' I found David in his sleeping-bag stretched across the cabin seat dead to the world. I removed my sleeping-bag from under the seat and quietly shut the door. Patrick called to me from the top of his truck. 'Up here, Fran.' He was hanging over the canvas roof. 'Put your foot there, that's right. Now give me your hand.' He swung me up. 'Best place up here. The canvas is like a hammock and you sink into it and the snipers can't see us. Goodnight, Fran and God bless.'

We were back on the road well before dawn, now dressed in our UN flak jackets and helmets. Conversation dulled, partly because David was half-asleep, but also because the noise of the engine didn't encourage chit-chat. We passed a lot of empty dug-outs and just before midday, came upon the Norbat camp.

Norbat were happy to see new faces and welcomed us into their mess tent with considerable *bonhomie*, offering us bread, soup and cold meats. Speaking English to Patrick, they discussed our strategy for entering Brnka. An hour later, we moved out again, this time with an Armoured Personnel Carrier and a UN Land-Rover both provided by Norbat leading the way, flying the UN flag, and another Armoured Personnel Carrier bringing up the rear. The Norwegian soldiers were cheerfully hanging out of the vehicles getting themselves a tan. Only when they pulled themselves back inside and the hatch was sealed did I realise that we were about to enter Brnka. The Norwegian officer in the UN Land-Rover negotiated the convoy through three checkpoints and into the town. At first sight it was not dissimilar to our own city. Many of the buildings were reduced to rubble and we had to deal with the problems of craters by driving on the pavements. We were stopped at a further checkpoint. This time things did not seem to be going so smoothly. After about an hour, Patrick walked back to our vehicle.

'We're having problems with the military officials. They are demanding half the food for their soldiers which only leaves us half for the refugees. They won't let us move on until we agree.' He repeated what he had said in English for David's benefit.

'Fuck the bastards,' muttered the erudite David.

'Norbat is on the radio to their own HQ asking what they advise.'

'How many refugees are here, Patrick?' I enquired. We had not seen a soul since entering Brnka apart from soldiers.

'They estimate about 150,000 including the locals.'

'Where are they?'

'I gather a good many are imprisoned in the schools, some of which are very close by.' A machine-gun distracted us and

Patrick leapt into our cabin. Then it was quiet again except for the rumbling of tanks on the outskirts of the enclave.

'So what do we do?' asked David.

'We have no option, but to sit and wait.' We spent the rest of the day sitting in the cabins of our trucks, as the Norbat soldiers had told us on no account to lower our windows or get out of the trucks. Patrick flitted between the trucks with information on how negotiations were progressing – or not progressing – and encouraged us to be patient. By the evening my need to urinate had become as powerful as my sense of frustration. It was all very well for the men, who just opened their door and pointed, but as I indicated to Patrick, I needed to squat. 'Just go round the back of the truck, I'll watch the soldiers.'

'But the drivers in the truck behind will see me,' I remonstrated. However, the pain of controlling my muscles far outweighed my modesty.

Again and again permission was requested for our convoy to continue to its previously agreed destination. The soldiers refused. I wondered how the starving refugees behind their barricades must be feeling, knowing that trucks laden with food for them were standing only metres from their catering hut. The enemy soldiers had made sure that they knew, and were apparently deliberately taunting them, raising their hopes, only to smash them. Eventually, some time after midnight, a compromise was reached after twelve hours of discussion. We were allowed through the barricades. The UN soldiers from the APC stood guard round the trucks while we unloaded. We climbed up onto the roof canvases to fall into a deep sleep as dawn was breaking.

Next morning, the trucks were driven off to be refuelled, as had been agreed between the enemy soldiers and Norbat. I was sitting on the side of the road when an open UN jeep passed by, and then reversed to stop beside me. I watched the blue-capped soldier look at the ID pinned to my flak jacket.

'Want a lift, Fran?' he offered with a heavy accent.

'Where to?'

'Up the road to the school.'

'Are you going to see the refugees?' I noted from his ID badge that his name was Buino and that he was an UNMO – a United Nations Military Observer.

'Yes. Jump in unless you've got something better to do.' I jumped and we started off.

'What are you doing here?' he asked me.

'Interpreter for the convoy.' I hoped that Buino would not decide to speak English! My command of the language was extremely basic.

'Where are you from?' I enquired.

'Holland. Here we are. Do you want to come in?' Buino nodded to the guards on the barricaded gates and we passed into a school playground. 'I'll be about ten minutes.' He walked off past the twenty or so enemy soldiers standing around in groups of two or three smoking cigarettes, their Kalashnikovs at the ready. I sat staring at them and they stared back at me suspiciously. I opened the jeep door and got out to stretch. I could feel the tension in the air. One of these soldiers could be the man who had killed Mo when he had been zig-zagging up the mountain to draw their fire away from the rest of us while we were living in the cave. My heart beat loudly. The soldiers were young and tired. Their green combat uniforms were streaked with mud, the barrels of their guns black.

'Can I go and look through the window?' I shouted to the nearest group. They shrugged their shoulders, so I moved slowly up to the walls of the school. Nothing could have prepared me for what I saw through the window. I was reminded of countless battery chickens squashed together. Women and children, old and young, hundreds of people, or so it seemed, lying on top of one another in a classroom which must have been meant for thirty children. Some lay in their own excrement: all were filthy and skeletal. The stench must have been horrendous. Fortunately for me the windows were closed so I didn't have to smell it. Dead hollow eyes stared back at me through the glass. There was no noise, not even the sound of a child crying. Just breathing seemed to take all their energy.

'Hey, come away from there,' someone shouted, and I turned towards the jeep and retraced my steps. Buino returned and we drove out.

'Want a coffee?' I could not contemplate either food or drink, so I refused.

'Can you drop me here?' I asked when we were a little way down the road. 'I'd like to walk for a bit.'

'Sure – but there's a café up there. I could bring you anything you want.'

'Thanks, but no.' I wondered when Buino had last seen a woman to socialise with.

'Go on, live dangerously,' he joked.

'Please, I'm sorry – just let me out.'

'OK. Don't get your knickers in a twist.' He slowed down. When we had stopped he tried to reassure me. 'I didn't mean anything by it, I just thought you'd like a coffee.'

'I'm sorry, I didn't mean to be rude. But I'd better get back to the convoy.'

'Suit yourself.'

And I left him. As I walked back up the road I heard sporadic shelling. Buino and the other UNMOs were unarmed. I wondered if they ever felt secure. I realised suddenly what a hopelessly impossible situation it was for the UN. No matter what atrocities were perpetrated, what horrors they came across, they were unable to take sides and unable to take any real action that could affect the war.

When I got back to the convoy, Patrick and the drivers had

202

returned and were sorting out food rations and litre bottles of water to be divided between the trucks.

'When do we leave?' I asked.

'The sooner the better as far as I'm concerned,' said Patrick. 'Mind you, it should take half the time going back.'

'Why?'

'Being empty means we can go faster and there's unlikely to be any trouble at the checkpoints now that we aren't carrying aid.'

'Mission accomplished as you might say.'

Patrick grinned – 'I won't go as far as that till we're all home in one piece, safe and sound.' Patrick was staring into my eyes. 'Are you all right, Fran? No, you're not.' He put his arms round me. 'What's up?'

'I've just been up to one of the schools,' I blurted out.

'You saw the refugees?'

'Yes. They're living in the most appalling conditions. You wouldn't leave cattle like that.'

'They're alive at least.'

'Hardly,' I mumbled miserably. 'Isn't there anything we can do for them?'

'No,' he replied firmly. 'We're under the auspices of the UN here and there's nothing whatever we can do. We have to keep a low profile.'

'But it's evil.'

'It's war, Fran. War does not discriminate between good and evil, adult or child.'

'But they're innocent. They're not part of this war. I wouldn't imagine that any of those people have ever picked up a gun.'

'It is always the women and children who are the innocent victims of war.'

As he said it, I remembered Mamma being hurled into the

back of the truck outside our village hall, like a dead animal. Where was she, what had happened to her?

'Mamma could have been in that room.' The dull ache was back.

'No, Fran, come and sit down.' Patrick pulled me down onto the grass verge, and without releasing my hand he continued, 'I've been meaning to tell you this for some time, but the opportunity – well – there never seemed to be the right moment.'

'The right moment to tell me what?'

'About your Mamma,' he said gently. Sorrow lurched from a dull ache into agonized longing.

'I've been attending the UN briefings these last months,' Patrick continued.

'You know where Mamma is?'

'Fran, it was confirmed that a truckload of women and children from several villages including your own were driven into the woods, thirty miles east. They were shot.' I felt numb. Patrick could not possibly be talking about my Mamma.

'No, Patrick. That couldn't have been Mamma. It must be something recent. My mamma was taken over a year ago.' Patrick put his arm round my shoulder.

'Fran, they found a mass grave. The victims were definitely from your village. It's been established that they were all shot in the head the same night they burnt your village.'

The dormant ache in my heart had been anaesthetised by hope. Now it overflowed. Wave upon wave of suppressed agony shuddered into life, lashing at the wounds I had so long concealed by turning a deaf ear and a blind eye to what I now knew beyond doubt to be the truth. Mamma was dead.

CHAPTER FOURTEEN

Looking back, I think that I had really known for some time that Mamma must be dead. But until one hears otherwise, the sliver of hope lurks deep within the heart.

In one way, Patrick's news brought relief. The unknown is always frightening and at least I now knew for sure. In his concern for me Patrick had decided that I should make the return journey in his truck which would bring up the rear of the convoy this time. I was amazed at how fast the heavy trucks could travel when they were empty. We rattled along the road and had no trouble at any of the checkpoints. The enemy soldiers peered inside and waved us on once they had ascertained that they were empty. Norbat escorted us out of Brnka and as far as their camp where we bade them farewell.

It was late evening. We had been making good progress and were not far from our city when disaster struck. We were on a winding mountain road. David was setting a fast pace in the leading truck. Patrick had eased up knowing that we were nearly home, so our truck was quite a way behind the rest of the convoy. Afterwards Patrick admitted that this had been a bad move. As we slowed to approach a bend he changed down. The gear locked as he struggled with it and we ground to an ignominious halt.

'Bloody hell!'

'What's happened?'

'I think the clutch has gone.'

'What does that mean?'

'It means, dear Fran, that this old crate isn't going to move. Wait here.' Patrick grabbed a torch, flung open the door and leapt out of the cabin. I heard him tinkering under the belly of the truck and I looked around. It was too dark to see much, but I must have been more frightened than I realised. Every tree looked like a soldier in camouflage. Patrick re-emerged. 'I'm not a mechanic, but I'm pretty certain it's kaput.' He turned on the engine again and tried putting the truck into a different gear, but to no avail.

'Shit. What the hell were the other drivers doing? They're meant to watch in their mirrors.'

'It's not their fault,' I defended them. 'We were slacking behind.'

'But they must have noticed that our headlights had gone. Damn it!'

'What do we do now?'

'The rule is that we keep the doors locked and stay inside the vehicle till help comes.'

'It's going to be a long night.'

'Sorry, Fran, it's my fault. I should have kept up with the convoy.' I remained silent.

'What's so stupid is that we're only twenty miles from home.'

'Let's walk it,' I suggested. 'If the vehicle can't move, the soldiers can't steal it.'

'How long have we been here?'

'About half an hour.'

'OK. We'll wait another half hour and see if anybody comes back for us. Meanwhile I'll get the towrope out of the back just in case.' I must have dozed off. The next thing I knew Patrick was tugging at my sleeve. 'Fran, I'm not happy marooned here.

If some trigger-happy drunken soldiers appear, we'll be in deep trouble. I think that we should start walking up the mountain to the left, keeping the main road in sight. That way we are going in the right direction for the city and we can spot anyone on the road. We'll need to take our backpacks.'

We strapped them on and started to climb. Patrick going ahead and me following silently in his footsteps. It was a moonless night. In a couple of hours we had reached the summit and could see the road winding downhill across a gorge in the valley and zig-zagging up the other side. I was tired and my legs were stiff from the climb. Progress was slow. Scrambling down rocks into the gorge was daunting and Patrick was limping badly. His bad leg was obviously giving him trouble.

'Patrick, can we stop for a while, my leg muscles are killing me.' He was a little way ahead and retraced his steps.

'Good idea. Let's look for cover.' We found a crevice and I collapsed onto the pebbles. Patrick threw off his backpack and squatted down, rummaging inside.

He found what he was looking for. A huge bar of chocolate. We laughed.

'Do you remember the first time you gave me chocolate?' I asked him.

'I'll never forget it. You were such a funny little scrap, snivelling there in the snow. You quite touched my heart.' He gave me a quizzical look as we began to dig into the chocolate. 'We can't go on meeting like this, Fran,' he chuckled.

We laughed. I thought back to Patrick's superb co-ordination when he had glided away from me on his skis after giving me the chocolate all those years ago.

'Where did you learn to ski?' I asked him.

'In Switzerland – St Moritz. My parents belonged to the Combined Army Ski Club and we went there every year in the Christmas holidays when I was a kid.'

'Was your father a professional soldier, then?'

'Good heavens, no. But he is a Colonel in the territorials. He likes playing soldiers. He's a lawyer by profession. I think he hoped I would follow in his footsteps, but it wasn't my scene.'

'When did you realise you had a vocation to be a priest?'

'It wasn't something sudden. I was at a Catholic boarding school run by monks, so the monastic life was part of me from the time I was a very small child. I don't remember a time without it. You know the Jesuit maxim "Give me a child for the first seven years and he is mine for life." You might say that it was congenital. What about you?'

'Mamma was the Catholic in our family. Dadda was agnostic.'

'Did your mother practise?'

'Oh, yes. She took me to church every Sunday.' I paused. 'Are you still a priest, Patrick?'

'Yes.' He said the word so loudly and so defiantly that it seemed to echo across the gorge.

'Were you a priest that time I first met you skiing?'

'I was training then. I hadn't been ordained.'

'But if you are a priest, how come you are driving aid into our city?'

'The Bishop gave me special permission. Comfort Aid is a Catholic charity and they desperately needed someone to accompany them who spoke your language fluently. They advertised in a Catholic newspaper and I responded.'

'But how do you come to speak our language in the first place?'

'My mother is from here. She was determined not to lose her roots – our roots too – so she brought me and my brothers up to be bilingual. We used to come here on holiday in the summer to visit our grandparents.'

'Are they still alive?'

'No, thank God. They died in a car crash when I was a teenager.'

'I'm sorry.'

'Don't be. I couldn't bear to think of what they would have gone through these last few years if they had still been alive.'

'Do your parents realise that you're still alive?'

'They realise now. After I was shot and while I was in hospital the Comfort Aid workers went back to England and had to say that they had no idea what had happened to me. I had just disappeared as far as they were concerned. There was no means of communication from here during the siege as you well know. I think that's part of the reason I behaved so badly when you took me back to the tomb and I stole the food. It was a sort of semi-breakdown. I had been so busy being pleased with myself for helping poor unfortunate people that I didn't recognise my own frailty. I never realised how much my family and friends meant to me. It was a hard lesson to learn. I hadn't realised I was so dependent. I didn't recognise my arrogance, my pride. I lost hope. I lost faith.'

'How did you come out of it – the breakdown, I mean?'

'A few days after you had thrown me out, I met Assad. I was at rock bottom, living in a bombed-out building. If I had had the guts I would have committed suicide but, as you know, courage is not my forte.' Patrick smiled wearily. 'Anyway, when Assad saw me, rather than turn his back on me, he came over and asked how I was doing and I told him to bugger off. He stood his ground and simply told me how sorry he felt for me as I had spent my life living a lie. His pity infuriated me but it got me thinking. It had been so easy to come here to help and then disappear back to the comforts of my own country. It made me feel good. When I came round in hospital and realised that I was stuck here and was going to have to live the life of a refugee like the rest of you, I resented it. I didn't want to be part of your war. I think that Assad must have been looking for me, because a few days after he had found me in this bombed-out building, he asked if I'd like to go up to the forward first-aid station with him. Assad was a very perceptive young man. He realised that it would be therapeutic for me. So I spent all the hours God made, working up there and when I realised that Assad had forgiven me for the way I had behaved, I knew that I could forgive myself.'

I was intensely moved by Patrick's story and by Assad's part in it. Eventually I said, 'I'm glad you have forgiven yourself, Patrick. What will you do now?'

'I was going to tell you. I'm returning to England with the next Comfort Aid convoy.'

'When's that?'

'Some time towards the end of this week.' It was now Tuesday.

'Will you come back?'

'Some time, Fran. But not in the near future. Now that I have discovered all this about myself, I need somehow to build on it. I have to take time just to *be*. Before I was shot I was so busy doing that I didn't have time to be – I think I was too scared to face myself. Now that I know the truth about myself I need to find strength, I need to go away on retreat.'

'We will miss you.'

'And I shall miss you. But some day I'll return. Maybe when the war is over.'

'Can we keep in touch?'

'Of course.'

'How do I stay in touch with you, Patrick? There's still no post.'

'Use Comfort Aid. I'll write to you and there's a fax machine in the office for when the electricity's back. I'll arrange it all before I leave. We'll fix up a PO box for you at the office.'

I felt bereft.

'Assad's left me and now you're going.' Patrick lay down beside me on the pebbles and gently stroked my cheek.

'Don't be frightened, Fran. I felt just like you do when I woke up in hospital and found that all my colleagues had left and gone back to the UK without me. But you're not alone. You have Ben and Edwina.'

'And I had Mo, Adjin, Gregor and Assad.'

'You'll be all right. You're a survivor.'

'Assad once said that we were both survivors, but he didn't make it.'

'No, he didn't.' Patrick lay back and closed his eyes and we drifted into unconsciousness. The sound of goat bells jerked us from sleep as the dim grey light of dawn appeared. It was cold and I felt deeply and miserably alone. My future appeared as bleak as the dawn as we began to climb the last mountain before the city. It was as we reached the summit and were debating whether or not we could rejoin the road in safety now that it was daylight that we heard the laughter of the soldiers. They were sitting on boulders beside the road. There were twelve of them, their Kalashnikovs resting on their knees, unshaven, unwashed and probably highly undisciplined. We threw ourselves flat behind some sparse bushes.

'Renegade soldiers,' Patrick whispered. I nodded. Supposing we had met them during the night on the road. Suddenly, from nowhere, a child in a checked smock appeared driving her goats. She could not have been more than ten years old. The soldiers caught sight of the child and called her over, appearing to be friendly. For a minute or two all seemed well as they chatted to her. She turned back to her goats and I saw one of the soldiers slowly and deliberately swing his gun to his shoulder and take aim. I thought that he was aiming at a goat. After all, they looked as if they needed a good meal as badly as we did. Patrick must have had the same thought for he, too, seemed unperturbed. Only when the shot rang out and the child spun around and fell to the ground, did it dawn on either of us that she had been the target. I was on my feet but Patrick restrained me. The goats had fled.

'No, Fran. We can't help,' he hissed. The soldiers were picking up the agonising blood-bespattered little body. She was far from dead. The soldiers placed the dying child across the narrow road carefully positioning her. Patrick had his arms around my waist. He was holding me in a grip of steel.

I could hear the child sobbing with pain.

'We've got to help her,' I hissed.

'No, Fran!' I struggled in Patrick's arms.

'I know courage isn't your forte, Patrick,' I spat out, 'but even you can't be that yellow!' His grave eyes were moist as he freed me.

'What can we do against twelve guns, Fran? Believe me, if I thought we could save that child, I would be the first down there. If you think you can help her, I won't stop you.' I hesitated. The soldiers had left the child in the middle of the road and were now hiding behind the boulders. I wondered what on earth they were doing.

'It's a hijack,' Patrick told me in a low voice. 'Trust me, Fran.' We lay in the shadows. Time seemed interminable. The child had stopped whimpering and lay still on the tarmac. My recklessness had subsided into frustration at my own power-lessness. The minutes passed. Sun had broken through the early morning mist when we heard the drone of a vehicle. We could see a Land-Rover snaking up the mountain road. I looked at Patrick in desperation. He put his finger to his lips but I couldn't have screamed even if I had wanted to. The roar of the engine came closer and then we could see it directly below us. I noted French number plates. There was only one occupant. As he rounded the bend he saw the child and jammed on his brakes, tyres squealing.

The soldiers crouched behind their boulders. The driver did not get out straight away. Perhaps he sensed an ambush and was trying to make an impossible decision. Get out of the van or try to drive around the tiny body. Eventually, the driver's door opened. A man in a bush-shirt and khaki shorts clambered out. To my amazement, instead of walking directly to the child, he leant into the back of the vehicle and emerged with a couple of cameras. Patrick gasped and whispered 'I know him. He's a French journalist. He used to come to the UN briefings. Oh shit! Get back in your vehicle, man, and drive on.' But the man was squatting beside the child, taking photographs. As far as I could see he had not taken her pulse or made any other effort to find out whether or not she was still alive.

'Bloody journalist,' I muttered. It all happened so quickly. A shot rang out. It missed the man and he leapt towards his Land-Rover. A second shot and he fell between the child and the vehicle. The soldiers came out from behind the boulders. One of them walked across to the child and shot her in the head. A second soldier shot the journalist. They were talking, laughing and lighting cigarettes. The soldiers gathered around the Land-Rover to inspect their booty. One of them removed himself from the group and went over to the journalist to wrench his cameras out of his hands. The soldier had to tug at the cameras. The journalist lay there, grasping them even in death: a true professional. After they had finished their cigarettes, the soldiers picked up the two bodies and threw them over the edge of the road and down the mountainside. Six of them clambered into the hijacked vehicle and drove off. The rest ambled off up the road away from the city. Patrick and I just sat there, speechless. Totally drained. Patrick eventually said:

'Oh, God!' His face was ashen.

'I'm sorry I said you were a coward.'

'I am, but that wasn't what was stopping me going down there.'

'I know that. I'm sorry that I thought it was.'

'Forget it. It's not important.' I put my head between my knees.

'You OK?' Patrick asked.

'Yes. I was wondering when this is all going to end and how much more suffering there has to be? I can't take much more.' Patrick edged over to me, squeezing my arm.

'Fran, you're so strong. Much stronger than me. Look at all the horrors you've been through. I do believe that one day there will be peace here and then you'll be able to look forward, instead of back.'

'I haven't always been strong. It's the war that has made me what I am and I don't like what I see in myself. Assad once told me that he didn't like what he saw in me.'

'I don't believe he meant it.'

'I don't know. I think at the time he did mean it.'

'What do you see in yourself that you don't like?'

'A terrible hardness. If Mamma could see me now, she would be horrified at the way I have become so callous. Mamma was so gentle and kind.'

'You're so wrong, Fran. Your Mamma would be very proud of you.' I felt my eyes prick with tears. I tried to restrain them but they poured down my face. Perhaps it was reaction to the murders of the child and the journalist. Probably it was the thought of Mamma.

Eventually we scrambled down the hillside to the road and peered over the edge of the mountain to see if there was any sign of the bodies.

'It's too steep,' said Patrick. 'Let's head for the city and we can inform the UN.'

We had given up any thought of keeping to the mountain but had covered only a few miles of the road when I heard the sound of an engine behind us. There was no real cover, but as the vehicle came over the summit we saw the familiar white of the UN.

'They'll pick us up,' I said confidently.

'They won't, Fran. They're not allowed to give lifts to civilians.'

'Not even in an emergency?'

'Not even in an emergency.'

'Fuck that!' I leapt into the middle of the road, waving my arms frantically. The vehicle had little choice. A cheerful face peered out the window. It was my Dutch friend from UNMO.

'Shit, Fran! You had me worried there,' said Buino.

'You must give us a lift,' I begged and started to tell him what had been happening since we had left Brnka. 'You are going to the city, aren't you?' I wheedled. 'I know it's illegal for you to give lifts but couldn't you just turn a blind eye this once?'

'Yes, I'm going to HQ. Hop in. Oh! by the way this is Ted, my colleague.'

I had not noticed Buino's passenger. We shook hands and I introduced Patrick to them both. We could have been attending some business meeting. Nobody would have guessed that Patrick and I had been witnessing brutal murder two hours earlier. Buino drove us to UNHQ, where Patrick disappeared into the office of some Major for debriefing while Ted and Buino took me to their canteen for a meal. I was starving and I had my first plate of hot meat and vegetables in years. The first I had had since leaving Mamma. I had a second helping. Then I told Buino and Ted about Ben, Edwina, the twins, Vedra and B.B. When Patrick eventually joined us, I had been given six silver foil dishes to carry home to the basement.

Patrick arranged for the truck with its broken clutch to be

towed back to the city that afternoon. I went straight home. The excitement at my homecoming made me feel as if I'd scored a winning goal in the World Cup. They jumped all over me and B.B. was so overcome that little drops of piddle dribbled out of him as he pushed his way between the exuberant bodies to smother me with licks. Everybody was talking at the same time.

'We have electricity for two hours between 3 a.m. and 5 a.m.'

'We can turn on the light.'

'Of course, there's a blackout but it doesn't affect us because we don't have any windows.'

'We got up and played charades last night. It was great.'

'What's in the six silver trays, Fran?' They'd been so delighted to see me that they hadn't even asked about what I'd brought.

I told them, adding, 'B.B. do stop piddling.' It was so good to be home.

With electricity restored, albeit for only two hours a night, life took on a new dimension. Different areas of the city had their two hours of electricity at different times. The Comfort Aid offices had electricity between 8 p.m. and 10 p.m., so Patrick worked in the evenings for the next few days. His impending departure generated gloom amongst us, but we went about our routines – soup kitchen, standpipe, washing and the rest – with feigned cheerfulness. Shelling was intermittent as was sniper shooting. There were rumours that the politicians were meeting in Geneva and that President Yeltsin had proposed an international conference in order to unify diplomatic efforts to agree on a proposal for peace. The US had also come up with a new plan, which reportedly might involve some redrawing of boundaries. The rumoured shift in the balance of power seemed to be forcing new political initiatives but as yet these had had no effect on our daily lives.

At the end of the week, on the day before Patrick's departure for England, I decided to walk over to the Comfort Aid office. B.B. and I wanted to spend the last evening with him. Patrick was in the office with three of his drivers who were just leaving.

'Am I intruding?' I asked as I put my head round the door.

'No, come in Fran. Hello B.B. We're just in the middle of an emergency. Tara, the girl who keeps this office ticking over, has run away with her boyfriend. I have twelve hours to find a replacement. I don't suppose you know anybody?'

'Don't think so. What are you looking for?'

'Well, officially it's a matter of someone coming in on a daily basis to check the mail, write a few letters, deal with faxes and have the beds made up for the next group of Comfort Aid workers. They are arriving in six weeks.'

'Presumably Tara got paid for this?'

'Of course. We bring it over in deutschmarks.'

'I think I do know somebody.' I held my breath. Patrick glanced up from his desk.

'I could do it,' I said, trying to sound assertive.

'But, Fran, can you work a computer?' Why did he have to ask about computers?

'No I can't. But I can learn. I can write letters and I can make beds.' Patrick looked dubious.

'Can't you try me out for six weeks?'

'But you can't speak much English.'

'I'll learn that too – and I can always take the mail down to the UN to get them to translate. Please, Patrick. It would give me a job and we'd have some money coming in to look after the children.' He was wavering. I pursued my advantage.

'Surely I'd be better than some outsider. After all I'm a

217

Catholic. I know what this charity is trying to do. You know I wouldn't let you down and . . .'

'Fran!' Patrick held up his hand. 'Come and sit here,' he pointed to the chair in front of the computer. Obediently, I sat, B.B. curled up at my feet. How was I going to convince him that I was not some flibbertigibbet moron as far as running an office was concerned. 'OK Fran, you win. But I want you here at eight o'clock tonight for your first computer lesson.'

CHAPTER FIFTEEN

Patrick and I embraced for the last time. I couldn't look him in the face. I should have been expressing my gratitude for all his help, but I could only think that he was going. Assad had left me and now Patrick was going too. I had lived with the imminence of death, I had watched my friends being cut down by violence. I had accepted the finality of their deaths but this was different – Patrick was alive and he was choosing to leave us; choosing to return to the peace and comfort of his own country. A sense of betrayal had been ignited within me. I had presumed that Patrick would stay with us for ever and this had brought a measure of security. But he had chosen to abandon us. Sorrow enveloped me. Patrick kissed me gently on the forehead and limped towards the truck. We smiled without joy. We clasped one another, a moment filled with silent promises of love and resentment. Patrick climbed aboard his vehicle without looking back. I stared as the convoy disappeared down the road growing smaller. It turned the corner and vanished. A silent scream rose in my throat. Who was going to leave me next – Ben, Edwina, Vedra, the twins?

But Patrick had left me with a job and he had taught me enough about the computer for me to be able to do what was necessary in order to keep the office running. Every evening between 8 p.m. and 10 p.m. when there was electricity, I would write letters on the computer. But none of my letters could be posted because the people I was writing to did not have addresses. I wrote many many letters to Assad. The office became a haven from loneliness and a retreat from reality. One evening Vedra asked if she could accompany me.

'No,' I barked.

'Why not?' She persevered.

'You'd be bored. I go to the office to work.'

'I could watch you on the computer.'

'Absolutely not,' I snapped.

Ben took Vedra's side: 'What harm can she do, Fran?'

'I don't want some bloody kid looking over my shoulder.' I realised that the room had gone silent. Vedra looked defeated.

'B.B. hasn't had a walk today,' Edwina was trying to change the subject.

'So bloody what? Why doesn't someone else take him? Why do I have to do everything? It's not as if he's my blasted dog. Why don't some of you take him out instead?'

I stormed out into the street. I hated the lot of them. I reached the office and I wrote a letter to Assad. The following day I relented and allowed Vedra to come with me to the office. I showed her how to work the computer. Between us we composed a letter to Patrick telling him how much we missed him and asking him to send some deworming pills for B.B. in the next convoy.

'Do you think his Bishop will read this?' Vedra giggled.

'No, you idiot, this goes to the English office of Comfort Aid, not to the Bishop's palace.'

Vedra was going through the drawers of Patrick's desk. 'Stop snooping.' She had extracted a file. 'Put that back.'

'Look at this!'

'For heaven's sake, Vedra, do as you're bloody told.' I grabbed the file.

'Why are our names in it?'

'What do you mean?'

'I can't read English, but I can read our names.' I grabbed the file but Vedra snatched it back.

She flicked it open under my nose. 'Look!' Vedra was quite right. All our names were listed with our dates of birth. 'Why would Patrick have done that?' asked Vedra.

'How should I know? Give me the file.' I looked more carefully and realised that the file contained copies of reUNite registration forms.

My irritation was subsiding and I explained to Vedra about missing minors and about reUNite which tried to link them up with their families.

'Does that mean Patrick has registered us as missing minors?' she asked.

'Looks like it.' I was remembering what Assad had said to me just before he was killed about the UNHCR wanting to find places of safety for the little ones. He hadn't wanted to give our address to the man and woman at the UNHCR office when we had gone to give them the names of the dead women we had found in the cave for fear of reUNite coming to take the twins and Vedra away.

'Will reUNite separate us?'

'They have to catch us first,' I said lightheartedly.

'Well, it shouldn't be too difficult. That looks like our address.' She pointed to the second page.

'Shit! What did Patrick think he was doing?'

'I suppose he thought he was helping us. I don't want to go into some refugee camp for orphans, Fran. I want to stay with you.'

'Come here, you rat-bag.' I cuddled her. 'You're not going to be put in any refugee camp or any orphanage. I think we'd better get back home now.' I wanted to tell Ben and Edwina about Vedra's discovery as soon as possible. If necessary, we would have to move. There was absolutely nothing that I wouldn't do to keep us all together and if we had to live on the run so be it. I knew that I would give my life for Vedra and the twins no matter what happened. I cursed Patrick but I also remembered a story he had told me about a soldier who was finally coming home after years fighting in Vietnam. The soldier had called his parents from San Francisco airport.

'Mum and Dad, I'm coming home, but I've a favour to ask. I have a friend I'd like to bring home with me.'

'Sure,' they replied, 'we'd love to meet him.'

'There's something you should know,' the son continued, 'my friend was hurt pretty badly in the fighting. He stepped on a landmine and lost an arm and a leg. He has nowhere else to go and I want him to come and live with us.'

'I'm sure sorry to hear about that son. Maybe we can help your friend to find somewhere to live.'

'No, Mom and Dad, I want him to live with us.'

'I'm sorry, son,' said his father, 'but you don't know what you're asking. Someone with such a handicap would be a terrible burden. We have our own lives to lead and we can't let something like this get in the way. I think you should just come on home and forget about this guy. He'll find something.'

The son had hung up and his parents heard no more. A few days later, however, they received a phone call from the San Francisco police. Their son had died after falling from a building. The police believed it to be suicide. The grief-stricken parents flew to San Francisco and were taken to the city morgue to identify the body of their son. They recognised him but to their horror they also discovered something that they hadn't known – their son had lost an arm and a leg.

Patrick had pointed out that most of us are like those

parents. We find it easy to love people who are good-looking and fun to have around, but we don't like people who inconvenience us or make us feel uncomfortable. I vowed that whatever happened to the kids and whoever came for them, I would stand by them and defend them at no matter what personal cost to myself – and 'inconvenience' was likely to be putting it mildly.

Some days afterwards I was walking down the road and passed a bombed-out church. I noticed people going in, mostly women, with their heads covered with scarves. It must be Sunday and they would be going to Mass. If things had been different, that was what Mamma and I would have been doing. I wondered if Patrick was celebrating Mass back in England. Suddenly I was engulfed in loneliness. I must have stopped and I was staring at the church when a voice from behind me said 'Will you come in with me?' I swung round. She was an ugly old woman dressed in the traditional black of widowhood. Her hooked nose was too large for her wrinkled, pitted face which looked as if it had been chiselled. She was severely stooped and consequently had trouble looking up into my face. She put out a withered arm. Wordlessly, I helped her up the steps of the church and we went inside. I gasped. This was like no church that I had ever seen. The roof had gone, presumably blown off and the wall behind the altar had crumbled away so that we could see the mountains behind. The pews were riddled with bullet holes and the marble was no better. The statues were either cracked or headless and the aisle was pitted with large holes which one had to edge around. I was no stranger to gutted buildings but this one glowed with the light from literally hundreds of candles flickering along the remaining walls which were covered with photographs. Photos of children, photos of grannies, photos of husbands, photos of lovers, photos presumably of every parishioner who had either died or been killed. The ugly old woman led me to a bench. Mass had begun and the women knelt in prayer while the men stood at the back glowering self-consciously. I wondered what they were all praying for. The end of the war? The safe return of loved ones? More electricity? A short sermon? I bowed my head wanting to be part of the fellowship and yet unable to think of anything except my friends who had died while I had been left alive. As far as I was concerned, God had messed up. It was I who should have been dead.

I heard the priest say 'Peace be with you' and thought the words an absurd irony. The congregation were offering the sign of peace to one another with kisses and handshakes. The ugly old woman turned to me: 'Happy Easter,' she said. She lifted my hand and placed a painted egg in my palm. I was flabbergasted. There hadn't been chickens in our city for years. What was she doing with an egg in her bag? I stared at the egg in disbelief. I could not remember when I had last eaten an egg. It must be Easter Sunday! I turned to thank the old woman, but she had gone. The pleasure I experienced in just holding the egg was beyond words. I kept staring at it and turning it over. The service finished and I sat on alone in the candlelit church. Perhaps God hadn't messed up after all. I looked at the egg and wondered if it was hard-boiled. I shook it and listened, turned it into my other hand. I tapped the shell and then banged it impatiently against the pew. If it was raw, I would lick it up. As the shell splintered, I saw the white of a hard-boiled egg. To make it last as long as possible, I decided to recite five Our Fathers between each nibble. As far as I was concerned, this was the most precious Easter egg I had ever received or ever would receive. I left the church, fully restored, and made for home.

As soon as Ben heard my footsteps he came out to greet me. 'Fran! have you heard the news?'

'No, but do you know what day it is?'

Ben ignored my question. 'They've released our people from the detention camp.'

'Well, that's a step in the right direction. Is this a political initiative or a gesture of goodwill to fit in with the season?'

'I don't know. My source just mentioned that they had sent UN medical teams in to assess the situation in the camp and that trucks left before dawn to bring our people out. What season is it anyway?'

'It's Easter. Easter Sunday.' By this time the twins and Vedra had joined us. Easter Sunday meant nothing to them, partly because they were Muslims. Ben sat them down and regaled them with the story of Good Friday, the Crucifixion and the Resurrection on Easter Sunday. Vedra and the twins had recently been given paper and paints by a recreational centre that had just been set up for street children. They had been giving full expression to their creativity and the results were stuck up on the walls, next to Mo's postcard of Zanzibar.

'Why don't you paint pictures?' I suggested. 'Vedra, you do the Crucifixion and you, twins, you do the Resurrection.' My suggestion was greeted with enthusiasm and the room suddenly turned into an art studio as Edwina and I decided to make Easter cards as well. In the evening, when the children were preparing for bed, Edwina and Ben approached me.

'Fran, we thought we'd go up to the park to see Edwina's family and Assad. B.B. could do with a walk.' It was getting on for eight o'clock, the time I would normally go to the office and write a letter to Assad. I hesitated.

'Please come with us, Fran,' pleaded Ben. 'After all, it's a special day and Assad was the one who wanted us to stay together as a family.' I was about to tell them that I wrote to Assad every day, when Vedra bounced up from the mattress she shared with the twins. 'We all ought to go and see Assad,' she said indignantly.

'You just want an excuse to stay up,' laughed Edwina.

'No I don't,' said Vedra. 'We were all part of Assad. Not just you adults.'

'She's right.' Vedra won her point and we all made our way up to the park. The little ones decided to take their Easter pictures to place them on Assad's grave. I took my memories.

Routine is an essential part of war, however tedious. Routine creates a security which helps one to endure the day. It breaks up the endless nothingness. We always performed our chores in the morning and in the afternoon we would send the little ones to the recreation centre. Ben was still working in the warehouse, whilst Edwina now worked every other day in the soup kitchen. While we were never short of food, there was little variety and no meat, fruit or vegetables. Although shelling was infrequent, snipers were still a danger near the front line. I had to be careful when taking the washing down to the river.

The UN and the police were still maintaining road blocks on the periphery of the city, but these did not affect us. Now that the weather was better, the children took advantage of the lighter evenings and played outside, whilst Edwina and I took the chance of a chat indoors.

'What will you do when the war's over?' Edwina asked me. The question came as a shock. We had never dared to look into the future, never dared to think about what we might do afterwards. Perhaps we had never dared to believe we would be alive.

'I don't know.' Somehow the savagery of war had left us without initiative for the future. 'Perhaps I'll write a book now that I know how to use a computer.'

'You have to learn to spell first,' she grinned.

'What will *you* do, Edwina?'

'I want to go to university.'

'Oxford or Cambridge?' It was a joke we had shared with Patrick, who had always insisted that there were only two universities worth attending. We laughed. Vedra appeared at the front door of the basement, her face puckered in distress. Behind her was a tall man in a dark suit. 'That's Fran,' Vedra pointed at me. The man edged his way through the door and came towards me offering his hand. I ignored it and waited.

'My name is Elvir. I work for the Red Cross.' He produced his plastic ID card, but my eyes were blurred and my mind was racing. Vedra had gone to stand behind Edwina.

'What do you want?' I asked rudely.

'Please, there's nothing to worry about.' The man paused as if expecting me to reply, but his very presence raised alarm bells. 'We would like you to come down to our office. Is there a Ben Sahovic here?'

'Why do you want to know?'

'We would like to talk to him.' The man paused. 'You do know Ben Sahovic?' How did they know about Ben?

'He's working.' That was all I was prepared to say. The official saw my reluctance and said with a half-smile, 'I knew your English friend Father Patrick. You're not in trouble, Fran, but we can't talk here. Would you and Ben be prepared to meet with me and my colleagues in the Red Cross when he returns from work?'

'What do you want to see us about?' The man glanced quickly at Edwina and Vedra.

'I can't discuss it here but I'll give you my card with my name and address. I'll be in my office until ten o'clock tonight. Believe me, it will be to your advantage to come and see us.' The man turned to go out, almost falling over the twins who were sitting on the basement steps. I stared after him. Vedra burst into tears and flung herself into Edwina's arms. The twins held each other's hands and looked bewildered.

227

'Don't let them take us away,' howled Vedra.

'Nobody's taking anybody anywhere,' What the hell did the man mean? What would be to our advantage?

'I'll kill myself if they separate us,' Vedra sobbed.

'Don't be so dramatic.' What the hell was it all about?

'Come on, kids, get washed and we'll get supper ready.' Edwina had always been good at creating a diversion. 'Ben will be home soon. Vedra, wipe your eyes and feed B.B.' Ben walked in ten minutes later and we sat down to supper, everybody trying to tell him what had happened.

'I won't bloody go,' Vedra said truculently, 'nor will the twins, will you?' The twins shook their heads in solidarity.

'Calm down, everyone.' Ben popped the last piece of bread into his mouth.

'We could move to Fran's office. They won't find us there,' said Vedra.

'Stop jumping to conclusions,' said Ben. 'For all we know they might be rehousing us.'

'Oh sure. The Honeymoon Suite in the Hilton Hotel, perhaps?' The twins giggled at my sarcasm.

'Well, we're not going to find out sitting here. Come on, Fran. We've got nothing to lose by going to the office. Have you got the man's card?' Ben turned to the little ones and said solemnly, 'I promise you that we'll do everything in our power to keep you with us, even if I have to pretend I'm eighteen so that I can adopt you.' The unconditional love and the trust in their eyes must have pierced Ben's heart. Mine fluttered with fear and apprehension. I had understood both the nature and the severity of the situation, for I knew that if Patrick had given our names and dates of birth to reUNite the Red Cross would almost certainly have them too. Ben hadn't a hope of passing himself off as eighteen.

I gave the man's card to Ben and we set off to walk to the

address we had been given. We walked a good way in silence. Then Ben spoke gravely.

'Fran, if I cannot keep my promise to hold on to the little ones, will you and Edwina go away with them? Somehow I'll get out of the country. I'll go abroad and get a job and when I'm eighteen, I'll come back and find you. As soon as I possibly can, I'll come back for you. I do promise you that.'

I could only take in the fact that Ben was probably going to leave us. My eyes brimmed. 'Please, Ben, don't you go as well.' I stumbled on beside him, panic-stricken. 'Don't leave me.' Ben paused, his peaceful face was strained as he looked towards the distant mountains. 'Hopefully, it won't come to that, Fran. Come on, there's only one way to find out.'

We arrived at the Red Cross office and were shown into a reception area. We asked for Mr Elvir and were kept waiting, which did nothing to calm my nerves. Mr Elvir finally appeared. He had discarded his tie and his dark suit was crumpled. His informality worried me. I introduced Ben and we were shown into a luxurious room with soft armchairs and a coffee table. Not at all what I had been expecting.

'How do you like your coffee?' Mr Elvir seemed to be trying to put us at our ease. 'My colleague Mrs Jowlitz will be joining us. Ah, here she is.' An attractive blonde woman swept into the room, greeting us with a smile as warm as her eyes. 'Good to meet you both.' She was holding two files. We all sat down.

'As I told you earlier,' Mr Elvir began, 'I knew your friend Father Patrick. Before he left the country he brought your situation – your plight – to our attention.'

'Plight?' Ben interrupted. 'You make it sound as if we've got some sort of problem.'

'I'm sorry, that was the wrong word to use. I was referring to your circumstances. My colleagues and I were sent your files by reUNite and have nothing but admiration for you both.'

'Then why are you going to take the little ones away? We look after them. They're well cared for and well nourished and they have told us that they definitely do not want to be placed in a refugee camp.' My outburst did little to relieve my feelings. Mr Elvir appeared somewhat ruffled.

Mrs Jowlitz intervened. 'I think there's been some sort of a misunderstanding.' I stopped her.

'We understand perfectly. What you don't seem to understand is that we're a family. We take care of each other. We don't need your help or anyone else's. I don't care what Father Patrick told you. We were managing perfectly well long before he . . .'

'Fran,' Ben cut in, 'that's enough.' But I was far from finished and was about to start a further onslaught when Mrs Jowlitz rose to her feet and approached me with such a broad smile that I was startled. She moved my cup of coffee, perched herself on the table beside me and clasped my hands.

'Fran, we're not here to take the children away from you. But unfortunately, it was because of the children that Mr Elvir felt unable to confide in you when he came to see you earlier today. The children are not going to be quite as fortunate as you and Ben.' Mr Elvir's words came back to me – 'Believe me it will be to your advantage.'

'Would you kindly tell us what all this is about?' said Ben. Mrs Jowlitz proceeded to open the two files she had brought into the room. From each one she produced a photograph. She gave one to each of us. I saw the colour drain from Ben's face as he looked at his. I dropped my eyes and stared at the print I was holding. The fountains of childhood memory that had been silted up by pain burst forth. 'Dadda! It's Dadda.' The walls of anger crumbled within me as I glimpsed hope. Endurance had conquered and borne fruit in the life of my father.

'He's alive?' I groped blindly for words, hardly daring to hope.

'Very much alive, Fran. Your father and Ben's father were released from detention camp last Sunday. They're in poor health, but with rest and decent food, they'll be back on their feet within weeks.'

'When can we see them?'

'They're being debriefed at the moment. I'll drive you both over to see them tomorrow.' Mrs Jowlitz was sharing our joy.

'Do they know we're alive?'

'Yes, we have informed them.' Ben and I fell into each other's arms weeping, our exultant happiness fulfilling and surpassing the longing for peace in every human heart. Our empty souls were freed from the slavery of self-inflicted blame. I savoured the sweet gentle warmth of hope that eclipsed all past suffering. Our war was over.

I sat at the computer in the office, Baked Bean on my lap. Tenderly I fingered the photograph of my father. I wondered how Dadda would feel about having four daughters.

I began to type a final letter to my dearest friend.

Dear Assad,
Tomorrow, I will be with Dadda . . .